Global Deadline

SARAH GERDES

RPM Publishing

Coeur d'Alene, Idaho

Copyright © 2018 Sarah Gerdes

All rights reserved.

ISBN-: 978-0-9992743-9-2

Library of Congress cataloging-in-publication data on file

Printed in the United States of America

First American Edition 2018
Second American Edition 2023

Cover design by Lyuben Valevski
http://lv-designs.eu

ALL RIGHTS RESERVED. NO PART OF THIS BOOK MAY BE REPRODUCED OR TRANSMITTED IN ANY FORM OR BY ANY MEANS, ELECTRONIC OR MECHANICAL, INCLUDING PHOTOCOPYING, RECORDING, OR BY ANY INFORMATION STORAGE AND RETRIEVAL SYSTEM, WITHOUT WRITTEN PERMISSION FROM THE PUBLISHER.
P.O. Box 841 Coeur d'Alene, ID 83816

Global Deadline

FACT

The systems you are going to read about are real. The software that controls the underlying manufacturing processes for the food we eat, the drugs we take, the financial institutions we use, the clothes we wear, even the cars we drive are created and managed by these systems. It takes one slip of the finger on a computer keyboard to impact an entire product, cripple an industry or decimate a nation.

It's not a matter of *if* this disaster will occur. It's a matter of *when*.

CHAPTER 1

Austin slid her right hand around the back of her sparring partner's neck, feeling the soft bristles of his hair as she curled her fingertips along the line of muscle running behind his ear, grazing the tip of the white uniform. She caught a faint smell of cologne, mixed with sweat, the aroma appealing. If she had been in a crowded dance club, a drink in one hand, swaying to the tempo of the music, the gesture would be very close to a move of seduction. In this environment, it was anything but.

She hoped to get the maneuver right this time. It was a Friday night in San Francisco and instead of being at a club, she was perfecting the art of neck breaking.

Her instructor, Sean McLemore, a fifth-degree black belt, had seen her action from across the room. He called out, stopping her, collapsing the distance between them, his glide more catlike than human. She released her partner and bowed, clasping her hands in the traditional greeting she was required to give her superior.

"It's the back of the hand, sliding across either the front or the back, like this," he instructed, taking her palm and moving it below her partner's ear. "When it gets to this flat section, grip the chin with the palm and fingers of your other hand, like this, and pull as hard as you can. You need the right speed and force to get the desired effect."

That effect was a broken neck of course, Austin thought. She nodded, subdued, aware it was the second time she'd made the error.

Her instructor stood back, giving her a nod of confidence. Last Tuesday night, he'd surprised her by telling her the instructors had agreed she had *earned the right* to learn to break an opponent's neck as a fifth section, two belts below a black.

"It's all about control, and you have a lot of that," he'd told her. It was also about the ability to paralyze an attacker or explode an internal organ using a palm thrust to the chest.

Austin adjusted her position, made eye contact with her partner and waited until he nodded. She immediately placed her right foot next to his left, as she curled her right hand around his neck, cupping his chin with her palm and holding her fingertips tight. With a slight amount of pressure, her partner's head and body began to turn. It was all done in slow motion, as not to inflict actual damage.

Again, her instructor paused her.

"What did you miss?" Austin looked at him blankly. If she knew that, she wouldn't have missed anything. "You must put your heel behind your attacker's foot, destabilizing him so the twist of the neck throws him back and over your foot, like this. He was supposed to fall as you broke his neck. Try again." Before she could retry, her name was called. An assistant instructor motioned to her from an open window in the outer room. Austin made eye contact with Instructor Sean and bowed, receiving his permission to leave.

"Austin, I've got Leonard Campbell on the line," her assistant Jackie said with the pacing of a tamer talking a lion down from pouncing. "And before you hang up, just hear him out. I wouldn't have put him through if it wasn't serious."

It better be.

"Austin, it's Leonard, I'm sorry to call you but…"

"What do you want?" she broke in, glancing at the doorway.

"Aren't endorphins supposed to make people happy?"

"You stole my largest client," Austin replied coldly. This wasn't some junior flack trying to get in the business. He was the man who wiped a half a million from her books last year. "Make it fast."

"I've got a situation, and I have a proposition to you."

"You need another one of your extracurricular problems fixed before your wife finds out?" She hoped her insult would propel him off the phone. The silver-haired professional was as handsome as he was unethical, and he used both to his advantage. Sadly, the state of the social situation in San Francisco was one wherein box seats for the opera were more important than self-esteem, and his wife stayed with him, ignoring Twitter and keeping her chin high when she showed up at the winter galas.

"Austin, Blendheim Pharmaceuticals, the seventh largest in the world, is in crisis. People have died. I have the account for their public relations. You have the expertise in crisis communication and the staff. It's a perfect match."

Austin watched the students in her class separate and listen to Instructor Sean's comments. She was missing it, talking to Leonard Campbell, the patriarch of investor relations firm Jones and Campbell. Seer and revelator to the big five investment firms, oil barons and certain sons of former presidents. Her firm was good. Excellent in fact. But good enough to have Leonard call her on a Friday night? It didn't add up.

As annoyed as she was, she pulled her eyes away from the class and stared at the bamboo shoots on the wall. "You want us to come in and save you?"

He paused one second too long. "They've been clean for twelve years, no issues, no problems. Growth through product development and diversification giving double digit returns."

Her irritation faded, replaced by a little bit of wicked glee. The only reason he'd be calling her is because he was screwed on two fronts: getting the job under false pretenses and now having to do the actual work.

"I'm listening."

"It's big, as in millions."

And I'm not going to split it.

"If my company does the job, then it's my company who gets the money and the credit." No offer could entice her to remain anonymously behind the scenes.

"Come on, Austin," he said as smoothly as if he were dropping ice in bourbon after dinner. "We've been acting as Blendheim's agency since they went public. We could staff up in the area of crisis communications, but it would take time."

"Too bad I'm not in the temporary staffing business," she said, her irritation returning. "You've got deaths and that means lawsuits, an inevitable investigation and government hearings. Quite a complex situation for you to handle."

"You're being unreasonable," he protested, not quite pulling off the confident note. She could almost see a bit of sweat dripping down the side of his sailboat-racing tanned face.

"You're mad because I'm calling you out for not making an honest referral? Please. Do you really think I'll slink in the backdoor, do all the heavy lifting and when it's done, let you walk out the front, arm-in-arm with the CEO? Thank you, but no."

"You're still pissed I took a client, but you returned the favor by poaching Asa, who was my best account manager, which you knew. We lost two clients because he left."

"Which didn't total the amount of loss I took when you pulled your under-the-rug maneuver."

"Bury the hatchet and let's move on," he suggested. She remembered the rage she'd felt when her client dropped her for Campbell's firm.

"You better get going, Leonard," she suggested. "You've got about sixty hours before the market opens and your client's stock is going to flatline. Who broke the story by the way?"

"A reporter named Garrison from *The Weekly*, who happened to be on morgue watch at Stanford University Medical and used a hearing device to catch the ER chatter. Got on the Internet, checked with other hospitals and had his scoop hours before anyone else."

Impressive. "He must have picked this up last night around eleven."

"How'd you know that?" asked Campbell, surprise audible in his voice.

Because anyone in the business knew that to make the early bird papers the story had to be in by midnight, *idiot*. And, if her colleague knew half of what she did about a crisis situation, he'd be peeing his pants right about now.

"Goodnight, Leonard," she said, shaking out her legs. Her hips were sore from the Tai Chi Chung forms she'd learned in her self-defense class the day before.

"Wait — wait. I'll conference in the VP at Blendheim."

"No deal. VPs aren't going to cut it at this level. I work directly with the person who makes the decisions and that's the CEO. To be completely clear," she continued, "if I take this, I do the crisis management. You keep the day to day investor relations. No mixing of the two, and this contract is mine." Leonard huffed away his last ploy. If he had another choice, he wouldn't have called her in the first place and they both knew it.

"Not to add any undue pressure, Austin, but this one's big."

"Aren't they all, Leonard?"

"No, Austin. I mean the money. They have a threshold of several million."

Her eyebrow raised in unison with the corner of her lips. A couple meant two million, a few three and several four. It would pay off the last of her debts, and give her a cushion going forward.

Moments later, Austin took a call from a very distressed CEO, Luther Mackelby. She gave him her terms, he accepted, and a half hour later, she had gotten dressed and sent out a group message to the four directors in her firm. They would convene in the office in thirty minutes, pulling the first of what would likely be several all-nighters. With one client, she'd eclipsed the total revenue for the previous year. And it was going to be worth every dime.

CHAPTER 2

The crystal chandeliers of San Francisco's Pan Pacific Hotel's grand ballroom chimed softly with the bustle of the room. It was Monday, 8:25 a.m., with the press conference scheduled to begin in five minutes. Austin suppressed a smile of satisfaction as she looked at the gold inlay on the walls and reflected how far she'd come from standing on the sloping, deteriorating docks of the Jersey waterfront. In six years, she'd graduated from defending waste spills, accidental food contaminations and executive affairs to the white-collar world of product recalls and stock manipulations. Not bad for a girl with nothing more than a brand name prep school on her resume.

If Dad could see me now. A flash of his devastated image appeared in her mind's eye; her rejection of the family business the turning point in their relationship. His decline, then suicide, both blamed on her. It had taken thousands of miles and years to distance herself from the pain, but she'd made it, mentally and financially. At least her uncle applauded her success, even if he didn't agree with the vocation. That was enough.

As the reporters entered the room and took their seats, she thought about Uncle Ramon, her father's brother. He had been her surrogate dad, with all the positive and negatives.

"Doesn't it bother you to represent companies accused of death and destruction?" Uncle Ramon had asked, his thick, Latin accent mocking her.

"No company intentionally creates a product that's going to hurt a consumer," she said with a laugh.

He'd taken a long draw on his cigar, blowing the smoke through the palm-sized leaves from the elephant ear plant that draped over his desk as he often had when she was a child. "These companies require an attorney, not a public relations person."

"The verdict of public opinion is far more powerful than any courtroom," she'd countered, knowing how often judges were influenced by the often fickle temperaments of their voters.

"I believe it's something more."

Austin hadn't answered. In truth, she was addicted to the adrenaline more than the money. She loved the intense, all out bursts required to create a national blitz and huddling with top-notch ad agencies for the production of spots to save a company. She also gloried in the small victories, like getting a prejudiced reporter to return a phone call, listen and change an opinion.

It all kept her mind occupied and her schedule overfilled. No time to think about the past.

"After the mill burned down, you could have rebuilt it, Austin. That's what your dad wanted."

"It's not what I wanted," she said, tired of the conversation. It was always about the money with him, she thought. She didn't need to remind him that other vocations paid just as well as tobacco and liquor; death and destruction.

"You can't run forever," he chided. "Nor must you do it on your own."

There was no one else. Her mother and sister had blamed her for her father's suicide, saying he pulled the trigger due to a broken heart.

"I have you as my backstop when I need emotional support," she said, her mood lifting. "Besides, it's very satisfying to save a company from closing and helping thousands of people keep their jobs when a manufacturing mistake is made."

"Bad company, bad people."

"Romo," she said, employing her childhood nickname for him. "Accountants and front desk workers don't need to suffer when the company does."

"I'm not worried about them. I'm worried about you. These press people hound you for information and once you give it to them, they disappear, only to surface again like sharks when blood is in the water."

"They have a job to do, just as I do. It's nothing personal." In fact, it added to the excitement. Anyone with an internet connection could represent companies who were doing ok. It took real skill to turn around an entire population's perception of a firm in trouble.

"Cameras in place," said the male voice in her earpiece, abruptly ending her recollections. The man at the back of the ballroom waved his hand. Today, she was here because her new client, Blendheim Pharmaceuticals, was accused of unintentional deaths due to tainted drugs.

Luther Mackelby, the short, stout CEO of Blendheim Industries, strode to her side at the edge of the stage. Lee Ching, the VP of engineering, looked uncomfortably stiff in his suit. He stood just behind his boss.

"I'll cue you to end the conference," Austin reminded Mackelby. When her man at the rear gave another wave, she signaled back, and he dimmed the lights slightly. The room fell silent and she touched Mackelby's elbow. The two men went to the podium, the CEO behind the mic and Ching to his left.

"Ladies and gentlemen…" Mackelby stuck to the script she'd written. He began by apologizing to the families, the loyal customers and investors for the accidental, drug-induced deaths. It was a mirror of the press release that had been distributed within hours of taking over the account. Mackelby then gave a full history of the situation, starting with the drug manufacturing process, just as they planned.

As he spoke, Austin scanned the packed room of reporters recording, note-taking or typing directly into laptops. Two days ago, she'd never heard of

Blendheim Industries, the drug Lucine or the manufacturing process. Four million dollars later, she knew it intimately.

"You said the error was machine made," said a reporter with a voice sounding like two pieces of sandpaper pushing against one another. "Can you prove it?"

Austin zeroed in on the face of Clive Garrison from *The Weekly*. Given the scoop, he'd earned his place in the front row. Looking at him now, he was an odd cross between a panting dog eagerly waiting for a bone and a handsome, FBI agent receiving instant news in his visible earpiece.

Yet he was neither. Garrison's story was legendary. When he'd been young, good-looking and connected, he'd graduated from UC Berkeley, married a Nob Hill socialite and drunk away most of her inheritance before he started spending his own trust fund on the cute skirts located up and down O'Farrell Street. He got the boot from her family, was disinherited from his own and wound up in the SFPD lock up for scoring a gram of cocaine. Waiting for his attorney, he overheard two cops talking about a married politician from Woodside, a male escort and GoldMember's strip club. Garrison's cell phone was out of battery, but he had two quarters in his pocket. With one, he called a friend at the *San Jose Mercury News* who told him to pitch the editor of *The Weekly*. With the second quarter, Garrison called *The Weekly*, promising to write a story as an exclusive scoop if the paper paid his bail.

The story appeared the next day.

From there, Garrison turned into a full-fledged gossip junkie overnight, filling the pages of *The Weekly* with stories from San Francisco's underworld. He frequented places where the person he wrote up and took down fit his editors' agenda; republican, male, unscrupulous and preferably white.

In other words, people just like him. Who better to sniff out a scandal than someone who'd experienced it first hand?

Of course, the man was well-dressed enough to blend in at the right clubs or doctor waiting rooms without causing a stir. She read his filings here and there, more for the entertainment value than anything, but she had to give him credit. He'd evolved from a hack with a good writing style to a serious reporter with glimpses of brilliance peppering his latest pieces. Still, she wondered why the editor bothered to have him come at all. It wasn't as if *The Weekly* was going to cross the line and start covering corporate affairs.

Garrison seemed to be enjoying his presence at the press conference, as though he knew this was the majors and was bound to hit a homer his first time at-bat.

He was a nice looking man, thought Austin as she listened to Ching take over the explanation of the manufacturing process, especially considering he had a ten-year dark period of indulging in too many vices, legal and illegal. The lines on his forehead were present, but not overly deep. He was blessed with greenish-grey eyes set under light-brown eyebrows, the color of his hair. His face was only a little full, which Austin hypothesized was more from late nights and too much soda, because his neck was tight not layered with the skin from too many steak dinners at Morton's. One day of clean living would lean him out. His expensive Herringbone jacket hung nicely on his shoulders, the Brooks Brother's shirt laying against his neck was upright. A shame his appearance didn't match his personality.

Austin turned her attention to Ching, listening to the script he was reading, still fascinated by the beautiful simplicity of the underlying manufacturing technology.

Hundreds of ingredients in minute amounts were measured and poured from perpendicular holders into small mixing vats run by automated machinery. Each one was blended and mixed an exact number of times, then poured into the clear drug coating. After being ushered through a cleansing process, automated hands selected samples from rolling conveyer belts. Finally, the drugs were funneled into a metal container that counted and poured pills into plastic bottles. The drugs were documented, labeled and loaded into the warehousing docks for inventory and shipment.

"Once word of the deaths emerged, engineering discovered the input ingredient level was inconsistent from the time of the order to when it arrived at the manufacturing center. In short, the numbers within the software system were incorrect. The result was the .0008 differential."

Ching paused and cameras flashed, his eyes squinting at the discothèque effect in front of him. Austin pushed the pager in her right hand sending a buzz to the man. He began again. "We traced the code back to the specific production cycles," he continued, in a prescriptive tone. "These systems have worked without fail for the last twelve years, therefore we aren't sure of the reasons behind the sudden change."

A dozen reporters called out for questions that Ching answered equitably. Process improvements, personnel checks, mischievous intent; all suggestions were ruled out by Ching's undaunting reliance on the facts of a tried and proven drug manufacturing process.

Austin depressed the button on her pager again. The clock was running down against the morning news hours, and she needed to hit the east coast feeds. Mackelby needed to take a few final questions.

"So, you are saying these fatalities are due to an error in the manufacturing process," said Garrison loudly. The man's eyes glinted with focus, his voice clear and strong. "Would you agree with that?"

Austin saw the trap before Ching did, but she couldn't step on the stage to cut off an answer.

"It's possible," responded Ching.

"So, it's *possible* that you might have had this same problem for years, but since no one died it wasn't caught?" he pressed. Unkept, definitely. Wicked smart? Absolutely.

An uncomfortable lull had fallen over the room, as though the other reporters realized Garrison's line of questioning was sound and were giving him a respectful amount of time to get an answer.

"It's unlikely that could be the case," Ching answered.

"But you have to acknowledge it *is* possible." Austin shifted from one foot to the other. *Say nothing,* she willed to Ching.

Ching thought momentarily and responded honestly, "Yes. I suppose it is."

The room went wild.

CHAPTER 3

Garrison's white teeth were more like fangs glinting from the victory of getting Ching to admit a gaping hole of liability. Others smelled the blood of a wounded animal and began shouting questions over one another, not waiting for either executive to answer. Billions of dollars in value, wiped out with a simple, three-letter word. Yes.

"What about product side effects?" asked Bernie Jax, the senior medical reporter from *The San Jose Mercury News*. "What has been logged and filed so far?"

"Maybe multiple deaths previously unattributed to your products are out there as well," suggested Annie Hansen from *The San Francisco Chronicle*, talking over the last part of Jax's question. "How many other products are potentially tainted?"

Ching was overwhelmed from the sheer volume of noise. Mackelby seemed torn between maintaining professional stoicism and hiding his shock. Austin visualized the stock cratering and the thirty-day bonus she'd managed to include in the contract evaporating with each passing moment.

In two strides she was beside Mackelby, standing directly in front of the cameras. The noise level lowered briefly with her appearance and her distinctive voice rose above the pandemonium in the ballroom.

"The systems Mr. Ching mentioned are approved by the FDA," she said with a voice of professional authority, "and are in use at every pharmaceutical company certified by the government both here in the States and in the European Union."

"And you are?" asked Garrison, cutting over the others. She knew him, but he didn't know her. That was helpful.

"My name is Austin Marks and I'm responsible for communications at Blendheim." He tried to talk over her but she raised her voice and glared him down. "To suggest that flaws of the type we recently encountered have been ongoing would be to imply that nearly every firm in the entire pharmaceutical industry is producing faulty drugs." She spoke slowly, precisely, and reasonably. "Furthermore, manufacturing companies in more than seventeen industries also use this software, so an implication that entire industries are using a common thread of software with critical deficiencies would be incendiary and irresponsible. Most of them are in the Fortune 2000. That includes Boeing, one of the first companies in the world to adopt this same software when it produced the 777."

The impact of her rational words had a dulling effect on the crowd. The blood hunt had been momentarily called off.

"Mr. Ching said it was isolated to specific lots," said Bernie. "Can you detail the process and specifics?"

Austin looked at the man who she considered friendly. Now and then she threw him a tip on a story that was bubbling up from Silicon Valley. He returned the favor by giving her soft-ball questions, if, and only if, it wasn't going to put his professional standing in jeopardy. It was how the game was played, and everyone on the inside of the media circles knew it. They needed her and other PR flacks just as badly as she needed them.

"Of course," she began, her voice still firm. She paused, giving the reporters time to put hands to laptops and ready thumbs for rapid texting. "Product lot numbers and points of distribution were identified, the suppliers notified and all retailers in the supply chain removed the product from the shelves before stores opened this morning. And although earlier batches passed the quality tests, Blendheim has removed *all* its products until random samples can be tested and validated. The FDA has approved this course of action, the most aggressive of its kind in the history of pharmaceuticals."

"Removal doesn't equate to victimless," interjected Garrison. A good soundbite, Austin thought to herself, but Garrison's competitors in the room were unlikely to print it.

"Nor am I making any such suggestion, Mr. Garrison," her comment momentarily shutting his mouth. He was evidently surprised she knew his name. "That's why we have already started the process of reviewing the production cycles of all Blendheim drugs for the last five years. The other major pharmaceutical firms with the same systems have also voluntarily agreed to do the same thing as a precautionary measure." In effect, the entire industry was reviewing their own systems at a terrifying rate, but she wasn't going call those firms out by name.

She made a point of glancing at her watch before she left the podium and the audience took the hint. If they were going to make the nine a.m. spots, the stories had to be filed in less than ten minutes.

Her job done, Austin sidestepped off the stage, catching Mackelby's arm as a ground-shifting shake occurred. Above her, the large chandelier swung back and forth. The reporters in the front row were already on their feet.

As she and Mackelby exited, she kept her hand on his elbow. "Slowly," she uttered, her lips barely moving. She didn't want to tell him that walking faster made him look guilty, or afraid, despite the fact that others were employing the same life-saving instincts. "Eyes open. Don't wince."

"Ching's comment could be a billion-dollar screw-up," he muttered.

"Let's hope thoughts of personal safety are taking precedent over his last words."

They joined a mass of other people winding through the ballroom conference area, down the escalators and out through the main lobby, clogging up the front doors like flour pushing its way through a sieve.

"I should fire his butt and shoot that prick Garrison," he continued. Austin coughed lightly over the last few words. Even low-grade microphones picked up comments unintended for the general public.

She led him through the throngs of people to his car outside. As Mackelby ducked his head under the roof of the black town car, he turned to her.

"Was it strange no one asked the name of any of the systems we use? This is the Silicon Valley after all."

"The shake didn't give them the chance." She told him they'd talk after the news reports and firmly closed the door. Even without the earthquake, the press would soon be chasing other firms behind the source of the problem at Blendheim. Her client would be reduced to a mere victim of a systems glitch caused by sloppy engineers.

Austin felt eyes on her and she looked around. Garrison. He was standing outside the hotel, staring straight at her. They made brief eye contact, and she gave him a nod and a smile. He'd done his job, good for him. He tipped his head to her in response, acknowledging her. She'd won this inning.

She hailed a cab. Soon enough, Garrison would be hunting down another story, his debut in the majors only getting him to second base.

A cab stopped and she got in, already checking her phone. Her team was nearly done with the first round of Blendheim customer testimonial ads, set to begin airing within the hour. It would be followed up with a full-court press tour of the major broadcast outlets and on-site visits to the manufacturing plants. Blendheim's stock would rebound on the promise it wasn't their fault. Of course, Leonard Campbell was going to be furious. Several of those software firms she'd implicated were his clients, and he'd feel stabbed in the back.

Actions and consequences, she thought. And if it all turned out, her first international crisis would catapult Mark's Communications from the earthly sphere of public relations to celestial levels. And she was going to make sure her star shone the brightest.

CHAPTER 4

Garrison rubbed his jaw and shifted the weight from one leg to the other, his bony rump aching, a not-so-gentle reminder it had spent more time on chairs than at the gym. The perfectly proportioned figure of Austin Marks had hovered protectively near her client until he was safely within his car. Her crème Chanel suit and shoes matched her briefcase. She had probably called ahead to the Pan Pacific to color code her outfit with the walls.

He'd noticed her left hand resting on the car door. There was no wedding ring, but a tasteful brown leather watch with rectangle face peeked through the sleeve of her jacket. Bedat Number 7 he guessed, probably scored from some love-struck boyfriend for Christmas who was gone by New Year's.

Garrison subtly rubbed his cheek, massaging out the cramp from the stale piece of Nicorette gum that helped him make it through the conference. Death held no appeal unless combined with a scandal, and scandals were his specialty at *The Weekly*.

But not for much longer. He'd been writing hard-hitting investigative pieces, but his editor had rejected most of them.

"Serious doesn't sell our paper," Kell repeated. "Sleaze does. Make it a mixture if you must, but don't forget your audience."

Garrison swirled the lukewarm coffee twice, lifted the cup to his mouth and using the liquid to drench the gum, then started chewing again. He had to economize while he saved his money, and Nicorette was expensive, but it was paying off. He'd had his classic jacket dry-cleaned before the press conference, so he looked respectable and felt gratified when Austin had given him the head nod. In truth, it had surprised him. Women who looked like her didn't typically recognize men like him.

Or at least, they hadn't, for a long time.

Things are changing, he thought to himself. And that had started well before he'd nailed Ching hard, right in the middle of the forehead. Word of Garrison's line of questioning would get around and it was only a matter of time before a real paper took a chance on him. He had all the strengths of a good investigative journalist; just enough honesty to make a story accurate with equal amounts of amorality to not care who he hurt in the process. Sure, he'd uncovered some good stories, but most were a cross between a gossip columnist and Geraldo Rivera-like investigations. And though it made for Enquirer-readership numbers, plumping up the already obscene profits of the paper, it wasn't the tough news to get him hired into a Pulitzer caliber company.

Today had been a whole different world. It marked his first appearance with a room full of investigative reporters who never deigned to look his way, as if the stench of scandal would rub off on their own editorial aspirations. That pompous Bernie Jax and his cushy corner office at the *News*, lobbing the soft ball question at Austin so he could get better access from the flack the next time around. *User liability*? Please. To add insult to journalistic integrity, Jax had phrased the question in order to give Marks enough time to give a reasonable response. She was probably sleeping with half the reporters or giving them free dinners along with invites to cocktail parties.

He inhaled the cool fall air. When the doorman had hailed a cab for her, he'd waited until her back was turned before he scoped her out from head to toe.

Austin was a looker. Her olive skin was peppered with a few dark freckles and smile lines spread at the corner of her eyes and on her forehead, as though she'd spent a lot of time in the sun as a teenager. Her shoulder length blondish hair was cut angular, along her jaw line, giving her an edgy look while still appropriate for her age.

He started walking to the office, still thinking of Austin Marks. The doorman had practically tripped over himself to shut the cab door. She handed him a tip, thanking him; polite, concise and all business. Clive wondered if she really was as oblivious to the doorman's ogling as she seemed to be. It then made him wonder about her personal life and any skeletons in the closet. No-one was ever as pure as they seemed.

Before he reached his building, he spit his gum out and rubbed his right jaw before unwrapping a fresh stick. As long as he was digging, he was going to add her to his list and see if he could find a bit of golden-covered gossip in her pile of dirty laundry.

Just one last good story, he told himself. That's all it would take to launch himself one rung higher on the journalistic ladder. Woodward and Bernstein. And Garrison. He smiled at the thought. It sounded good.

Inside the cab, Austin ran through the scenarios about what to do and where to be in the case an earthquake. She couldn't recall anything about staying in a car or getting out, so she just watched the traffic as it made its way slowly down Sansome. If it was her turn to go, she was going to get crushed regardless.

Another tremor hit, followed by a tremendous crash. The cabby made eye contact and her chest constricted, the momentary silence within the automobile filled with wailing, first from police cars and fire trucks, then from people. In seconds, traffic in front of her stopped. The cab wouldn't be going anywhere.

Anxiety moved downward to her gut, clenching. She hoped it wasn't her building coming down on her team. She banished the thought as reason asserted itself. The building was the shortest skyscraper in the financial district, not large enough to make that kind of massive sound.

She paid her money and got out.

Austin watched her steps as she hit the speed dial on her phone. After a few tense seconds, the phone picked up.

"You OK?" Austin asked.

"The building shook several times, but this old frame held up," Jackie answered, sounding as unperturbed as ever. "Not even a picture fell from the wall." Austin wasn't sure what had occurred in the woman's life to give her the stability of a ballast, but she made it through the roughest of storms without any qualms at all.

Jackie informed her she'd already told the group to pack their laptops and head outside until the word was given employees could go back in the building.

"Can you see anything from where you are?" Jackie asked her. "All we heard was a really loud crash."

"I was in the cab and have no idea what happened. Give me another thirty and I'll be there."

Austin worked hard to get through the crowd, constantly merging with the flow of professionals exiting the high rises. She moved off Market, taking a side street to connect to Mission and nearly ran into a mass of people who had come to a complete stop.

Looking up, Austin stared wide-eyed at the site in front of her. The Metropolitan. *Impossible.* It had been up only a few months.

Steel, concrete and broken glass were piled into a mass of jutting angles. A plume of smoke drafted into the air, carrying the screams and sobs of those lucky enough to make it out of the rubble alive. Dust was carried on the wind, a blast hitting her like a wall as she approached.

As she neared the decimated building, she covered her mouth, breathing shallow. A man was screaming for Carlos as he craned his head into jagged, dark openings in the rubble. The man's panic increased until a police officer grabbed his shoulders.

"But my brother's in there!" he yelled, pushing away the officer.

"We'll find him buddy. We can't have you get hurt if something else falls."

The man ignored the officer and started picking up blocks of concrete as if he were going to single-handedly unearth the person he sought.

Austin watched the macabre scene in front of her deteriorate until her eyes started to burn. The air was getting worse with every second, and she struggled with feelings of guilt. She wanted to help, pausing, looking around like all the others watching, but didn't have a chance.

More officers came into the area, arms raised, shouting for the people to get back, away from the wreckage.

"I'm no attorney, but the company that built this is going to be in a world of hurt. Can you imagine how many people died?" said a woman behind her, her voice raspy from the dust.

Soon, the painful whines of steel being cut became more effective at dispersing the onlookers than any warnings from the police.

Austin left, taking Mission, walking as fast as she dared. She swallowed, feeling the dirt particles in her mouth. Tragedies often made for a crisis and that made for good business.

I'm not going to get my pass to heaven with ideas like that.

In the next thought, she gave herself a break. Criminal defense attorneys didn't run around hoping for a person to be murdered in order to represent the defendant. But when deaths occurred, they were hired, and nobody judged an attorney. Her business was a part of reality, just like an earthquake.

CHAPTER 5

It had taken a while, but Garrison finally made it back to the dilapidated offices of *The Weekly*.

Once in his publisher's office, Garrison got his marching orders.

"You got your scoop, now get back to business," Kell ordered. "Our readers want fodder to share at the water cooler."

"And lawsuits don't sell," Garrison retorted, doing a fair imitation of Kell's thick, Welsh accent.

"That's right!" yelled Kell in response.

Garrison grinned, making straight for the kitchen. He poured himself a cup of stale coffee and went back to his grey-speckled cubicle. He asked Max, his intern, to run up a file on Austin Marks.

"Looking for?" asked the twenty-year old grad student, his fingers already typing the name into Google. Max had the metro-sexual look down, man-bun and all. Not that it would matter which way Max's sexual wind blew. He was a wizard at finding obscure information, his expensive UC Berkley education giving him all the access and inroads the "real" journalists used.

Garrison flicked his head. "Anything."

"Nice!" the intern purred, leaning towards the screen. Max had already found a photo and enlarged it on the monitor. "She say yes?"

"I'm not looking for a date," Garrison replied before he took a swallow of coffee, grimacing before throwing the cup in the trash.

"It wouldn't hurt." Garrison backhanded Max's head, hard enough to warrant a yelp, but the intern continued pulling up additional photos, enlarging each in a slideshow format. "Why is she always lurking behind people?"

Garrison peered closer. He'd hit the golden age of forty and noticed a marked difference in his eyesight over the last year. If it wasn't for that deductible he'd have already gone to the optometrist.

"Doesn't want to be in the spotlight," Garrison concluded, remembering how she'd ducked off the stage as soon as she could.

"Why? Any woman looking like her should be front and center, at least in this town."

"Go to her website." Max's fingertips clicked at the keys and Garrison read the tagline at the top of the site.

"*Clients are the focus, not us,*" Max said out loud, as if Garrison was incapable of reading. "Catchy." Max's approval irritated Garrison. He didn't want his helper liking his person-of-interest. "Let me guess. You want to know who she's sleeping with and how much money she's making?"

"I want it all. Everything you can get." Garrison sat down at his cubicle, ignoring Max's chuckle. If he was in his early twenties and got paid for prying into the lives of others, he'd laugh as well. But he wasn't. He was playing catch up for twenty years of screwing around. Austin Marks had diverted the attention of the reporters, taking away from his victorious moment of getting Ching to admit culpability. He should have had more than a fractional second to enjoy the spotlight.

"What she'd do to get you going?"

"Not much, other than representing scumbags for money."

"Plenty of people do that. Why don't you go down to the strip club? Probably easier leads."

Garrison twirled his pencil in thought. "She looks way too young to be representing a billion-dollar firm. She's not even in her mid-thirties, I bet. She had to do more than sleep with a few people to get this far."

"Maybe she's good at what she does?" suggested Max.

"Maybe she has something to hide." Garrison unwrapped a piece of Nicorette gum, adding it to what was already in his mouth and threw Max a stare. The kid saw his look and focused on his screen.

"Deadline. Dirt. You got it."

Years ago, Austin had accepted the truth of her vocation. Bad news was good for business. It was also good for distractions.

Today is full of bad news.

A brief, uncomfortable wave of guilt swept through her frame. She hadn't asked for anyone to die, just something large enough to cause a distraction.

She was still walking, her offices in view when her phone vibrated. Austin saw the caller ID and immediately answered.

"The first news report just hit," said Luther Mackelby, his relief apparent. "The announcer quoted me on the history, Ching's comment about the systems, but the only image they showed was of you, stating the industry is reviewing their own products. Then it was an immediate switch to the earthquake."

Austin grimaced. She never, *ever* wanted to be on television if she could help it. It was a stroke of terrible luck she'd had to step up to the podium and worse to be on film.

"I'm sorry Luther. I saw no other way to stop the damage than to intervene." He dismissed the need for apologies.

"If you hadn't done it, I might be looking for a new job right now," he said, not entirely joking. "The stock decline has evened out, just like you said it would. It could have been worse."

"A lot," she agreed, thanking the God above for the blessing of the earthquake once again. She wanted her bonus, and that was tied to the stock price. She didn't care what caused it to go up.

That's going to be my second trip to the hot place. With her next thought, she added a prayer for the families of those killed or injured.

The conversation turned to the FDA and congress. "Nichele is doing a fine job with our general counsel and the people at the FDA," Mackelby was saying. "She's already got my legal team reviewing the statement you created, and my supporters in the Senate and House have started making the rounds."

"Are the executives ready?" Mackelby confirmed his secretary had just received a rough schedule and travel arrangements for the group were nearly finalized.

"They'll be in San Francisco in short order. Before you go, I want to say thanks, Austin."

"Wait on that Luther. We're not out of the woods yet." She figured it was going to be at least another thirty days before the stock had fully returned to pre-crisis levels and she got that bonus.

"That's what I've told the board."

CHAPTER 6

Highway 101 runs southward from San Francisco, through Burlingame, Menlo Park then Palo Alto, mini cities that branch off the main freeway. Hidden in the rolling hills are the enclaves of first generation technology millionaires, protected behind enormous trees and gates with laser security systems. Closer to the freeway sit the venerated venture capital firms, the entities who supply the money for risky start-up ventures. To the serial CEO's looking for investment, these firms are the drug for their entrepreneurial addiction.

From these groups are board members chosen to advise executives through the treacherous business environment. Planned board meetings cover financials, hiring and strategic plans. Special board meetings are rare, and when they are called, invariably are in response to something bad. Today Royce Slade, president and CEO of Dolphin Software, called his first ever special board meeting.

Bad was an understatement.

Royce downshifted his 1986 Porsche Turbo as he came upon a Volvo. Then he gunned it, nimbly sliding his black comet through an opening left by a truck. He had been in the middle of his annual insurance health checkup at the doctor's office when his phone went off. It was with no small amount of irony that the doc asked him to turn to the left and cough as he read that the CEO of Blendheim Pharmaceutical had laid the entire blame of the deaths from Lucine on several unnamed vendors. Any bit of digging would implicate Dolphin. Their software was the backbone of Blendheim's operations, just as it was for over two thousand global organizations. By the time Royce was out the door of UCSF's medical center, the other board members had cleared their schedules and were heading toward Silicon Valley.

He depressed the accelerator until the speedometer hit 100. The car was the first material possession he had bought with his financial success. It was a symbol of overcoming adversity, achieving the unachievable. Of winning.

He'd already called his wife Tracy, a shrewd counselor whom he'd come to value as an advisor during their three year marriage. After briefly describing the crisis, she made a brilliant suggestion. Royce made a single tweak of his own. By the time he entered the board room, he felt confident in his pre-emptive strike. Unfortunately, it seemed the group was already polarized by a philosophical chasm.

Kendrick Mellon, a conservative sixty-something whose fund had investments from the Harvard Trust, was arguing for pulling back all sales and marketing programs.

"Anything aimed at creating more awareness of the company is going to draw a consumer backlash. Why would we take that chance?" he asked the assembled group.

Royce nodded at Kendrick, confiscating the open seat next to him. Mellon came from the Warren Buffet generation that dictated organizations stay out of the limelight at all times, not just when a scandal broke. If this wasn't done to Kendrick's satisfaction, entire lots of stock in his fund might be dumped tomorrow morning, and the rest of Wall Street would follow suit.

"Kendrick is right," joined in Sharon McKenzie, the only woman on the board. "Our competitors will do everything they can to create fear in the marketplace. And gentleman," she paused, never once wasting an opportunity to emphasize her participation in the elite male group, "all it takes is a couple of market leaders to dump a vendor. Once that happens, we will all be looking for new board appointments."

"Disagree," said Rakesh. "Make proactive statements like Blendheim did this morning." Rakesh Gupta represented one of the original angel investors, known for placing money into risky investments and using aggressive and controversial strategies to take a company to market. "We double our marketing forces to show we are as solid as our track record indicates."

Kendrick looked like he'd heard that Pearl Harbor was a deserved strike. "When a half-dozen people have died and we could be responsible?"

No one responded. If Rakesh was going to lead the battle against Kendrick, the others would let him. Most had direct investments from Kendrick's fund outside of Dolphin. They had reason to stay on his good side.

"The key word is *could* Kendrick," said Rakesh. "We've reviewed the code and we're ninety percent sure we weren't responsible."

"It only takes one percent to get pregnant," Sharon said dryly. Rakesh steeled his gaze at her with the unadulterated look of disgust, but she was preoccupied, basking in Kendrick's approval.

"Do we need to let someone go?" Kendrick suggested.

This was it. The opening Royce was waiting for. "We don't need to let go of talented executives who've created a fantastic product," Royce began, his confidence capturing the attention of the entire room. "What we need to do is make sure our distributors trust in our product, preventing competitors from wooing away our clients."

"And how are you going to achieve this?" asked Sam Michaelson. Royce anticipated this from his attorney and silently thanked him. Sam had become the youngest managing partner of Grayford Strong, the second largest buyout firm in the country, at forty-one due to smarts, not his looks or pedigree. For now, Royce knew he was willing to hit the ball into Royce's side of the court and see what he returned.

"We take away the opportunity for Dolphin to be the scapegoat in the future."

"How is that possible?" asked Kendrick.

"Retain the very firm handling Blenheim's crisis." It took a moment to sink in, but Rakesh looked as pleased with the idea as Kendrick was appalled.

"Give money to the agency who laid the blame at our feet?" Kendrick asked.

"Precisely," continued Royce. "I know for a fact that Mackelby got a hold of Austin Marks at karate class. She negotiated a deal with the CEO within the hour. That meant she had one day to work on the strategy and another day to create a series of ads which are now already on the air. She controlled what the media saw, heard and reported. This woman, and her firm, have that kind of influence. Very few American presidents are so lucky with their own press secretaries."

"What if Kendrick is right?" Sharon asked, looking at Kendrick first. "If the whole thing melts, then what?"

"Then," paused Royce, delicately lacing his long, tan fingers on the table, "it's potentially the fault of the service company hired to represent the firm. After all, many a shareholder lawsuit has been filed against the law firm, consulting firm, and even public relation firm that failed to serve the *'best interest'* of their client."

The entire room was silent as each member digested Royce's response.

"Doing unto others, is that it?" concluded Kendrick for the group, obviously unwilling to say anything that could be misconstrued in the future.

"I'm simply ensuring the financial and shareholder goals of this company will be met," explained Royce smoothly. "And hiring the best crisis communications firm in San Francisco is the most prudent strategy to employ at this juncture. I'm calling for a vote so we can make the necessary financial budget allocations."

"What's the name of the agency?" asked Kendrick with a note of resignation in his voice.

"Marks Communications. Led by the founder, Austin Marks. Potentially the smartest person in this entire affair."

CHAPTER 7

"This is it?" asked Garrison, picking up the paper Max had put on his desk. It had been all afternoon and there was little more than a timeline of Austin's appearances in San Francisco and her client list. "I could find this myself." It wasn't exactly true, but he was making a point.

"The woman is a ghost," said Max defensively. "There's this last page," he said, grabbing another sheet from the printer.

Garrison scanned the document and grunted. Max explained that he'd paid a few hundred bucks to a background checking service used by dating services that culled physical addresses, former employers and even neighbors. From this, the only physical address to appear had been in New Jersey, and that was six years old. Her current address was listed as an office downtown and a post office box.

"The only write up on her is also from New Jersey when she purposefully got in the way of someone's fist," Max explained, leaning back in his chair. "Apparently, they were after her client and she took the hit for him." It was only a paragraph, alongside a picture of her and another person on the ground. "She did the noble thing," Max said, his voice carrying a hint of admiration. "Austin Marks is a relatively common name, and I looked at hundreds of photos of weddings, graduations, but can't find her anywhere."

"She could have changed her name," Garrison said. That meant more digging.

"On it," Max said gruffly, not from anger, but because he'd missed something so obvious that Garrison caught.

"Or, she could be gay," Garrison hypothesized, remembering her obliviousness to the man at the hotel.

"No. Way," said Max with confidence. "Look at that woman. Her eyes. The way she dresses." Garrison wasn't going to disabuse Max's innocence with the reality that many beautiful women preferred lipstick.

"You give me her address and I'll tell you if you're right or not."

Max handed it over. "Going old school?"

"No law against following someone."

Garrison turned to his computer. There had to be something on this woman. Life for Austin didn't start in Jersey with her getting clocked. He'd keep going until he had her complete story. And the first chapter was going to begin this evening.

"Garrison, where's my article?" bellowed Kell.

"On it!" he yelled back.

He turned to his computer and started typing. He'd crank out his usual fluff for the paper, but he now had a new mission. The start of a series on a woman who spent her life behind the scenes. No longer.

When Austin walked in to the lobby of the office building, she found her employees strewn around the open space separated by two-story stone columns. Each person had their laptop and cell-phone, working one, or in some cases, both simultaneously. None looked worried that the hundred-year-old building, constructed of marble imported from France, was going to come rumbling down.

Asa commandeered the corner of a coffee table, with his three team members around him. His ocean-blue button-down shirt fit snug against his well-proportioned upper body, the slight sheen of the high-thread cotton silk blend highlighting his flawless skin. If the public relations industry wanted to create a pinup calendar, Asa would be the African American chosen for the job.

He should be on the large billboard for the Gap off Embarcadero. Not that she would ever get close to giving him that kind of compliment. He already knew it.

Nichele Mayer, another director and Austin's first hire, sat with her team members on a couch. Austin had initially thought romantic sparks would fly between Nichele and Asa. After all, Nichele was an exotically beautiful Eurasian with a 'bit of Native American' as she liked to say, a perfect match for Asa's tall, urban look.

Austin's hypothesis had been right. Sparks had flown alright, just the wrong kind. Nichele saw right through Asa's charm, shooting him down hard and fast. Assigning her rejection to jealousy over his recruitment and salary, Asa had rebounded with the grace of a boxer who'd won the match but was still smarting over losing a round. They got on well enough, as long as they weren't on the same account. Susan, the third director, sat along the inset window at the far wall with her staff of two. She was more round than tall, ivory white skin against muddy brown hair, the combination unintimidating. She was the perfect individual for working with the government and public policy world, environments that bored Austin to death. Darren, the last director, was sitting on the windowsill, his two team members on the floor, laptops on their thighs.

"Your uncle has called my cell phone twice," Jackie told Austin. She nodded, heading to a corner and called him back. He answered on the first ring.

"I'm fine," she assured him quietly. "It's San Francisco."

"Yes, and the Metropolitan went down not far from your offices." She looked out to the street, watching professionals go in and out of Starbuck's as though nothing had occurred.

"And our old building barely moved," Austin replied calmly. "Can I call you later tonight, Romo? As you can imagine, we're in the middle of the Blendheim affair right now."

"Good press already, I see."

She smirked. "How in the world would you know?"

A soft laugh chided her. "Costa Rica carries this channel called CNN." She gave him verbal loves and returned to her team.

The group remained in the lobby for another hour until the city Marshal announced people could return to their offices. The afternoon passed in a blur of follow up media interviews where Austin was the silent party with Mackelby. It wasn't until 3:30 p.m. when the last analyst call for Blendheim was over that Austin took a break.

Asa joined her in the small kitchen. "You ever heard of a company called Interface?" She shook her head, chewing her apple. "They are the company that built the Metropolitan. It was their architect and plans, their building. I just got off the phone with the CEO. He wants to hire us."

Bad things are good for business, she thought again, and swallowed. "That was fast."

"He said they had already budgeted this year for a crisis communications plan and knew all about our work. Do you have any idea how much they will pay?" Unlike her, Asa's objectives had very little to do with helping the needy. He'd probably already run the numbers, figured in a cut for his bonus, and knew the visibility of the project would be a major bullet point on his resume. He didn't bother to mask his agenda; prestige was why he defected from Leonard to come to Marks. And money. She was extraordinarily generous with her employee compensation, giving account leads a healthy override on every dollar brought in.

"You're up next for a client," she said. "Can you handle the load?"

"Absolutely," he answered with confidence. "Our planning project for Demoine wraps Thursday." His ego pushed him right up to the limit of arrogance. She knew the schedule better than her own team and had no doubts about his ability to take it on. She was just goading him on.

"Then you better schedule that call," she said, suppressing her smile. He gave her a crisp nod and was gone. Asa was adept with managing tough clients even if he periodically evidenced a bit of chauvinism. Her mostly-female staff had strongly opposed Asa's hire, contending that women build stronger relationships with the press and governmental community affairs. But Austin had trusted her gut and asked her staff to put their prejudices aside long enough for the man to prove himself. The number of positive press mentions for his clients had at first equaled, then surpassed his peers. With respect came a tolerance for his attitude.

Asa's only other fault lay in his hips, or rather, the word among the media of his inability to keep his trousers up.

"Just don't let it interfere with current clients," she'd warned. "And don't double dip in the press. You won't know the meaning of being blackballed until it happens to you." To her gratification, Asa had been quick to understand that if he slipped up once, he'd be gone.

At 4 p.m., Asa dropped off a two-page dossier on Tom Montegue, Interface's CEO, and his firm. Asa was in Austin's office, sitting across from her, waiting for the call from Interface to come through.

"Before we start, great job on the latest systems upgrade," Austin told Asa, grateful they benefited from his value as a technologist, in addition to account manager. "It's demonstrably faster and the user interface to back-up all the data is fantastic."

"Back-ups are important things, as is hosted email. Never want to be prisoners to the physical servers here at the office."

The phone rang as Jackie sent through the call.

"Asa said I need to come up immediately," began Montegue, as though he were continuing a conversation he and Asa had been having. "Do you agree?"

"Los Angeles," mouthed Asa.

"Yes," Austin replied. "Asa's team will start booking appointments with you and the mayor, the head of the San Francisco Police Department and potentially the office of the Attorney General. It won't take long before lawsuits will be filed by a multitude of entities. We have to get all the players together to talk strategy or we will be relegated to the sidelines."

"Can you assemble your top executives up here for training?" asked Asa. "They'll need to be ambassadors for existing customers, distributors and local media in your territories, and you have many."

"Our executives are booked weeks out."

"Understood, but here's the challenge---" Asa tried to explain.

"Austin, is that really necessary?" cut in Montegue. Asa turned a shade of red, his full lips ground together into a thin line.

"Yes, it is," Austin said firmly. "You are going to have entities from Jakarta, where you built the Bank Tower, to Brazil where you put up the Lupeke Mall, all questioning your firm. On top of that, you will have building managers dealing with those trying to cancel leases or cut a better deal. Your team needs to prepare and proactively address every situation."

"I'll have them up there Wednesday."

Asa lifted up a piece of paper and she gave him a nod to speak. "Tom, based on our conversation, I went ahead and started to create the blueprint of the crisis plan we will follow…"

Austin listened to Asa's plan. He must have a lot of confidence Montegue was going to sign at whatever price she put on the table. "I've already got the team writing the scripts for call centers we use. They cover the three continents that will address citizen complaints or concerns—unless you already have a telemarketing group?"

"We're a construction firm," Montegue answered in a tight voice.

"We'll have a hundred people trained with our messages that can be up and running tomorrow morning," Asa continued. "I'd also advise you get in touch with the CEO of your primary insurance provider."

"Our corporate attorney thought the whole point was to delay payouts as long as possible. Why not wait until the claims start filing in?"

Asa used his hand to gesture that Austin answer the question.

"First, the insurance firm will assign an investigator," Austin began. "This person will want to determine if, when, and what type of construction fraud was committed. As long as the insurance company is faced with the prospect of paying up, their buzzards are going to fly around the carcass in search of a weak victim. *We* have to learn what *they* learn at the same time."

"Our attorneys aren't investigators," Montegue stammered, his voice now vacillating between disbelief and anger. "They handle contracts." Austin looked at Asa. She wanted him controlling the account and managing the client.

"This isn't about putting off payments," Asa said firmly. "It's about controlling information."

The CEO started to argue about the details and she inhaled. They had no time.

"Tom, the more we communicate, the lower the risk that investigative reporters will come searching for new data. We must be proactive so they understand we are on it." She thought of reporters like Garrison, who would be lurking on the corners for just such information although she doubted he'd be covering something as mundane as an earthquake.

She heard Montegue yelling in the background to his assistant, telling her to track down the CEO of the insurance firm.

"Yes, Stenson Black. GreatLife. Get him."

Austin thought the name sounded familiar, couldn't immediately place it and got back to the present. The truth of the matter is that something had caused the building to drop when all the others around it were still standing, intact. *Why* wasn't her problem, any more than the Tylenol crisis public relations team was responsible for a deranged person tampering with the pill containers. Her job was to get the facts and work out a solution.

Austin turned the conversation to their financial arrangement.

"Tom, we work on a twelve-month contract; the time it takes to deal with the crisis, the follow-up and preparation for future issues. The fee is six and a half-million, half due up front and the remaining paid out in equal monthly installments."

Asa quietly pushed a client list across the table to Austin, accompanied by a wink. Interface was a St. Louis-based behemoth with $3.4 billion in revenues. It took six regional presidents and a slew of vice presidents responsible for business development and project management to handle all the work. Interface could handle the fee.

"We can jump on this now or wait," she offered. "Of course, the longer we, or any firm you hire, waits, the more expensive the program will become because the environment you face will be that much tougher."

"Does your contract have a breach clause?"

He's in. Negotiating with men was so predictable. They always wanted what they couldn't have.

"No," replied Austin. "A breach on our side is nothing more than our clients giving us a 30-day notice."

"How often has that happened at Marks?"

"In six years of business, not once."

"Send it over."

CHAPTER 8

The call finished, Asa leaned back in his chair, his eyes fixed on Austin.

"Where'd you come up with that figure?"

"It's what the market can handle," said Austin, her voice as flat as her lip line. One paid more in times of desperation, and Montegue was desperate. "It also didn't hurt that I listened to what you told me about how much Campbell charged his accounts. I had no idea how significantly we were underbilling."

Asa nodded, eyes squinting. She knew coming to her firm was just another stepping stone in his career path, and he would one day leave, going to another, or start his own. He'd take every bit of learning he'd gained with him. The reality didn't bother her in the least. There were certain people who were climbers, social or financial. Asa was both. Even with his future departure a certainty, the timing was not. She knew he'd stay around as long as he kept learning and making money.

Austin asked Jackie to assemble the team in the conference room, and Asa to provide a summary of the project. "They are likely to give some pushback on the client load," she warned him.

"It's why I came here," he said with confidence.

Once in the room, he gave the group the overview. It was Susan who spoke first.

"My group and I will be stretched since the government will be involved."

"Can you do it?" asked Austin.

"With enough hours and money, anything can be done."

Asa turned to Nichele. "Taking Interface will certainly impact us," she offered. It was her team who had been up around the clock working with the agencies to churn out the Blendheim ads. Nichele opened the project plan on her laptop. The group was quiet as Nichele's eyes scrolled down the page, calling out the major milestones left to hit. "We'll need a lot of extra hours for the next two to four weeks, but it's doable."

"Then you have carte blanche," said Austin. "The three and a quarter up front will cover it."

"Did I hear that right?" asked Darren. Austin nodded, knowing they were all figuring out their share of the revenue.

"Austin, one thing I didn't have time to ask about was bonuses." Austin applauded his strategy. He was using money as the tipping point for motivation among his peers. It was another reason Leonard had been so angry he'd jumped ship.

She glanced at him then around the room. "I was thinking we start with bonuses for everyone when the first money comes in instead of after. Just this once," she added with a wink. She was sure her accountant would be slightly paranoid, but between Blendheim and Interface, their cash flow would be assured for the next few years.

The response to her comment was vigorous head nodding and a few glassy-eyed stares.

"Let's get going then."

At six p.m. Austin's phone rang. Only one person called her at this time.

"Hi, Karen."

"Have you been flattened like my breasts after nursing?" asked her best friend without missing a beat. Austin issued a burst of laughter, causing Jackie to peek her eyes just above her station. She always knew when Austin was on the phone with Karen; spontaneous outbursts were the norm.

"Look at the time! Of course, I feel flattened. Besides, why aren't you sounding stressed out? You're closer to the Met than I am."

Austin picked up the framed photo that showed Karen in all her glory on the side of Mt. Rainier, her freckles popping from her cheeks and nose, her shoulder-length red hair forever getting stuck on her pink or gold-colored Juicy-tube lip gloss.

"Nope. I'm at the beach house," replied Karen.

"Oh right. If I had that home, I'd be there all the time too."

Austin thought Karen had lucked out in life. She'd been born tall and lanky, with equally long fingers. She'd started playing gigs at clubs as a teenager, talking her way past the manager long enough to sit at the piano bench. Her talents had put her through college, while she pragmatically turned to the more lucrative field of software sales. Her first employer went public a few years after she'd joined, and the second was acquired within two years from her start date. She banked the money and continued to play a few nights a month for fun.

In the photo, Karen was standing beside her then-boyfriend, now husband, Dirk. He was two inches shorter than Karen and smiling like he'd won the lottery.

Austin thought he had. Karen met Dirk at one of her gigs, and they'd become great friends. He was a kindred artisan spirit, crafting custom furniture, eking enough money to live and travel, which they did even as the relationship was platonic. When Dirk developed testicular cancer, she offered to put him on her life insurance. That meant getting married.

"Are you crazy?" Austin had exclaimed at the time. "You guys aren't even sleeping together."

"He's a good guy," Karen had responded. "He needs the insurance. Besides, a marriage license is just a piece of paper." They decided to tell no one about the marriage, lest they offend either one of their parents.

Karen helped Dirk through chemo and in the process ended up falling in love. Karen maintained marriage was still only a piece of paper, but Dirk's more traditional family wanted a wedding, so years after the fact, they had a formal affair at the San Francisco Cathedral. One kid arrived and they had another on the way, thanks to some sperm Dirk froze before his therapies started.

Austin told Karen about her new client acquisitions; the only female she knew who was secure enough in her own financial situation to understand and appreciate the accomplishment.

"Any good cuts among the new clientele?" She meant cuts of meat. Man meat.

"Ribeye only. I'm looking for filet," countered Austin.

Her friend dismissed that with a snort. "If you spent less time in the dojo learning how to break someone's neck and more time in a short skirt, you might get somewhere."

"Sure. I'll stop going on Friday nights and the heavens will open, raining down men."

"Look, you've earned the right to be happy," her friend said, her voice still playful but now sensitive. Karen had an ability to use honesty to cut through Austin's emotional layers without offending her. "Just find someone's who's not as boring as dry toast, will ya?"

Austin promised. In the quiet of the room, her eyes burned hot, and the muscles between her shoulder blades bunched to the point she was sure she felt individual knots rubbing against the back of her chair. The sun had long since set behind the downtown skyline, covering the city with a grey that wasn't entirely gloomy.

She liked the city at night. A different town came to life when the married demographic left for the suburbs, leaving the inner core empty for the singles who filled yellow cabs that darted around the narrow, one-way streets with the zeal of lightening bugs.

Tonight, she wouldn't be among them.

She rubbed her neck. *Not that I am on any other night,* Austin thought, leaning back towards the computer. Then she remembered her last boyfriend, and felt at peace. She'd rather have no man than experience that level of pain again. With a determined attitude, she refocused on her computer. Nothing bad came from that black device on her desk.

CHAPTER 9

As Royce watched the wood paneled garage door silently slide up, he was comforted by the sight of his wife's Lexus in the bay. The car was an extravagance, just like the garage door. The difference was that she had put both on her personal American Express.

He appreciated Tracy entered their marriage with some of her own money and that she spent it on items she really wanted. He stopped short of admitting his pride was hurt when she'd come home with a gift similar to, and often nicer than one he'd purchased for her.

"You can buy me things that are small and round," Tracy often said, lifting up her fingers. *Like more rings*, he knew, *each one worth more than the last*.

They made a good team, he and Tracy.

Royce drove his car into the garage, turned it off and waited until the door settled onto the black and white checkered floor to get out. Six cars, one for every occasion, but as Tracy joked, one vehicle short of a week's worth.

He remembered a time when life was simpler. The money wasn't flowing as freely as it was now, but neither were the demands and pressures of running a public company. Those were the trade-offs, he thought, getting out. This is what he'd wanted since college; a home in Woodland Hills, CEO of a public company, a gorgeous wife and a fleet of cars.

Hearing him come into the house, Tracy emerged from the hallway bathroom, fingers behind her ears. She was putting on perfume, a habit she had before he came home. At first, he'd been flattered, interpreting it as a sign that she was dressing up for him, ready for some action. After a year or so, he'd figured out that it was just in-bred in Tracy. Somewhere, someone had told her that one must be presentable every moment of the day. Heck, she probably put perfume on at 10 a.m. in the morning before tennis.

Don't complain, he told himself. *Better to have a woman who takes care of herself than not at all. Good body and good mind.*

Tonight, he needed her good mind. Tracy's intelligence was validated by the Oxford degree she kept in her credenza drawer. She'd even done their taxes the first few years of marriage until he'd told her he'd rather pay the accountant than have her take the time.

They were perfectly paired in every way…but one.

There were no little voices greeting him at the back door or the sound of running feet. It was Tracy's singular failing, thought Royce, but he couldn't blame it totally on her. In his arrogance, he'd thought he could convince her kids were in their future, or that she'd suddenly manifest a motherhood gene. The opposite had happened. Tracy had become less interested in a family and ever more focused on the life he, Royce Slade, had designed. Homes. Events. Fancy dinners with a room full of acquaintances. He tried to turn it off, but every so often, he wished for two sets of young eyes, full of undiluted, unadulterated love and innocence greeting him. That's when he thought of Elaine.

Not now. Now I need the tough-as-nails, cold-and-calculating Tracy.

He and Tracy dined at the marble counter and Royce told her of the board agreeing to her idea.

"You should have seen Kendrick. He looked like he was going to swallow his testicles." Tracy laughed. "Just like you said he would, I might add," he said, tipping his beer bottle her direction. Her smile continued as she placed her lips against her wine glass.

"I told you that you didn't need to call Elaine. Her value to the company has long since passed."

Royce nodded his head, knowing anything else he said would be misconstrued.

"I should be back at the office, alongside my engineers, overseeing and supporting my team." He caught her look, the feeling he had for one woman instantly transferred. All he could think about was her lips around him, stroking him and doing nothing more that gratifying his desires.

"I know what you're thinking," Tracy said, running her tongue around the rim of the glass before setting it down. Royce's heartbeat increased in speed when she stood and started undressing. Stripped to her bra and panties, she swiveled the bar stool towards her and smiled.

"I think you need some moral support to sustain your first, long night, don't you?"

Thirty minutes later, as he fastened his shoelaces and picked up his keys, he glanced towards the bedroom. Tracy was in the shower, her life completely unchanged by the events of the day. She had her tennis clothes already laid out. Two hours in the evening ensured she slept well and kept her legs trim. It also set him free to go back to the office where he needed to be.

He revved the engine, heading down the drive. The image of Elaine came to his mind again. She wasn't just a former love. She had been his co-founder, the creator of the original Dolphin Software twelve years ago when it all started. She had been with him and in love with him until he'd pushed her away.

Royce merged into traffic. In five minutes he'd be at the office. He could only hope his lead engineers could figure out what really happened to the software over at Blendheim, because if he couldn't, Royce would have no option but to track down and call up Elaine himself, and beg her to come back.

That would be one way to start a fire in his homelife, a flare up he didn't need right now. He was already feeling the heat.

CHAPTER 10

Tuesday at 4:50 a.m., Austin and Mackelby were on the phone with the east coast analysts and press. She'd taken a caffeine pill to give her the lift that three hours of sleep couldn't.

As Luther answered questions, she listened, clarified where necessary, and multi-tasked, rapidly typing responses on blogs, texting reporters and instant messaging with Mackelby's on-site assistant. By six, a very weary sounding Mackelby asked her how long this pace was going to continue.

"Another day, maybe two," she replied, reiterating it was less hectic than normal, by virtue of the fall of the Met. "This afternoon and tomorrow we will go through more trade press."

Asa and his team were working at their own frantic pace, writing, editing and placing the scripts and releases and booking appointments for the next few days of Montegue's life. Jackie brought in food and Austin ate while the phone was on mute, getting up only to use the bathroom.

At four, Austin finally removed the earpiece, laced her fingers in front of her chest and stretched.

"Going to class tonight?" asked Jackie.

Austin nodded. "Only for an hour," she answered, exhaling as she slowly lifted her arms over her head, leaning as far back as possible, curving her spine. She couldn't miss training, especially on a day like today. Her body needed a break as much as her brain.

"You going to get much sleep?"

Austin smirked and shook her head. "Probably not," she admitted. The 24-hour media wasn't sleeping, neither could she.

After a tough class, Austin sat down in her car, drained. She'd learned the essentials of how to break a person's shoulder from three different angles. It was worth it. Beyond the practical application of the techniques, the way she figured it, the investment of ten thousand a year was a cheaper alternative than seeing a therapist or joining a health club. She'd dropped two pounds for every five hundred bucks she'd spent and the exercise helped her cope with the drawers of emotional baggage she kept carefully shut.

A minute after she started the engine, Austin received a text from Jackie.

"Are you freaking kidding me?" Austin said out loud. She deftly cut in front of on-coming traffic on Sansome, missing a biker by inches. "It's just a phone call," she said to herself, repeating Jackie's words.

Austin activated the Bluetooth and placed the call. "Hi Royce, it's Austin Marks returning your phone call."

"So glad you found the time to call me back," he said. She instantly thought he didn't sound like a man who drove a Prius to take a JetBlue flight. She imagined something closer to a Gulfstream and car to match.

"I understand you are close to achieving your black belt," he remarked, and she pressed her lips. He was either creeping her or Jackie had told him where she'd been. Both were uncool.

"Good for keeping away the bad guys," she replied. "I was told you are interested in becoming a client?"

"Yes, but first, I'd like to thank you for not mentioning our name specifically during the press conference. I was discussing it with the board, and we have a few ideas I'd like to run past you, in person. Since you're in the middle of working with Blendheim, how about we have lunch towards the end of the week?"

"Jackie owns my schedule, so if she can find a slot with your assistant, then we'll make it happen."

Austin drove westward along Market Street, then left onto 17th Avenue, a street lined with side-by-side, three-story flats with single car garages. Her apartment was on the west side, one of the few homes with trees in the front. She pulled her car into the driveway and manually lifted the garage door, thankful to see an open space.

Not that thankful, she thought, briefly subdued by a sense of loneliness when she saw the space beside hers occupied. Someone was having a sleepover, and Austin was the person everyone counted on as being flexible when asked to move her car so their friends could stay overnight. She wouldn't regret leaving behind the communal car-sharing arrangements when she upgraded her living situation. She pulled down the garage behind her, jogged up the stairs and closed the front door behind her.

Not very aware of her surroundings, thought Garrison as he watched from his parked car. He'd followed Austin from the karate studio, easily tailing her in the light traffic. From the clothes she wore and the car she drove, Garrison had expected her to live in the Marina district, a place filled with former college frat boys and sorority girls, complete with sand volleyball courts that paralleled the paved biked path that stretched from the Embarcadero to the Bay Bridge. When she drove right through it, he figured the journey would stop at the lily-white neighborhoods of Russian Hill or Presidio District.

That didn't happen either. Austin continued to the predominantly Spanish occupied Mission district, mildly surprising him.

Just as she pulled up to what he assumed was her home, Max had called him with Austin's birth name: Austin Carmichael. She'd changed it just before she got her first job in New Jersey.

"Go rogue," Garrison encouraged. "Orphanages, divorce files, anything under that name." Now, as he waited in his car, Garrison received an email from Max.

When I'm right, I'm really right, Garrison thought smugly.

Austin had attended prep school in London and that took her through graduation at sixteen. Max found photos of her winning an equestrian event. Horse riding was an expensive sport. An announcement in the paper identified Oxford had accepted her and the start date. Max had learned she'd been accepted and registered, paying the first year in advance, as required. But she never showed. The registrar had a note of 'death in the family.'

Reporters like him had a motto to live by and it proved true time and again: where there's money, there are secrets. Austin Carmichael Marks reeked of money. And that meant big secrets.

Austin Carmichael Marks. Carmichael sounded foreign, and he thought of the color of her skin. Spanish? He knew many Mexicans who had blond hair, due to the early German settlers. Maybe that was part of her background.

He rolled down the window an inch. The air by the bay was a full ten degrees warmer than up on the foothills, where the fog of the ocean crested and hovered. It was said San Francisco had at least eight different eco-systems, and this determined where each ethnic group lived. Here, in the flats, the homes were generally rented out to multiple occupants, who sought to live economically in the most expensive city in the country.

Garrison watched the street. What was a woman of her affluence living in a flat, several streets off the main drag, and within spitting distance of gangs? It didn't make any sense.

He rummaged through his glove compartment, finding his objective. He opened a week-old bag of beef jerky, staring up at the three-stories, hoping Austin would make her presence known, and that he'd get some kind of view into her world.

CHAPTER 11

After a quick shower, Austin sat down behind her home office desk. She pressed the play button on an Internet radio station and caught up on the Blendheim news reports, answering emails from reporters and other items from Asa.

She found a paragraph-size write-up announcing Campbell's firm was getting into the crisis management business. *No time like the present.* He was still in an idiot, and an old one at that. The crisis business was a young-person's game, ideal for those without relationships, hobbies or the desire to have a life.

"As I've often said, when things are bad, business is good, and Leonard," she continued, speaking directly to his professional picture on the screen, "you like the easy life way too much to mess around with this industry. You don't have the stamina."

It was after midnight when she finished. She entered the kitchen and removed a plate of leftover pea vines and barley shaved noodles from the fridge, not bothering to heat them up. The garlic was strong, but she had no need to fear her bad breath would offend someone in the bedroom.

Then why is the notion bothering me a bit more than usual? Because I don't have anyone to share my little triumphs with, like landing Interface.

But did anyone else in her company have a partner? She considered the romantic status of her employees. No. Not a single person in her office was married or had children. Susan had the glimmer of a serious relationship, but even he was living in Paris, working on a two-year consulting project.

Only Asa had an active social life, and that was more about conquests.

Austin went back to her email. Just one more check on the news feeds then she would go to sleep, she promised herself. At no time did it occur to her to look out the window and down below.

Garrison had a perfect view to Austin's third-story apartment. The screen from her computer lit up her face, shining an ethereal hue upwards, ghostlike. Her hair was pulled back, so he could see her long neck as it dipped into the collar of her leopard print top.

He leaned over the center console of his Acura, a parting gift from his wife who wouldn't deign to keep the thing when their marriage ended. Thankfully, the heated seats worked when the engine was off. When he leaned back, he dropped his pen between the floorboard and the seat.

He cursed. That was going to be a pain to get out. Had it been any old ballpoint, he would have let it go. But this wasn't. It was a digital voice recorder pen that looked like a Mont Blanc. It was identical to the real version, but on one end it held a chip that recorded up to two giga bites of information. He'd never come close to using the 128 minutes of record time the baby held, but for seventy-seven bucks, he couldn't pass it up.

Garrison wedged his fingers between the metal bar and the floor, snagging the pen with a fingernail that needed trimming. *Gotcha*! Since he was down there, he curled fingers around something larger. The small amplifier he'd picked up from the Internet, buying in to the marketing tagline of being 'the PI's choice.' He'd totally forgotten about it. The small disk was only the size of his palm, and not the most robust. It had a range of maybe a couple hundred feet. The earphones were ugly, silver things, but in the middle of the night, it wasn't going to matter. Private cops didn't troll the Mission District like they did the Presidio. But hey, it was here so he might as well put it to use.

He set it up and listened to the clicking of her nails against the keyboard, the soothing music playing in the background.

Garrison glanced at the time. Did the woman ever sleep?

Garrison propped the handle between his folded arms, leaned back the car seat and adjusted his headset, comfortable in the folds of the warm leather.

"Dating service. *Right*." The thick sarcasm in Austin's voice jolted Garrison out of his slumber. It was now after one. He shook his head and adjusted his arms, checking the voice recorder. Nothing on the playback other than typing, until this. "Unreal," he heard her mutter. "Bloody Uncle Ramon. That's what I need right now. Two clients in serious trouble and he keeps pushing me to find a boyfriend."

Garrison shuffled his rump, tempted to turn on the car but decided against it. He didn't want to have the cops called on him.

"Are you *serious*?" he heard her say. He squinted in the dark, seeing Austin's face clearly through the glass. "Ramon, *what* in the world did you sign me up for?"

Garrison moved his cold hands to type the word into his Notes. *Dating service. Uncle Ramon.* No Uncle had turned up on Max's search.

The woman needed a life. He'd give it another five minutes and then was gone.

An electronic beeping caught his attention. Someone was calling her at one-fifteen in the morning.

"Yeah, noticed that you were on IM. You saw what I forwarded you?" Austin's laugh was a low, full-chested sound with a higher lilt at the end, like she was getting away with something. Unexpected, but not entirely unpleasant.

"Who else?" She paused then said, "And who comes up with a name like Midnight Blue other than a Silicon Valley entrepreneur?" Another burst of laughter. "Besides you, he's the only other person getting on me all the time. Very funny, I know."

The changing screen threw a blue sheen on Austin's face, then another page of white. She was going through different web pages on her screen. "Yeah, I couldn't help checking him out. But who knows what my uncle put in my profile.

Can you imagine the crackpots that will get sent my way? I could end up on some missing person's file." More laughter.

Garrison typed Midnight Blue into his device. Sure enough, a dating site for the wealthy and desperate.

"Oh, I see it now," Austin said, leaning forward to the screen.

Garrison looked down at his phone, reading through the information, scrolling along the main page as Austin verbalized what he was reading. A solid twenty-five g's to sign-up and only the men were charged. What a racket.

He heard Austin promise she was absolutely not going to give it the time of day. She had too much work, too many distractions and no interest in being pursued by a man who couldn't get a woman on his own.

"Karen, why don't you look at it for me and see what you find?" she suggested before she laughed again. "Sure. Tell me if you find any beefsteak," she said with skepticism. Austin spent a few more minutes behind the computer before the light disappeared at the familiar clicking sound of a laptop lid closed. Austin stood, her figure briefly outlined. Garrison sat forward in his seat, ignoring the cold leather. He typed out another short text to Max before he started his car and headed home.

CHAPTER 12

After Austin unlocked the office door at 6:30 a.m. she went straight to the coffee machine. She loaded up a double espresso, stopping to pop a caffeine pill.

"You're going to be sorry later," Jackie warned, entering just as Austin was pouring a cup.

"So will you. I said you didn't need to come in."

"I want good coffee so I had to arrive before you, and once again, you beat me." Austin laughed. Her attempts at coffee resulted in a great smell but it tasted like dirt. She spit it out, and handed over the container to Jackie, who promptly put it in the sink and started the water, shooing Austin out of the kitchen.

Austin laughed and followed her orders. In her office, she looked at the time, calculating how long it would be between the meteoric rise from the energy pill and the inevitable crash and burn. Last night she'd only managed a few hours of sleep, and even that had been restless.

That morning, she and Mackelby had a series of ten-minute calls with reporters from the trade magazines and he was a guest on two podcasts. By 8:30, he was off and she was receiving a compilation of press hits from her team. By nine, the wire from Interface cleared the bank and she notified Asa. At ten, Jackie brought her a juiced up mineral water and a granola bar.

"What's Midnight Blue?" she asked Austin, her eyes twinkling. Austin cocked her head then figured it out. Her uncle would have used her work email address, and Jackie had administrative privileges.

"My uncle took my romantic life in his hands," Austin explained with a sigh, taking a bite of the bar. Jackie raised her eyebrows and rolled her eyes.

"Of all the times…" Jackie said, shaking her head.

"No kidding."

"Well, it was two years of barely hanging on, then the setback which-shall-not-be-discussed, and then an upward tick in business for the last two. He probably figures you're financially stable, so why not? But it might take a while to find someone *suitable*," she said, putting the last word in air quotes.

Austin glanced at her computer. "More on this topic later?"

"I could do it for you," Jackie offered.

"Sure," Austin laughed, relenting. "You and Karen can both be dating trolls for me." Thankfully, when Uncle Ramon had created her profile, he used her physical description along with information about her work, but withheld the name of the company and hadn't uploaded a photo of her. "As of last night, my profile hadn't posted because I have to approve what Ramon wrote."

"Was it good?" Jackie asked.

"It was accurate. Don't know if that qualifies as good, since I can't see the competition."

"It's the norm of modern dating," Jackie said.

"I don't *care*," Austin replied, a mock wail in her voice. "It's more stressful than being on the line for millions of dollars in contracts, which, by the way, I need to get back to."

"Great. It's settled then. I'll check out the site in my spare time. At some point I may want to get on that site as well."

"You go for it," Austin advised. She had enough to do without adding the distraction of a dating service. When Jackie left her with a stack of press releases to approve, Austin forgot all about Midnight Blue.

She cracked open a window. When the owner of the building offered to change out the windows for something modern and glazed and more secure, Austin would have none of it. She loved being able to actually have a window in an office and theft wasn't a concern. They had no cash and her staff used laptops.

The only items of value were a server rack and computers housed in a closet, but even that was probably low value.

A visual of Asa leading their last team meeting came to her. They were still distant, but at least respectful. When he was hired, the others had been threatened by his aggressive approach to landing clients. Over time, they had to grudgingly credit him with helping bring the company to another level of success; he was unemotional, a trait that seemed to give large companies comfort during times of crisis.

If only he was as steady outside the office as he was within, Austin thought again. Well, he was only twenty-eight.

Austin went back to her work, unaware of the set of eyes on her.

It took Garrison an hour of going between floors on the building adjacent to Austin, his story of wanting to take pictures easily accepted by the security guard when shown his press pass. The guard helped him find an unoccupied corner office on the seventh floor and left him. Garrison, quietly chewed his gum, watching Austin go through the motions of her day. He absently picked up his Red Bull, annoyed when only a few drops hit his tongue. He was beginning to wonder if he had the stamina to keep up with her schedule, and it had only been twenty-four hours.

His only accomplishment was satisfying his editor. He knew Kell would fire him if he missed a filing, so before leaving the office, he'd penned a witty and pointless piece on the general manager of the Forty-Niner's and the birthday party he put on for his wife. It was gross, he'd told Kell, which guaranteed it would run. The party had included a male stripper urinating on the stage in front of a crowd that included the mayor, and that was only the beginning. Garrison hadn't been there, but one of his former college buddies-turned high-falutin' restaurant owner had sent him a few screen shots, most unprintable.

Kell had been giddy with excitement, sure the manager would be forced to resign his position and the mayor would spend the next week justifying why he was at the X-rated party instead of attending a charitable function for the Children's Hospital.

Garrison zoomed his lens in on Austin's screen. He couldn't quite make out the text, and short of putting a microphone in her purse, which would land him in jail, he wouldn't have any idea what she was saying. Even the cops had to get a court order for planting a wire.

After an hour, the security officer came by again.

"You are welcome to see my entire roll of digital pics if you'd like before I go," he said, but the man waved him off.

Garrison's stomach grumbled. Behind the building was Tommy Toy's Chinese, a place he hadn't frequented since before his divorce but now wasn't within his reporter's budget. Frankly, neither was Starbuck's at four bucks a cup. It was however, the obvious choice, located next door to the building where Marks had her offices.

He slid his long lens from Austin's office down to the Starbucks. The patrons consisted mostly of men in suits, checking their phones, texting, drinking or reading the paper. He looked at each person, hoping that one might work for Austin. He surveyed the tables and counters, then finished up at the bar that faced the street. A man sitting on the side, facing the street and closest to the wall, would be easy to remember. Unlike the other patrons, who wore ties and overcoats, this guy wore an olive suede jacket over a round neck light tan sweater.

"SoCal trash," he muttered, sure he was right in his assessment. No one from Frisco wore suede in the city. Come sunset, the fog would roll in and the light mist covered everything in sight, ruining the sensitive material. A text came through from Max and he immediately picked up the phone.

"Are you kidding me?" was all Garrison asked.

"Would I kid about something like this? Six and a half mil from Interface is what the man told me, and that's on top of the four for Blendheim."

Ten million in less than a week for helping solve problems. He bet the stock holders would really love to hear where their money was going.

"So," Max said, interrupting his thoughts. "You going to run with it?"

"I can't verify the numbers, but it will do the one thing she doesn't want, which is to put the spotlight on her."

"That's kind of mean," Max said hesitantly, as if he knew Garrison would swat his head if he were nearby. "She's not the person who has done anything wrong."

"No, not yet. But that's not the point."

"I don't think Kell is going to care about her revenue, but if you say so."

Garrison thought the kid might have a point. "Maybe a competitor will be righteously mad about this and willing to talk. Max, look up other companies who offer crisis communications in town. I'd like to see the list." He put away his camera, dutifully handing his visitor's badge to the security guard and wished him a good day.

"Come back anytime for more shots," the man said.

"Thanks man. I might just do that."

CHAPTER 13

Across town, Scott Petrano, the forty-four year-old deputy attorney general for the State of California left the Federal Building for a very late lunch. He nodded at the guards, who knew he'd be gone ten, maybe fifteen minutes, coming back with whatever food he could find from a street vendor. They also knew his wing of the building was working overtime.

Petrano speed-walked past City Hall and onto Van Ness and Grove. He saw a cart on Hayes, the vendor already starting to close down. He broke into a run, and once he arrived, Petrano convinced him a cold hotdog would be better than a fatality. The guy laughed, appreciating that Petrano was a regular. Expressing his thanks, he paid and started walking back, pulling the foil away from the dog. He took a bite with one hand and a swig of Coke with the other. At least the Coke was meant to be cold.

He took his time, needing the quiet. Over the weekend the Blendheim affair had been just another drug incident. Yesterday, the CEO made the standard public apologies and Petrano didn't give it much thought. He had a legal opinion on the mayoral succession to provide, a review of new plea agreement language for white collar criminals and shutting down an old power plant in the Potrero district. That Blendheim's manufacturing snafu caused a few people to die was unfortunate. It was a part of life, and his office rarely, if ever, got involved in those types of debacles.

Then his office had gotten an anonymous tip. Common enough and it would have gone into the round file had it not been found by William Cole, the tall, twenty-six year old who graduated cum laude from Berkley's BOLT law school.

Petrano took a sip of Coke as he contemplated one random act of fate and Cole's determination.

Truth be told, Cole's interruption had irritated him. His junior attorneys knew he took on one type of case: high profile vote getters that were short on time investment and long on public impact. Petrano loved prosecuting cases where public anger instilled the AG's office with a Robinhood sense of virtue for the small, unsung victim against the wealthy, corporate greed mongers. Over the course of his four year term, he had shared the glory with local district attorneys, creating a legion of loyal followers instead of fertilizing a group of potential political competitors.

As he finished his meal, he reflected on Cole. The kid had ignored his direct request and chased down the tipster anyway.

> According to the caller, John Doe, there is a high likelihood that the cause of the defective drug was a problem with the software that controlled the manufacturing process. Blendheim had originally insisted this to be the case and pointed to a systems provider as the root cause.

Although this was interesting, it certainly hadn't been compelling enough to make a case out of it.

> The caller said someone within Dolphin Software is working to sabotage the software files and in turn, impair select customers. When asked if Dolphin's executives were involved the caller was vague. He implied it was someone close to the executive team, but not the team itself. When asked if this was done by someone no longer with the company, he was also vague. This brings up the possibility of a criminal investigation, corporate espionage and technology terrorism.

Petrano had seen this type of exchange before. An informant gives just so much information and then backs off, either expecting or wanting someone else to find out the rest. It allays the guilt they may have felt in calling the attorney's office, since conclusions were drawn on the other end without giving away enough information to incriminate the people they might know personally.

> Doe sounded sure that another event would happen in the future. He also suggested that we should investigate the role of the software in the Metropolitan Building collapse.

Cole had underlined this part. Two separate and distinct types of events, each resulting in fatalities. One could have been planned while the other was a random act of nature. Petrano thought it was a stretch to think both were being orchestrated and linked by software.

Even so, Petrano could see why the tenor of the call caught Cole's interest more than the actual information. This was entirely too original and creative to be your 'good guy with a grievance' issue. Cole concluded the report with a character sketch on the caller and next possible steps.

> Doe sounded older, and quite possibly from an upper middle-class background. He spoke as though he was tired, the burden of this knowledge weighing him down. Based on the information Doe provided, it is the recommendation that we assemble a situational analysis of everything we know regarding both cases. We should be prepared to move it higher on the priority scale as it could quickly become a formal investigation.

Because he was always late getting back to his junior attorneys, they often went ahead on the preliminary stages of an investigation without his OK. If they didn't, nothing would progress. Case in point on this one. Had Cole waited for

Petrano's formal approval, he would have missed out half a night, and Cole wasn't the kind to sit. Cole was twelve years younger than himself. He was top of his class, thorough, ambitious and clean cut. He did two years of post-grad work with a federal judge in Washington before being offered the job with Petrano's office. The other hires in the office put in the hours for ego; Cole did it because he loved the job. Over the last year, Petrano found he gave Cole a bit more attention than the others.

Petrano jogged up the steps, nodding to the guards, and passed through security. Cole had found the perfect type of case to investigate. It was low risk with a high potential for success and commensurate glory. Just the way Petrano liked it.

CHAPTER 14

As the sun began to set over the bay, Austin sent a note of encouragement, thanks and praise to her team. The initial coverage on Blendheim had been mostly overshadowed by the media's frenzy of conjecturing why the Met had fallen, and all eyes had turned to Interface. It all added to Asa's pressure.

She had zero sympathy for the man. He'd wanted the account and the money.

Mackelby called as she was closing down her computer. "Do you know, Austin, that our hotline is full of doctors asking when the ban will be lifted? They don't seem to have any concerns."

"Nope, and neither does the market. Have you looked at your stock? The hedge firms are snapping up shares like they're going to sky rocket, and they probably will."

The final subject was the likely, forthcoming fall-out from the software vendors used by Blendheim.

"Ching can't replicate the problem," Mackelby was saying. "It could very well be it's our issue, as in, human data entry error. Too early to tell, Ching says."

"On the topic of Dolphin Software, Royce contacted me yesterday. He wants to talk about partnering up, and I'm going to meet with him to learn what's on his agenda."

"Do I need to come?"

"Probably not. I really don't see what we are going to talk about. We have one client, and that's you."

Across the street, Garrison was doing his best to lip read. He wasn't very good at it, and Austin wasn't making it easy, constantly turning her head towards the water and then back to her screen. He did catch two bits before he set up his small amplifier. The pharmaceutical company stock was up and Royce Slade wanted to meet.

"Only another hour today," Garrison told the security guard, who passed by again, waving. "Writing my piece now."

In fact, he was writing a piece, this one on Austin. The anonymous tipster had been specific on the money, source and dates of her new clients. Max was right, to a point, and Clive worked the piece so it appealed to those who dealt in the currency of gossip. It was like knowing the amount Ryan Seacrest had paid his attorney to defend himself against sexual assault claims; the dirty little secret people would love to discuss but never had the chance.

They would have it now.

Garrison finished the final paragraph and plugged his earpiece into the amplifier.

"I've just cleared your schedule," said Jackie, entering Austin's office. "Asa said the city wants a round of meetings tomorrow morning."

Austin looked at the clock. "When did this happen?"

"Out of the blue. Asa got a phone call from William Cole, over at the AGs office. Petrano's campaigning this year, remember?"

"That's a lot faster than normal." Garrison watched Austin grimace. It pulled down her cheeks, but only slightly. "Looks like Interface is going to serve as a launch pad for his formal race, and just when I thought it was going to be smooth sailing for us."

"Did you notice the meeting location for the Interface training prep?"

Austin leaned forward. "Am I reading this right?"

A tall, handsome black man walked in the room. "The San Carlos airport. What?" Asa said with a laugh. "You haven't taken a meeting in a private jet at the airport?" Austin shook her head. "As you requested, Montegue has executives flying in from all over the place, landing at SFO. We figured the best and only place to meet and have a confidential discussion was in the private plane of a board member. Everyone is being picked up in town cars and will convene in," he checked his watch, "approximately forty minutes."

"Thanks for another late night, Asa," she remarked, already packing her things.

Garrison watched Austin with growing interest. She was completely unaware of the man called Asa scoping her chest when her eyes were down.

"I don't expect it's going to be more than an hour," Asa said. "The execs will stay over at SFO and be on the first flights out so they can do damage control around the world while we meet with the city folks."

"Did Susan's contacts learn anything else about Petrano?"

"Cole contacted Lt. Nolebrow at the SFPD. That's all we know at this point." He passed her a sheet of paper. "This is for tonight."

"Thorough," she complimented. "Any concerns I should know about?"

"There's this Frenchman, Chabot. He's the head of operations and a real prick. I'm sure you'll know the perfect time to wield your verbal bat."

"Leave here in ten?"

"Meet you at the door."

Garrison snapped on the lens cap and collapsed the listening device. He decided to change the final paragraph on the piece, read it twice through and then sent it off to Kell. It was going to place Austin in the hot seat for once, and he was going to enjoy watching her bounce.

Only a time or two.

He hustled to his car, intent on getting to the airport. He needed to be in place, with his listening device set up. This, he wasn't going to miss.

CHAPTER 15

On the other side of the Pacific, a warm, light mist covered Elaine Sylvies, crinkling her sun-bleached hair into soft curls and turning light beads of sweat into rolling drops of water that ran down her taut, sinewy shoulders. Elaine dipped the graphite paddles evenly through the shallow water making figure eights as she propelled the single person kayak along a stream that eventually ended at a waterfall.

Over the last thirty months, she'd made the trek dozens of times. First with companions, then alone as her endurance and strength increased. She preferred rowing into town and back instead of taking her four-wheeler through the mud. The effort was as much to keep herself in shape mentally as it was physically.

She propelled the kayak under a bridge where tourists leaned over the edges, snapping photos of a view that stretched from the ocean to the mountain beyond. It was the image that had captured her imagination and inspired a move to the hills of Kauai after leaving Dolphin Software.

The more distance between the memories of me and that company the better.

As the current picked up, Elaine repositioned her feet against the Kayak's emerald green inner walls. She guided it towards the riverbank and beneath the overhanging trees that formed a natural arch providing a three-foot buffer from the white water of the rapids.

While her body pulled and struggled to maintain the forward momentum, her mind relaxed, focusing on the task at hand. She was dependent on no one, beholden only to herself; charting and recharting her destiny through the jungle.

"What are you going to do?" Royce had asked when she tendered her resignation. "It's not like Kauai is bustling with mental stimulation."

"That's the whole point," Elaine told him, placing the few items on her desk into a box. She'd been on auto pilot at the office for the previous twelve months, although she hadn't told him that. "My computer functions quite well with a satellite." Besides, with the stock options she held, she didn't really need to do a darn thing, and they both knew it.

"What about being a consultant?" he suggested. "You could travel all over the world, and I know you'd like that."

She shrugged noncommittally. Royce knew her decision wasn't about relaxing or traveling, but he was either in denial or hoping she'd volunteer more specific information as to why she was finally leaving.

Once she left, she gave a few friends her email, but no phone number. If they wanted to talk with her, they could do it by her preferred method of communication.

Elaine pushed the memory away with a stroke of the paddle. The only reason she was making the trip into town today was because the post office had notified her a letter had arrived. It wasn't from the company she co-founded however, it was a letter containing vague references to her departure from Dolphin, the current state of the company and potential problems.

It was then that Elaine realized just how out of touch she had been. Having not talked to anyone at Dolphin for over a year and reading only local news on her computer, she had steered clear of any major high-tech stories.

With a strong thrust she guided her kayak onto the narrow grassy area to the right of a thin waterfall. Her legs pulsed with effort as she made her way up the steep but solid wooden steps to her lanai. She stripped off her clothes, placed her waterproof backpack on the table, put on a light wrap and went to her computer.

"Wake up, Lucky."

The computer screen activated at the sound of her voice and a three-dimensional green and blue parrot yawned. "I'm awake," it said, indicating the screen had moved from standby to active.

"Run a search on all news to do with Dolphin in the last six weeks please."

"Are we digging up a relic from the past?" It was one of several automated responses Elaine had programmed the bird to respond with when she requested information on Dolphin. By the time she'd left, things had deteriorated so badly with Royce she had incorporated her mood into her new system. The negative responses generated by the computer were meant to dissuade her from checking up on the company.

It had worked wonders.

"Maybe," Elaine replied. "Hopefully it will be buried again soon enough."

The parrot squawked before it flapped its wings, circling inside the computer before disappearing while the search scanned the internet databanks for the desired result.

When Elaine chose this isolated location, it was an emotional decision. Exactly what she was not. Lucky was her companion, one that could only respond to questions involving specific data points. The beauty of this strategy was prevention from qualitative questions involving emotions. To those, Elaine still didn't have the answers.

Minutes later, the bird reappeared on the screen. "I'm baaack."

Elaine couldn't help smiling. She'd wanted it to have a life, a personality and a sense of humor. Technically, Lucky was neither male or female, leaving the gender up to Elaine depending on her mood.

"What'd you come up with?"

"Eight pieces by Dow Jones, AP and UPI."

"Summarize please."

"Dolphin is profitable—"

"Good."

"Founder Royce Slade and wife attend black and white ball—"

"Skip," Elaine said.

"Don't interrupt."

"Sorry." Elaine's programming attitude was coming home to roost, literally and figuratively. Now that she was in a rush, it occurred to her to go strip out the ad-libs. But she knew in another week she'd regret it and have to program everything all over again.

"Dolphin announces new product…"

"Skip."

"Blendheim has narrowed the possible causes of deaths down to several software providers. The complete list of software companies includes Abbot Software, BasicOne, Dolphin Software, ElegantForm…."

"Stop. Start from the beginning of the story."

Elaine listened, sitting back in her chair.

She sat in front of her screen, scanning the pieces one by one. Dolphin was potentially responsible for the deaths of nearly a dozen elderly people from the drug Lucine. The longest, an editorial, was in a small, San Francisco paper called *The Weekly*.

> This is not an editorial on the validity or truthfulness of the claims made by Blendheim. It is about the possibility that a piece of software is being blamed for killing innocent people. Granted, technology has given us many benefits—ATMs on the corner, cars that have digital maps on the dashboard, cellular phones to collect emails and make a reservation at the best restaurant. But if the downside of giving a machine the power to make decisions without human checkpoints is that one incorrect byte of information has potentially catastrophic consequences, from the safety of the car we drive to the ingredients of the food we eat to the drugs we take, shouldn't we all be a little bit more concerned about the

implications before continuing to rush headlong into developing more products that could just exacerbate the problem?

"Why the frown?" asked Lucky.

"What?" Determined to not fall into state of self-pity, Elaine had taken snap shots of her face smiling, frowning and a variety of images in between those two states. When her camera compared her desired face with what it saw on the screen, Lucky responded accordingly. "I'm fine."

"No, you're not."

"You're right. I'm annoyed I made you so smart."

The bird cackled and flew around the screen. It made her smile, even though she was still irritated.

If the problem was Dolphin's, someone had to be tinkering at the root level. Furthermore, someone would have had to remove the business rules coded in the production to accept discrepancies in the drugs. Computer intelligence could fail at any point, but it was more reliable than humans by far. The only answer was that someone had recoded the software to do all of this on its own.

But that was unthinkable. Just as crazy as someone knowingly wanting or allowing something as tragic as a dozen random deaths to occur.

Elaine stood up and made herself a Mai Tai. She swirled the straw in her glass and took a long sip. She knew lots of people who acted without morals to achieve a specific end. Look at Royce. He hadn't done anything illegal, he had just been amoral.

"But this," she said out loud, "is immoral in the best case and illegal in the worst." But to what end? If Dolphin did put out a faulty product, how many products…thousands… would be affected. The entire country. What had begun with smaller, regional clients had naturally evolved to global firms all of the world, in major industries.

But that was a ridiculous, conspiracy theory concept. Impossible.

As the screen saver turned on, Lucky's eyes closed for a nap and Elaine knew she needed to find out three things. One, what did Royce think of what was happening? Two, why had someone sent *her* information about Dolphin? And three, what was she going to do with it?

CHAPTER 16

Austin powered down her computer, slipped on her Burberry shell coat and accepted a protein bar from Jackie. Twenty-five minutes later, the cab pulled through the private entrance at the San Carlos Airport where executives parked their personal planes. The driver slowed and turned right down the smooth, obsidian black road, closer towards the Interface plane. If success were measured in terms of corporate jets, Interface would be a multi-billion- dollar conglomerate. It was a Gulfstream V.

I should have charged more.

A man wearing jeans, a maroon baseball hat turned backward and a casual pullover top approached the car. He glanced at Asa first, then Austin, awarding them both a brief nod.

"You the two with the public relations agency?" Austin nodded. "Let me get you settled." He gestured for them to follow him towards the aircraft. "The others are delayed, so make yourselves comfortable." With that, he waved his hand upward, towards the steps.

She made her way up the stairs and through the inset, mahogany galley. The bar was stocked with Perrier Jouet champagne and crystal glasses hanging upside down in their immovable holders. She chose a plush, white leather wrapped chair and Asa sat across from her, placing his briefcase on the couch next to him. She opened her computer, glancing at the plasma screen above Asa's head as her wireless came on line.

"How much?" he asked.

"Twenty-five, give or take," she replied. That was millions. Asa squinted in thought, probably figuring out just how long it was going to take him to be able to get a similar plane. He was a man who wanted to roll in style.

"A few more clients and you could afford one," said Asa, a tinge of envy in his voice.

"It's like boats, Asa. Don't own one. Have friends who do."

He smirked. "You've done a great job getting to this point."

"Just so you know, the trips I've taken on client's aircraft never included drinking champagne or watching cable on a high definition plasma. I was the one with my laptop open the moment the plane hit ten thousand feet. Pretty much like right now. The hired gun."

"Check it out," she said. She clicked on the television, looking for the Blendheim ads. It didn't take long to find one.

Asa turned so he could watch the screen. It was a fifteen second spot Nichele had constructed using a collage of Blendheim customers stating the products had elongated or improved the quality of their lives. The ad concluded with snippets from smiling employees in engineering, customer service and quality assurance, all pronouncing quality and life satisfaction as the reasons they came to work.

It was upbeat. It was convincing.

Austin reviewed her emails, one catching her eye. It was from the administrator of Midnight Blue. A tinge of discomfort coursed through her stomach. Her basic profile had been accessed. That meant either Karen or Jackie had approved and posted it for public consumption.

Someone has checked out your profile. If you want to learn more, click here.

Oh man.

Austin typed a short text to both Karen and Jackie with the news, asking who had selected the men for her to look at. Karen replied in the negative. She'd been too busy with a kid who had the flu to open Midnight Blue. Jackie acknowledged picking a few she thought would appeal to Austin.

Austin's heartbeat quickened. The very notion she was being virtually checked out was weird, like trying on a bathing suit in a dressing room that had a one-way mirror. Two more congratulations emails followed the first. OK, so three was good, *I think*.

She looked outside. Six men and one woman walking towards the plane. Were any of these men on the dating site? It was an intriguing notion.

Jackie was right, of course. She was never going date unless she set a deadline.

Check MB she typed, setting the reminder for midnight. That was when she expected to be home. She had a few more hours until she had to face her fear that her heart might get demolished again. Alternatively, she might luck out and find a man who was her equal, who believed in treating a woman right and wanted love as bad as she did.

Garrison watched the town car drive through the gated entrance to the private hangers, knowing he wouldn't make it past the security guard. He flipped the Acura around and tried to keep pace with the vehicle as it traveled south along the road adjacent to the covered hangars.

The visitor's parking lot was in an area designed to provide the best view for take offs and landings. Once he found an open space, he angled the vehicle in a way where he could watch the proceedings through his binoculars.

Austin sat by the window. Today, she wore a dark blue, slim pair of pants with a cropped jacked. It was modest, fashionable, and sexy all at the same time, reminding him of an ensemble his ex-wife would have worn.

Garrison opened the box containing the electronic pieces he required. The equipment was on loan from a cop who had gone astray with a male prostitute a few months prior. Kell wasn't interested in 'yet-another-gay-story,' about a white, married man playing on the other team, but Garrison didn't tell the cop that. He let the guy drone on, blaming his drinking and marijuana, along with a story about a wife and a kid on the way, then told him he'd use his compassion that night and not run the story.

His kindness would be exchanged for a favor in the future. Today he claimed that favor.

"No way!" the cop had exclaimed when Garrison asked for the equipment. "I'll get fired. You know it's only for governmental agencies."

"That presumes you still have a job to get fired from," said Garrison without emotion. "Don't worry. You'll have it back in a few weeks."

He assembled the miniature satellite with a microphone in the middle, plugging the end into an audio device. He was testing the machine as another town car drove up to the jet. Five men and one woman walked up the stairs and into the plane. By the time he had his earphones in, the conversation was well underway.

I'm sure this is how Woodward and Bernstein would have operated, he told himself.

"It had to be the products, not the people or the process," argued a man with a French accent.

"We understand Louis, but we must be clear on the best way to discover the reason this happened, assuming it can be found." Garrison knew the voice by now; it was Asa. With his binoculars, he could easily see Asa's unblinking eyes drill into the short, balding Frenchman. "At present, the media have already focused their attention on the quality of the materials used by misguided greenies."

"They are idiot, non eco-friendly zealots, using nothing more than their ignorance to justify their opinions." The Frenchman was rabid.

Garrison watched Asa lean forward, placing his elbows on his knees, clasping his hands together in an earnest plea. "Louis, it's a non-issue. The inspections were made on the buildings and approved. If we don't assist in the effort, you aren't going to have any buildings to build."

The thin-framed man's face turned an orange-reddish color, darkening the freckles on his cheeks.

"Louis, we must be transparent in our communications without being too revealing," clarified a stately woman in her fifties. "As the company's legal counsel, this is not only smart but lawful."

By now, Garrison had pulled up the corporate web site and was putting names with titles. Louis Chabot was responsible for all facets of construction. His butt was in a sling. The attorney was the woman.

"Chabot," said Austin, using what Garrison thought was a conciliatory tone. "This is not a personal attack on your team. It's about releasing information to the Attorney General. The sooner we communicate, the faster those heat-seeking missiles will look for another target."

"I'm assuming electronic is best?" asked a man with dark circles. Garrison looked down at his screen. Tom Montegue, the CEO. *Of course, he had dark circles.*

"Can you get the information to us first thing tomorrow morning?" Austin asked. Montegue agreed. Chabot pressed his thin, white lips shut and adjusted his glasses.

"That brings us to the next item: samples," Asa continued.

"I don't agree to supplying samples," said Chabot.

"Why not?" asked a third man.

"Come on already," Garrison muttered, wanting something juicier than rocks going to the lab. "Gimme something I can use."

"Original samples from the lab are necessary to be tested against those from the site," Austin said to Montegue.

That a girl. Pull in the honcho to get your way.

"Asa, what else?" asked Montegue.

"I've already heard from Devann Boggard, the investigator at GreatLife Insurance. He'll be on site for the duration, looking at Interface, but also the material manufacturers and the government."

"I don't follow," said Chabot.

"The government approved these manufacturers," Asa continued. "You only used materials that were approved. You weren't responsible for their creation." Garrison watched the heads nod in the room, all except for Chabot.

"You mean you want us to potentially turn back the entire green construction industry a decade by blaming this on the products we used? Absolutely not!"

"Austin, the green materials aren't limited to the Met," said Montegue soberly. "Marcus' team is everywhere. It's the future of construction."

"Okay," Austin began. "This discussion is centering on the products, and mostly, the cement, which seemed to buckle. Who produces it?"

A short silence followed, as though they knew where she was leading them.

"Sneaky woman," said Garrison out loud. "Another diversion tactic, just like Blendheim and the software firm."

"It could crater them," said Montegue, "and their firm."

"Then what do you prefer: their stock or yours?" Austin asked.

"You're one cold woman," said Chabot.

My thoughts exactly, added Garrison.

"You are welcome to find yourself an individual more empathetic, Chabot. Did you get to be a vice president with your charming personality?" Garrison held his breath. Her last word was said with a challenge. "So, what is it? Your company or someone else's?"

Garrison found himself nodding. "I'm on board," said Chabot with all the joy of getting a colonoscopy. Austin was cold, but she was also right. This was her job, to save the stock and the company, not to win friends.

And you don't have any from what I can tell.

CHAPTER 17

Garrison had heard more than enough and put away his equipment. Before he started his car, a vibration at his phone alerted him to a new message. It was Max.

More news.

Max had found seven other people with the last name Carmichael at Oxford in the three years prior and after Austin's acceptance. When he cross-checked all seven with the prep school, he came up with only one woman who seemed like she could be related to Austin. Max dug into his portable cooler on the floor of the front seat and opened a cold can of caffeine.

A picture came through. It was of a mousy-haired young woman, her nose too large for the frame of her glasses and her bony shoulders looking like a hanger for the cap and gown she wore. There was no resemblance to Austin at all. Another dead end.

Garrison was about to write Max a scathing text in response but stopped short when he received another text from his ever-determined assistant.

Tracy Carmichael. Older sister to Austin.

So? Garrison typed back.

Ready to heap praise on me? Max typed. Garrison grunted. He was going to heap a lot of whoop-ass on Max if he didn't get to the point of his texting. *Tracy Carmichael transformed herself into THIS.*

Garrison brought the device to his eyes and squinted, skeptical Max had the right person. A new nose, cheek implants or a good make-up job, the dirty brown hair color switched out to blond. The boob job wasn't over the top, but enough to graduate the woman from concave cavities on her chest to discernible mounds. Garrison had to admit, she was unbelievably attractive in her new manifestation.

And another

It was a photo of Austin taken from the recent Blendheim press conference. Max had put this picture next to Tracy Carmichael.

"Well tickle my ears," he said to himself. The two women now looked like twins, except that Austin's hair was cut into a sexy but professional A-line around her face. Tracy's shoulders were arched back, her hips front, as though standing for the wedding photographer meant posing on the runway. Austin, though unsmiling in the photo at the Blendheim conference, was poised; her eyes intense and filled with an earnestness.

Tracy Carmichael had literally paid to be transformed into the mirror image of her sister.

He continued staring at Austin's expression, and the more he stared, the more she looked like she was making a case, pleading for understanding as she gazed at someone in the audience….him?

Suuuuurre. She had stared at him during the press conference all right, but that was to make her points in an attempt to undermine his story.

A vibration alerted him to another text from Max with one last photo. This time, it was a wedding photo of Tracy. Garrison blinked, then slowly, holding his breath, he read the names below the picture. His heart stopped with shock then jumped up and hit him in the throat. He wanted to down a cup of whisky just to celebrate his good luck. Tracy Carmichael had the good fortune to marry none other than Royce Slade.

Collaboration? Wrote Max. Two women, one agenda. This was getting better by the minute.

He immediately pulled out his notepad and started the outline for a second story.

Elaine had tried to put the whole darn mess with Dolphin out of her mind last night, but it was impossible. Her tie to the company, to her baby, was indelible.

Just like my tie to that man had once been.

But no more.

She made herself some coffee and immediately started the task of breaking into the system she had created. She began by activating a false customer account she'd created early on. Elaine queried the list of paying customers, intent on using a working account to poke around the system. Fortunately, at least one administrator hadn't changed the password as recommended.

"Lucky, we are in the database," she said softly.

Theoretically, she hadn't broken any laws. She justified her actions by comparing it to opening an unlocked car door. She was taking a peek inside, but as long as she didn't take anything out or drive off, she figured she was safe.

She acted quickly and methodically, mildly shocked a more secure operation hadn't been put in place since she'd left. She hoped it would result in a short exercise to determine if the statements in her anonymous package were truth or lies.

But then what? What am I supposed to do with the information?

She started the executable to copy the latest software into the cloud. It was going to take a few hours, giving her plenty of time to consider her next steps.

Elaine went to the window, running her fingers through her hair, the warm breeze giving her no comfort. Even the image of the ocean beyond didn't settle her emotions.

Her journey with Royce began when she'd been a twenty-two year old Ph.D. student. She'd won a contest at MIT to solve the parking fine collection process, and he'd searched her out and offered her a job as the founding engineer of his new company—which was little more than an idea.

"Anyone who can make millions of dollars for Boston can make a couple for us," he'd reasoned, using a perfect balance of fact and flattery.

Elaine moved into the kitchen, got a mango and began slicing off the thick skin. Her winning project had been a good one. Every day, Boston gave out thousands of parking tickets and failed to collect. In desperation, the head of the traffic division appealed to the Engineering department at MIT to see if his students could come up with a solution to solve the payment problem.

It was Elaine's proposal that won, followed up by the code she'd written. In a few months, drivers who received the dreaded yellow boot on their tire could open their phone, pay the ticket and be given the code to unlock the boot. A message transmitted back to central, and a roving crew picked up the boots. It was immediate, it was foolproof, and it had been Elaine's first major invention.

Elaine put the mango pieces on a plate and went to the front porch, sitting in the hammock chair, remembering those first few months then years. After Royce outlined the idea for his new company, Elaine had summarized it in a sentence.

"It's document management software, but the document is really any object that's electronic."

"Exactly," he confirmed. "Once digitized or electronic, the author, version, history and any other data is cataloged and tagged, following the item everywhere in the system. Sophisticated workflows, with thousands of contributors and hundreds of steps, all perfectly managed, routing from one point to another, checked off, signed off and proceeded, all without the person taking a single step or printing a piece of paper."

Elaine began working on Royce's concept before graduation, skipping commencement to relocate to San Francisco. She'd been awarded patents on the process and technology while Royce got the funding. Nine months later they were ready for testing, and it was Boeing who used the unproven software in its 777. When the first 777 debuted to the market and took flight, so did Dolphin.

Suddenly an unknown software firm in Silicon Valley was on the front page of the *San Jose Mercury News* tech section, and like a heat wave, investors and Wall Street lined up at the company's front doors.

Elaine chewed slower, recalling Royce when he was at his finest. Lining up money and applying his business mastery, he went after any industry with multi-step processes, like automotive, aerospace and transportation. One by one, he signed up the largest firms, and like pins in a bowling lane, the other, smaller companies followed.

During this whole time, she and Royce had been good friends, confidants, then one day, they crossed the physical and emotional line of demarcation. They spoke of a future together, the company management being passed to a seasoned CEO and starting a family.

All that changed when Dolphin went public.

The beginning of the end, she mused, throwing the last bit of her mango into the jungle. It wasn't the travel schedule that stretched their relationship like a rubber band. It was the social aspects, none of which appealed to her. The more she resisted attending the events with him, the less time they spent together. He took up golfing, she started running. He attended opening nights, she hiked in the canyons. They grew apart, in the true and classical sense of the word. The physical infidelity occurred long after the emotional infidelity had begun.

She didn't blame him then or now. To deny someone else his dream wasn't right, and that's what she told him. Her resignation had come as a shock to her team but not Royce. It was time to move on, and she had, quite easily.

Now, she was being thrust right back into the world of software, and she wanted answers. For herself, her stock, and the knowledge that all was right on the mainland with the baby she'd created. She'd solve the riddle posed, and with any luck, Royce would never even know she was involved.

CHAPTER 18

At home, Austin took a quick shower, put on leggings and a tank-top. Her hair up in a towel, she sat down at the computer. Before she started typing, she had a call she had to make.

"What's the surprise? Guys are checking you out."

"Karen!" she said, a bit exasperated.

"What's wrong? People meet and hook up thanks to the greatest dating invention ever. Why not you? And for all that, I'm still not sure why you don't take Asa up on his offer at least once." Karen laughed. "He's waaayy better than dry toast. Besides, people who work together sleep together all the time."

"You know, there's the #metoo movement and at some point, it's going to come around for the #Mantoo movement, where women in positions of power seduce or coerce their male subordinates. That's long overdue and happens all the time, but not here. Not with me."

"You mean you wouldn't sleep with him even if he didn't work for you?" Austin had to laugh. For as much as Karen was a joy in her life, she lived by a different set of values. For Karen, getting into bed with a person was interesting in the same way driving a new car was interesting. There was no emotion involved; only the ease in which the gears shifted and the speed at which the corners could be taken.

"Not a chance," Austin replied.

She said goodbye then flipped open her computer, and seeing no urgent emails, she accessed the Blue Midnight site. She saw five new inquiries and her heart bumped.

She hesitated a few seconds, then clicked on the first one.

Garrison was running on fumes. He'd followed Austin back to the office, then to her apartment and paid a woman to move her car, faking a hip ailment. He set up his listening device while she was in the shower. He was now starting to feel more than a little sleazy by listening to her personal conversations, but he had to admit, he was hooked. When else had he had the chance to get the behind-the-scenes on a woman who had caught his interest?

This will be the last one, he promised himself.

By the time she got on the phone with her friend Karen, he heard every word. He munched on pistachios and winced at the jolt of caffeine from the Red Bull that flowed through his veins like the venom of a rattlesnake.

He wasn't all that interested in Austin's sex life unless it was going to help him, but he was beginning to wonder if Austin was a prude right out of the seventeenth century. Who didn't sleep with a fellow worker when it was convenient?

Garrison thought about that one. *Me, actually.* Too messy. The one time he tried it, it backfired, the woman complaining to everyone at the paper how she talked about a story idea and he stole it from her.

Kell had loved the story, right up to the point where his boss reamed him a new one for snaking it from under his co-worker.

"Sleep with the dog on the street," Kell had told him, "but have some class. Don't steal your co-worker's stories after you've slept with them."

Garrison watched Austin put the phone down and examine the blue screen. He wondered when she would get to the bait he'd set out for her.

"Jackie, did you review these at all?" Austin muttered out loud.

Garrison was happy the woman talked to herself. "Five-seven and one-forty? A wee-bit too short for my taste. Next."

Glad the woman had some standards, even if she did take on liars and companies with murderous tendencies. "Oh, now that's a picture for you," she continued. "Not into the bearded, lumberjack look no matter how interesting it might be to date a neurosurgeon. And is that even allowed in the ER?" Garrison coughed up a pistachio, snickering. "And in door number three we have…a red-haired pickleball champion who happens to be imported from Scotland, whose family has a coat of arms, and who is way…too…full of himself for me. And Karen asks me why I don't date."

She shook her head. "And you are telling me that each one of these men has a spare twenty-five grand?" she exclaimed. "They are obviously excluding the part where they are running drugs on the side."

Garrison grinned for a moment. This woman had a sense of humor, if nothing else.

Austin put both hands to her forehead, leaning over on her elbows, her hair falling forward, masking her face. She held the position in silence for several minutes. He turned up the sound to its highest volume and caught shallow breathing. Finally, she removed her right hand, leaving her cheek cradled in the palm of her left hand, scrunching her cheek. She slid her hair behind her right ear, and he heard the clicking sound of the mouse.

"This is it. The last one. Don't depress me." Two clicks later, Garrison watched her eyes moved up and down what she saw in front of her screen.

Don't be nervous. It isn't personal. Still, he held his breath.

"Not bad," she said. Garrison wished he knew what section she was looking at. The bloody questionnaire had a dozen pages of questions he'd had to fill out, along with several essays reminiscent of the SAT exams. He saw a curl on her lips, and she put her chin in her hand. Tilting her head, she laughed out loud. "Funny, too."

Garrison had no right being on the site at all. He'd called the vice president of marketing and pitched the story of writing an article as an undercover review of the best dating sites in the city. The woman agreed, giving him a trial run for thirty days, assuming he had a positive experience, and also requesting that he provide her feedback on how to improve their service.

"Good taste in books," Austin said. "*And* you hi-fly? Now that's something I could get into. Too many soft-bellied, wine-drinking snobs in this town. That stuff tastes like yack-pee, but no, I can't be honest with anyone about that, because I'll offend most people living in northern California. And you do get bonus points for admitting you hopped on the non-drinking wagon so we don't have to spar about wine. You've kept me reading this far."

Garrison spit out some Red Bull. *Yack-pee? And really? She'd put on a yellow jump suit and let the skin on her face whip at 70 mph? The woman is starting to kill me.*

"Married once. I have no problem with that. And I quote, 'She ran away fast.'" Austin let out a peel of laughter. Garrison had been truthful for the most part, because he really had no clue as to what the woman would be attracted to. It was a thousand-to-one chance she'd actually correspond with him anyway, so why not be honest?

He unconsciously set down the Red Bull. Austin kept reading what he'd written.

"I lost my money and found it again, like the drunk Irishman on a Friday night who expels his beer and potatoes on the corner, only to find it the next morning as he stumbles out for eggs and sausage." More laughter. "OK, that was…seriously…funny and gross at the same time."

She kept snickering and reading, mumbling a word, here and there. This time, he didn't even notice his own smile. He was too occupied waiting for her to object to one of his answers. When she came to the end of his profile, she let out a huff of air.

"What? No picture? Are you kidding me? After all that?"

Garrison felt his cheeks heat up. He shouldn't care what she thought of him. This wasn't about dating her. This was about entrapment, his intentions to engage her in a dialogue so he could get a story. She picked up her cell phone and dialed.

"It's me again. I know, but I lied. I got off with you and looked at the profiles Midnight Blue sent me. What a waste except for the last guy." She paused. "Okay, I'll wait." Garrison was unconsciously breathing quickly. "I know, totally your sense of humor. And no picture! What a tease!!"

Garrison noticed how she rubbed the tip of her index finger along the ridge of her bottom lip as she concentrated on what was being said to her. "I don't know, Karen. I know you're all good with email relationships, but you are the same person who married a friend just so he could have health insurance. The universe was on your side when you guys fell in love. That was meant to be."

Austin pushed back her chair and glanced over the monitor, out the window. "Oh, now that's just mean. No one is going to choose between a hot looking single guy and an anonymous one with a personality. What have I got to lose by pressing the button, you ask? My pride, for starters."

Please, just a few emails or instant messaging, Garrison thought, willing her to touch the reply button. It was right there. His new, personal email account he'd set up for just this purpose was ready and waiting.

"Didn't you notice that the one thing this guy didn't put down was his place of employment? He could be an attorney or heaven forbid, a gynecologist!" More laughter and then the sound he wanted to hear; the one of reluctant optimism. "Retired? Oh. Didn't think of that. But then, I don't want some rich, trust fund person. I need a guy who uses his brains. Hmm. You do have a point. How many guys would want a potential dater showing up at their place of employment just for a 'check-you-out.' Yes, I have always been attracted to older men, true, but not too much older. I can't see kids right away but that's definitely out there. Yes, I promise to think about it. Maybe an email or two over the weekend."

Austin gave her friend the kiss off for the night and worked for another ten minutes, the screen changing from the distinctive blue of the dating site to the odd, greenfield color of email. Garrison tried to stifle disappointment that she didn't press the reply button.

My best just wasn't good enough, he thought, the bitterness he associated with the old song flooding him.

"Starting the day with Petrano. That will be fun." Austin was reading her itinerary aloud. "Ah, Royce." Garrison jotted down the schedule, getting ready to pack it up. He was just about to shut it down for the evening when her screen went back to blue. He stopped his activity.

"I really hope you're not a crazy, demented or old and retired man, because you're the funniest person I've met in a long time, virtually or in real life. Here goes something. I hope."

A second later, Garrison got a ping in his in-box, alerting him to the fact that one of his "interests" had clicked on his profile. Long after Austin turned out the lights, Garrison packed up his gear and slowly drove down the street.

CHAPTER 19

Elaine was sweating when she hung up the phone. The constant breeze dried the moisture from her forehead but the fear remained. She'd never spoken with someone from the attorney general's office or to any attorney under these types of circumstances.

"Did you get all that, Lucky?" She stood up, walking to the breezeway.

"Squawk! Recorded," her electronic friend confirmed.

"How long was the conversation?"

The bird lifted its wings above its head to form a circle. Its eyes joined to form a large dial, its beaks separating to form a big and little hands on the dial. "Seven minutes forty seconds."

It had seemed a lot longer.

"Replay, please." The fact that Cole had gotten her number caused initial resentment but that emotion quickly gave way to a desire for knowledge. She wanted to figure out the information he wasn't providing her and the reasons behind his questions. First the letter, then a call from the AG's office?

"Elaine Sylvies? This is William Cole from the California AG's office…"

She listened as the recorder played back the conversation word for word. She had been surprised when he told her that he had a subpoena requiring she come in for questioning. When he said they could avoid that if she wanted to speak over the phone, and do so without legal representation, she made the judgement call.

Once she'd given her recorded okay, Cole tuned his line of questioning to past employees, specifically disgruntled ones.

"As in fired employees that were upset with the company?"

"For any reason," he'd responded. "They could be unhappy with something about the company and left on their own or were fired."

She couldn't think of anyone of importance who'd left, except herself. She told him she didn't currently associate with anyone from Dolphin, nor had she been particularly close to any of her coworkers. "When I left, it came as a surprise to most of the engineering team."

Why had she left? Was there something she sensed within the company that made her leave?

No. As far as she was concerned, the company and management were stable. So much so in fact, that she had not bothered to sell the bulk of her shares, only enough to buy a small house and some land on a remote part of a remote island. Her stock ownership was a matter of public record that could be accessed by anyone anytime, thanks to the internet postings of shareholder stock sales. She made the assumption he'd have already checked her stock sales status, which he affirmed.

Elaine listened to the rest of the recording as she made a cup of tea. He'd asked pointed questions and she'd provided honest and factual answers.

Elaine pulled up the attorney general website for the state of California. She had an uneasy feeling that her window to discovering the real problems at Dolphin was rapidly closing.

At his cubicle on the second floor of the federal building, William Cole reviewed his notes from the conversation with Elaine Sylvies. For a computer geek and a reputed recluse, Elaine hadn't been too bad of an interviewee, once the threat of having her fly to the mainland was provided. She also had a nice voice. The kind that made him think she'd stop on the side of the road to help someone who'd broken down on his bike.

Was she aware of the news and deaths? Was she aware that Blenheim had cast doubts on the software it used? Did she believe it was or is possible for someone to manipulate the software to produce a specific outcome?

"Well, I'm not sure if you've read how document management software works, but it's like a freeway. Any type of motorized vehicle can move on the freeway, get into accidents, disobey the laws, or crash into another car. The makers of the freeway aren't held responsible for the drivers who use the freeway of their own will." *Good analogy*, Cole had complimented her.

"So, Dolphin created the technology freeway and Blendheim is the car."

"Yes, and Blendheim installed their own off-ramp then gunned the Ferrari to 125 and went off the rails. It's not Dolphin's fault."

Cole tried another tact. "Could something be inserted in the software to cause—I don't know—a ripple effect—on the outcome? Is that possible?"

Elaine was quiet for a minute. "Anything is possible Mr. Cole."

"Call me Bill, please."

"Anything is possible," she said, avoiding his attempt at familiarity. "Boeing could make a plane designed to fail at 50,000 feet but it would serve no purpose other than to ruin the company."

"True enough. But in the end, the impact could be catastrophic." Cole waited for her to respond, which she did with complete silence. "Well, I think you've answered all my questions at this time Elaine. I'll be contacting you again if I have additional questions. But I appreciate your time on this issue."

He threaded his long fingers behind his neck. Elaine said everything while saying nothing directly. It *was* possible to manipulate the software, and in so doing, it would be possible to alter the course of the outcome.

Leaning back, he came to another more important conclusion. If she knew this was possible, he wondered if she was going to sit back and watch events unfold, or if she was going to try to intervene. Or he pondered, was she the magician behind the curtain pushing and pulling the buttons herself?

CHAPTER 20

"You look unusually energized for having such a long 24 hours." said Jackie, handing her a donut. "Sugar. Good for the mind and terrible for the body."

"Thanks," Austin said, taking a bite. "You're doing pretty well yourself."

Jackie smirked. "Client stock price increases are a wonderful reason to maintain a smile and energy. And there's also this." Austin glanced down at the paper. The customer survey results indicated the public at large viewed Blendheim as responsible, credible and trustworthy. The tainted drug was random, a manufacturing glitch.

"Unfortunately, there's also this article. It's what the donut is really for."

"*The Weekly*? Where in the world did they get this information?" She saw the byline: Clive Garrison. He was becoming a constant in her professional life. "Unfortunate, but not cataclysmic, and totally the type of thing he would pass along."

Jackie stepped closer, the cherry red locks brushing her cheek as she lowered her head. "Do you think someone in this office could have said something?"

Austin gnawed on her lip, reluctantly nodding. The six-sentence paragraph identified the total payment amounts from Interface and Blendheim. "Maybe someone got drunk at a bar and spoke without thinking," Jackie suggested.

"Time to reemphasize the confidentiality aspect," Austin said. Garrison was like a little mite that rested on a wall and fell on the shoulders of the unsuspecting. Then another thought struck her.

Leonard Campbell. He had the motivation to get back at her and he was amoral enough to reveal the information, but Leonard only knew the figures from Blendheim, not Interface.

Austin gave Jackie the paper. She didn't blame Garrison. He wrote a snippet from information that had somehow fallen into his lap. And she knew that rarely happened. Now she had to make sure it didn't occur again.

Jackie called the staff to the conference room. Austin described the piece in *The Weekly*, and Jackie handed it to Nichele, who read it and passed it to the person next to her.

"I'm going on the assumption that this information was unknowingly and unintentionally shared in a public place," Austin said, noting the pale faces before her. "It's not going to help anyone conjecturing how, when or where. My counsel is to stay focused on the tasks in front of you and keep your mouth shut."

"Anywhere and everywhere," added Asa. She glowered at him. For all she knew, he could have been boasting as he was thrusting.

Austin went back to her desk, glancing through the notes Asa had written up regarding the interview with Lt. Nolebrow and Chabot. All things considered, it could have gone a lot worse. One more day and then the weekend.

The weekend…

Her eyes flicked over her monitor to Jackie then back to the new icon she'd placed on her screen the night before. Not now, she told herself.

What I really want to see is a photo of that guy on Midnight Blue. Then it dawned on her she didn't know what city the man lived in. She glanced around her office one last time, opened the site and logged in.

No profile picture for him, but then again, her profile picture wasn't up. Perhaps he was as on the fence as she was.

Austin opened her photos and found a black and white from her as a teenager. She paused, examining her younger self. Her cheeks were full, zero crease or wrinkle lines, straight hair. She looked similar, but it wasn't a mirror image. No one would ever link that photo to her now. She copied, pasted and posted it.

Just before noon, Austin picked up her purse and hefted the concrete samples Chabot's office had delivered to her and left the building.

Austin met Tom Montegue in the modest, but comfortable offices of the State of California Attorney General's office.

"Unfortunate piece this morning about our fees," Montegue said, his voice low.

"Indeed," was her response. She should have known he'd see it.

"Good morning," Petrano said, walking in the room, his hand extended as he introduced himself. Behind him was a tall man who looked like he was in his late-twenties, with the body of a basketball player out of high school.

"William Cole," he introduced himself, shaking hands before they all took their seats.

Petrano spread out his paperwork and started in on the essentials. A building down. Multiple casualties. A combative chief of operations.

"An anomaly that could be an act of God, espionage or fraud," Petrano concluded, as eloquently stated as if he were before a jury, and probably as well rehearsed. "The state of California and the people of the city of San Francisco, want and need an answer."

Asa, you deserve a dinner on me. Her man had correctly anticipated Petrano's approach. Montegue was prepared and gave the perfectly crafted line Asa had written. After acknowledging the tragedy was in fact, a natural disaster, Montegue described the different suppliers, vendors and contractors who were being reviewed. Not just by Interface, but the SFPD, and Devann Boggard, the lead investigator from GreatLife Insurance.

Petrano asked a standard set of questions and if Interface was going to be putting up any other buildings in the city.

"If you are asking us to refrain from building as the investigation continues, the answer is no," Montegue said. "We won't, but it's a moot point. We don't have any buildings in cycle."

Petrano's eyes narrowed. "I'm looking out for safety not just in my town and state but others. Why won't you stop construction?"

"Because we have been building around the world for quite some time without an issue, in zones far more prone to earthquakes. Beyond our own engineering expertise, every permit has been issued by the proper authorities, up to and including the special division for environmental affairs in DC."

"You're covered," surmised Petrano.

Montegue replied, "You know a company can't build a bathroom in this country without a permit, nor is insurance available if one skirts the system. Know this: we are as shocked as you about why the building came down and my firm won't be in business if we don't get to the source of how it happened."

"I just don't want another Millennium Tower," said Petrano.

"Which was and is a totally different situation," inserted Austin. "The ground underneath wasn't stable, the building was up and level and only started to lean after construction."

"And I've got everyone from Joe Montana to Grandma Ree suing the building, the architect, every construction firm possible, and the city for issuing the approvals."

"But," Austin responded smoothly, "everyone did the job to the best of their abilities, and no one could have possibility anticipated what happened. That's why no charges have been brought or lawsuits settled. What are you going to do in this case, sue Mother Earth?"

Austin thought she saw a smirk appear on the junior attorney's face before he schooled his expression.

"So, if Interface isn't to blame, who is?" Petrano queried.

"As Tom said, an entire supply chain exists, from the inventors of the cement, to the concrete mixers, to those pouring the materials, all who had to get it right or wrong. And throughout the entire process, you had inspectors overseeing everything."

"Two things," Petrano said to Cole. "Inspection log and any other letters from the city. We are already chasing down the steel and inspection lists. What about the concrete?"

"Samples are being delivered to the testing sites today," Cole answered, looking at Austin for affirmation, who nodded.

"Call them to speed things along," Petrano told Cole. He turned to Montegue. "Since you are based in Los Angeles, I want someone with full authority available here while this is being investigated."

"And you'll have it. Austin has carte blanche to execute the program she sees fit under the circumstances. We want to see this through as fast and as thoroughly as you do."

Petrano focused his eyes on Austin. "It doesn't look good that stock holders have to pay so much for your services." Ugh. He'd also seen the piece in *The Weekly*, thereby proving her theory that the rag was read by the respectable as much as the unrespectable in the town.

"No more than the taxpayers who pay millions for their attorney general to go after red herrings. We have a job to do for a large court of public opinion. The only difference between you and I is that we come in before it's gone criminal."

"Let's hope it remains that way."

With that, Petrano stood up and walked out of the room with Montegue by his side, making his way down the long hallway. The junior attorney stayed behind. "Nice job at the Blendheim press conference."

"Thanks."

"Look, don't take it personally," he continued, his voice a little quieter. "Not all firms of your type are so helpful." Austin thought of Campbell. They gave people like her a bad name.

"I'll do all I can to help you. We want the same thing." Cole shook her hand again and they swapped cards. When Austin walked by Petrano's office, he looked up then down again, but she took Cole's advice. She didn't take it personally.

"That went better than I expected," Montegue said as he hailed a cab. She thanked him, confirming they'd catch up on the media coverage the following day.

As her cab went up Van Ness, then down Market and into the center of the city, Austin reflected on the meeting with Petrano. He'd asked for very little, demanded nothing, and didn't put out threats or ultimatums. He'd brought up the small piece in *The Weekly*, but even that had been an irritant, not a major issue.

It's because he's got what all AG's desire: to be first in line to file a class action lawsuit before the other states had the chance. He'd get the credit and the payout.

A national stage, just what he wanted.

The next stop was the SFDP. Austin was made to wait by security who required permission for her to proceed upstairs with the samples.

On the third floor, Austin met Devann Boggard.

"Pleased to meet you," said Devann, extending his hand. "GreatLife Insurance." She returned the shake and handed him the concrete. He began an immediate examination, and she held her breath. Had he put together their common clients, smaller, regional firms she'd represented that his firm had covered with insurance?

Lt. Nolebrow joined them moments later. Austin volunteered the name of their lab, identifying that Interface had approved sharing the results.

"This material has been used for years now, so we expect this effort to be a formality more than anything."

"You should be so lucky," said Nolebrow, though Austin could see that's exactly what Boggard was hoping.

She left, exiting the building, practically running into a man on the sidewalk.

"Pardon me," he apologized, steadying her from behind before she could utter a word.

"No, it was totally my fault."

She was intent on her destination, not even bothering to turn as she hailed a cab.

CHAPTER 21

"Hillstone please," he heard Austin say as she entered the vehicle. Garrison got in his own cab and gave the driver the same location.

When he arrived, Austin was already entering the restaurant located on the Embarcadero. He found a bench in the park in the shade, not far from the building. The small, metal object he'd dropped in Austin's purse was no more than a few millimeters in diameter and looked and felt like a nickel. He didn't entirely relish the notion of becoming her invisible shadow and tracking her with the GPS but she was his best route to success.

Just one final story on her and then I'll move on to other subjects, he repeated. *But I said that with the last one.* Hmm. He was finding her, and the stories, slightly addictive.

Garrison put the small satellite on his lap. His earbuds were already in, and he had a straight line of site into the Hillstone Restaurant.

"You must be Austin Marks. Royce Slade."

"Or are you going by the more judicious title of savior of the moment?" asked a second man.

"Unless someone really needs saving at this moment, I'm going to hold off climbing on the cross and have a bit of lunch instead."

Garrison smirked. *Good comeback.* Jerkoff deserved it anyway.

"Sydney Bennet, head of European operations," Royce said. Garrison popped a piece of Nicorette in his mouth as they sat and the waiter described the specials.

"The usual?" he asked Austin.

"Just crab cakes please and if you could put in an order for the bread pudding at the same time, I'd appreciate it."

"Interesting combination," Sydney remarked.

"Any food is improved with a bit of chocolate, and this is divine. I'd never thought of chunks of chocolate in such a thing, but it works."

"It defiles the original," the Englishman said.

"Or improves it. You should try the grilled artichokes with aioli sauce. Excellent as well."

"Jackie did say you come here often," Royce offered.

"This is about the only place where one can get a ribeye without the associated attitude." Austin pressed a lemon into her drink, waiting.

Garrison ignored the inane pleasantries, checking his email until he heard appetizers being delivered.

"Austin, we appreciate the strategy behind Blendheim, but it's flawed," Royce began. "For the last six days, we've been analyzing Blendheim's system and our own. Their engineers changed the software to the point it's completely customized. This comes from Ching himself. What happened was out of our hands and not our responsibility."

"Then I'd say if I wasn't prevented by morals, I'd have purchased your stock and wait to sell until after the rebound, which I suspect will happen in the next thirty days."

"If you want to purchase stock, and nothing prevents you from doing so, I suggest you do so in the next eight hours."

"Why's that?"

"Because by that time, you'll be representing Dolphin Software."

Austin's eyes remained steady as she chewed. "You already have Leonard Campbell as your PR agency."

"We want to prepare for a crisis, and that means enlisting your firm."

Austin took another bite. "You'd like an insurance policy, one wherein we tip you off and anticipate the media strikes against you? Not interested."

"Not at all. This is a true client situation, where Dolphin hires Marks for a long-term retainer-based engagement, starting with a simple crisis communications plan. Easy and straightforward."

This guy was smooth, Garrison had to give him that.

"It would be a month or two before I'd feel comfortable taking on another client."

"*Active client*, or one in crisis, sure," Royce emphasized. "But after creating a working document for us, your team could sit back and be dormant for months. Plus, you have the staff to handle the other services we need, like advertising." His words sounded familiar but Garrison couldn't place it.

"It's good website copy isn't it?" Austin asked, and Garrison found himself nodding his head. *Gotcha.* "Royce, you have an inherent conflict with Blendheim until your software is one hundred percent in the clear. In any case, the CEO would have to agree to the contract."

"Agreed on both counts," Royce continued, undaunted. "I'm proposing an annual retainer, upfront and guaranteed. Then a sweetener based on performance. So, if Mackelby agreed, would you sign?"

"I can't do a thing until it's in writing for me to review."

Royce produced a thin, yellow manila envelope from his briefcase that he slid across the table. "Here it is. Since you don't really have a motivation to take us on as a client, you will see another monetary incentive added for a decision made by Monday morning."

Sydney had little to say on the subject, finishing his lunch as Austin wiped her mouth.

"I'll take a look and we'll go from there. Sound good?"

Both men stood and shook her hand before she left. As Austin hailed the cab, Garrison continued listening.

Once she was out the door, Sydney took a drink and spoke. "Think she'll sign on?"

"Undoubtedly," answered Royce.

"She doesn't strike me as though she's hurting for cash. She could marry a guy, play tennis and shop all day long. Like the one you have." The silence was followed up by a quick, "just kidding. Tracy's sharp."

"For Austin, money isn't the hook," Royce said. "It's the challenge of representing us. That's what will get her."

"And tell me again why Leonard can't do the job? I heard him in your office as I walked by, arguing against taking her on."

Royce shook his head. "Leonard doesn't know the first thing about crisis communications."

"Okay, I understand we need Marks' expertise, but her argument is fair. Conflicts do exist. Why do you insist on her firm? There are others."

"Remember what I told you about the board meeting? Anything happens, Marks takes the fall not Dolphin."

"Her company flattens and we walk away clean."

"As Tracy explained, the media will be distracted. That might be all we need in a moment of crisis."

"As much as I instinctively don't like her, Austin doesn't strike me as a person who does anything for money, unlike me."

"You give eleven million to a person who's had her entire financial life ripped from her once already, and she'll take it."

"Did you say eleven million?"

"By Monday. You watch. The contract will be on my desk."

Garrison saw a cab pull up again in front of the restaurant, and Austin got out. The conversation stopped as she entered the restaurant and accepted her purse from Royce's outstretched hand. Austin left, but Garrison stayed put.

CHAPTER 22

Clive involuntarily hunched his shoulders as he watched the men. Slade was hedging his bets, which was interesting, but hardly a crime, unless of course, the funds going to Austin would turn right around and go back to her sister Tracy.

No, that was a stretch, even for my conspiracy-theory mind. Austin clearly had no idea this was coming, and for her to be in league with her sister Tracy, and Tracy telling her husband Royce to give the money to Austin, then back to her…Garrison looked up the stock and Royce's holdings. The guy was worth gazillions and the wife would get half in a divorce. Easier to just ditch the guy.

Scrap the sister-and-sister-screw-the-husband triangle.

What was weirder, Royce certainly didn't act as if he even knew his wife and Austin were sisters. Granted, Garrison had only been watching her for a couple of days, but she'd not brought up her sister's name once.

Instead, what might be happening was simple. Slade had a big, nasty pile of crap on his hands and needed Austin's skillset.

Then why am I mad?

Because they are intentionally setting Austin up to screw her. The underdog in him almost came out of his den, mentally fighting on behalf of Austin, but he pulled himself back on the chain. She wasn't innocent. She represented people who did bad things for living, just like attorneys.

"All is fair on the battlefield," he muttered, putting away his materials.

He went straight from lunch to the adjacent building, apologizing to the security guard.

"My computer with all the files melted down and I get to ask for a do-over. That okay?"

The ploy worked, and soon Garrison was back at his corner perch. He heard and watched Austin making calls. She was crisp, professional and helpful, even when she chastised Asa for his remark at the meeting about sharing information.

"It was a fair thought, Asa, but you do realize how you came across?"

He paused. "Like a pompous piece of male anatomy."

"Pretty much. Let me be the bad guy next time, okay?"

The lack of justice in the world is another reason why I'm mad. Tech guys getting rich, teachers being paid jack, people like him throwing it all away and starting from the ground up.

Thirty minutes later, he still had nothing and wrapped it up. He couldn't push the lies with the security guard any further.

"Where's my latest piece?" bellowed Kell as Garrison walked by.

"In minutes!" Garrison shouted back.

"Here," offered Max, his hand outstretched. "Life is better with some tar."

Garrison thanked Max for the cup of coffee and took a drink. It was lukewarm and bitter. He was sure he looked like death after the minimal sleep he got last night. But none of that bothered him as much as Kell turning down his last piece on the tie between Marks' crisis communication firms and the manipulation of public opinion.

"Why'd you reject it?" yelled Garrison.

"Defensible facts Garrison, whether it's hookers or the pope," Kell bellowed.

"Yeah, and I'll shove those facts up your behind," he said under his breath, causing Max to chuckle.

"Big man telling you to get a real story?"

"Nah. Just one with defensible and sourceable facts. Can you imagine?"

With his evening deadline looming, Garrison was going to rely on old school following and eavesdropping. At some point, something good was going to come through and he'd be ready.

Austin read through the contract while in the cab, and again at her desk in the office. The only ironclad section regarded mediation in the event of a breach of contract by Marks.

And since we have never failed to perform, we would never have to give the money back.

Could her team handle it? They'd be stretched, but her business had ebb and flows. In fact, client crisis' were like cold sores: where one flairs up another dies down.

Asa came into her office.

"Boggard called after you dropped off the samples. He told me a husband and wife team invented the concrete years ago and licensed it to three different manufactures."

Austin thanked him, already picking up the phone. "You ready for another client?" Asa stood still. "And no," she continued, "I'm not kidding, but it won't be your account. Also, I need to run this one by the attorney."

"I'm not aware of any other company in crisis."

"Not yet," she said with a wink. "I'll tell the team when I get the thumbs up."

"Susan and Nichele might balk," he warned. She shrugged, waiting for her attorney to answer, asking Asa to shut the door after him. Austin relayed the contract details to her lawyer, then scanned and sent the document. He reviewed the document and gave her the green light, pursuant to clearing it in writing with the attorneys at Blendheim and Mackelby himself.

"If you can do that, you'll get half the eleven million Monday."

Austin called Mackelby.

"Austin, I'll go along with you accepting Dolphin as long as we add an addendum to our contract that states Blendheim can cancel the contract at will, and without penalty, payments stopping immediately, no breach clause."

"That's fair."

Austin had her attorney modify their agreement. By the time the document was completed, most of her staff had left, and she wasn't going to sign until her directors were on board.

She vacillated between sending out an email and interrupting their evening or waiting a few hours. She opted to wait. A relaxing evening at home would be nice for a change.

CHAPTER 23

Garrison lifted the can of Red Bull to his lips and ten minutes later, popped an anti-acid and threw the half-empty container away. This diet of caffeine shots and anti-smoking gum was killing him. He watched the lights in Austin's apartment above and to his left. He had scored a better spot than he had the night before. No trees this time.

Austin appeared, a towel wrapped on her head. Her shoulders were bare, the white line of her towel stretched tight across her chest.

As he waited for the blue screen to light up her face, Garrison began accessing personal record sites. Some were free, others charged a fee. Normally, he'd have Max do this kind of work but it was past nine and Max was with his girlfriend, who was likely tugging on his man-bun.

Garrison went through what he knew: six years ago, Austin changed her name and moved out west. He used his access pass from *The Weekly* to get into the data files of property holders in the San Francisco area and got a hit. Austin Marks had once owned a property valued at $1.4 million. Status: foreclosed. Using the parcel number on the property, he accessed the county records.

"Holy, holy," he mumbled. Nearly four, full pages of listings for debt collectors. A contractor, mechanics, electrical, all associated with a construction project. He was starting to get amped up when he noticed a man's name was listed first on the line items, not Austin's.

Garrison entered the name of the man listed on the papers.

Oh, man. This is really bad. And really good.

"Hey, Karen." Garrison listened to Austin talk as he sped through the information on the screen. "Yeah, I had to take a gamble and post my photo. No, no response yet. I can't tell if he even saw it or not. Oh, it does? Where?" Garrison stopped his reading and opened up the Midnight Blue site. He accessed his account and saw the notice that a picture was posted. Sure enough, a photo of a hot, sixteen-year-old Austin was on line. Same nose, lips and facial structure. Unlike her sister, she didn't appear to have had an ounce of work done.

"Wait! The check just appeared on the screen," said Austin. "Does that mean he's looking at it? Right now?" Austin gave a little shriek. "I am breathing deep!" Austin's exaggerated exhales slowly reduced. "But right about now, he's realizing I put in a decades-old photo, thereby concluding I must be an out of shape bag. No! I'm not sending my bad vibes into the universe."

Garrison felt hot, then realized he'd turned his seat heaters on. What a relief. He didn't want to think he was getting all amped up for this woman.

"You know, if he's clever, he might put up something from his high school year book or college to match mine." Austin listened and laughed. "Okay. I promise not to sit and stare at the screen waiting. I think men can sense desperation through phone lines."

Austin changed the subject, telling Karen about the offer from Dolphin and that she hadn't told her staff yet. "They might have a collective aneurism," she predicted. "From the money or work, I don't know."

Austin's happy laugh sounded genuine, the vibrant pitch contagious. Garrison almost hoped she'd take the account and be successful. Then her sister came to mind. He couldn't completely disregard the nepotism angle. Silicon Valley was like a scatter-chart of past and former roommates, friends, lovers, bosses and relatives. Outsiders weren't welcome until they were somehow inserted into the formula.

Austin shut down the screen and disappeared from sight. He exited the notepad function on his phone and he was just about to start his car when he heard talking.

"Please, if this is meant to happen, let him be nice, and not crazy. Please allow someone in my life who will treat me right. Amen."

It was quiet then, in Austin's room and in his car.

Across town, Cole was lying on his bed reading. A piece of paper was on his lap, red with notes.

It was another tip, again about Dolphin Software. It was inflammatory and a bit crazy. "Not to mention completely defamatory," he said to himself. When he'd mentioned it to Petrano, he'd gotten what he expected. "Absolutely not," Petrano had said to Cole's suggestion of starting an inquiry into the software. "We have it in writing from Blendheim they customized their own software. As much as I want to nail them for screwing up, it truly might be a human input error. That will mean settlement costs but not maleficence."

Cole still tried to convince his boss. "Just an initial interview. To cover our bases."

Petrano regarded the junior attorney. "You're sticking your neck out, just this much," he said, measuring an inch between his forefinger and thumb.

"It will only be a flesh wound if I'm wrong," he said with a slight grin.

"Initial interviews and queries only. Within the confines of the law."

Cole called Elaine the following morning.

"Mr. William," she greeted him.

Cole laughed. "That's a first."

"What? You being called Mr.?"

"That's a formality most people don't use with me."

"Who would be rude to a person like you? Your picture presents a very good image."

"You've been doing some checking, huh?"

"It's only prudent." Cole thought he heard a smile in her voice. He hoped so. He enjoyed talking with her.

"You don't seem all that surprised to hear from me though. Can I have a minute?"

"Sure. What's going on?"

"I've got news and I need to ask for your help, if, on the off chance, you aren't already working on this."

"Ah, which means if I say no, you can't make me?" He allowed a cough, which was a half-laugh, the kind which admitted the truth without offering a word. "Okay. Go for it."

Cole told her about the latest tip, a conspiracy that Dolphin was behind the failures and it was at a core, software level. More would happen and the damage greater than the Met or Blendheim.

"We have no evidence at all other than the tip, so I can't call up anyone at Dolphin. My instinct tells me you have already been thinking about this since the first time I called you, am I right?"

"What leads you to believe that I have a care in the world when I'm surrounded by parrots and palm trees?"

"Fundamentally, Dolphin is your child who went off to college. Just because you talk doesn't mean you don't check on him now and then." Elaine laughed. "Also, if you'd wanted to sever the cord of civilization and Dolphin entirely, you would have sold your stock."

"That is true as well. I'll jump ahead a few steps and save some time. Let's just say I called up Royce. No one, not me, you or anyone is going to convince him Blendheim isn't responsible unless a substantial set of facts are delivered which confirm it."

Cole thought of Petrano's direct order. Initial interview only. "Can you help us determine if the problem is with Dolphin's software and if so, can you fix it?"

"Perhaps. If someone is on the inside, and that's the only way something of this magnitude could be pulled off, then they will catch wind of this immediately and change tactics." The neck that Petrano suggested he was sticking out just went a lot further.

"Agreed," said Cole firmly. "One last question, more for my own want-to-know. You left on good terms, you haven't sold more than enough stock to buy a bungalow on a relatively remote island and live a quiet life. Something more exists to this story, and one day, I'm wondering if you'd like to share it?"

"Maybe if you come for a visit, I will."

CHAPTER 24

Friday morning, Austin was in the office at seven-thirty.

"You taking it easy?" chided Darren as he rode up the elevator with her.

"It's Friday," she laughed. "Have any good plans for the weekend?"

"It was going to be my dog and the park until I got your email last night. Just want to say thanks. I'm genuinely pumped."

She gave him a smile. "You're welcome. You deserve it."

Last night, she'd decided to give the Dolphin account to Darren, assuming the rest of the directors were on board with accepting the company as a client. Asa would be annoyed, but he couldn't have all the high paying firms.

"And you?"

"I'll be at the dojo learning new ways to hurt people."

"Remind me never to get on your bad side."

Austin entered her office, her mind not on martial arts but on Midnight Blue. Increasingly, her thoughts returned to the anonymous man who had caught her interest. She hoped his looks matched his sense of humor.

Did she need Mr. Perfect body? Nope. She'd had such a man once before and the experience left her with a desire for honesty, morality and loyalty. If he had those attributes, a bit of a paunch on his middle wouldn't deter her.

At the morning meeting, each director gave a status report on their accounts.

Then Austin took charge. "Now let's talk about Dolphin. I didn't receive pushback emails but I want to make sure we are all on board before I sign the paperwork."

"Makes total sense until their software tanks," said Asa. "Perhaps it would be smart to wait a month."

"Then what? You want to take that account too?" asked Darren. No love was lost between the two men. Their personalities were as different as the color of their skin.

"You're just annoyed the account is going to be with Darren," interjected Nichele.

"Actually, I'm concerned that GreatLife was the insurer behind several small firms that Marks represented, most that predated me, but two since my time on board."

"They are a global firm," said Nichele. "Overlap is the norm."

"You're implying that Devann Boggard will be prejudiced against Dolphin because of our relationship?" asked Darren. "That's a stretch of major proportions. One had nothing to do with another."

Asa folded his arms in disagreement.

"I agree with Darren," said Austin. "It's a non-issue. The fact that we share clients is coincidence, nothing more." They'd all get large bonus checks, though Darren's would be slightly higher as the account lead.

The meeting broke and Austin focused on reviewing the changes to the updated interview schedule with Mackelby when a knock at the door caused her to look up. It was Asa.

"You really think this is the right thing to do?"

"I'm rather surprised you, of all people, are giving pushback. It's basically free money for you."

"Not complaining about that. I just have a weird feeling."

Austin raised an eyebrow. "You have feelings?"

"Ha," he said, his look black as he left.

Austin pulled up Blendheim's stock symbol. Three points higher than yesterday.

At one, she was eating at her desk when Darren came to her door.

"Have you seen Campbell's latest press?" Seeing she had a mouth full, he kept talking. "He's talking about cleaning up the public relations industry, reestablishing trust with the press."

Austin raised an eyebrow. "And someone is actually writing about it?"

"He got it into an article about conflicts of interest, which seems to dovetail to another little bit of unpleasantness. I'll send it to you now." A ping from her instant message came through. She opened and scanned the piece in the *San Jose Mercury News*. Six examples were cited where venture-backed companies had hired firms with potential conflicts of interest.

"Half the companies in this city wouldn't be in business if the rules of conflict were enforced," Austin remarked. "And ironically, Leonard failed to identify that at one of the companies listed, an employee of his is married to a vice president in marketing. Don't tell me that didn't sway who won the account."

"He's still bitter he lost Blendheim to us," Darren said, looking down at his phone, not bothering to mention Asa's defection. "Just sent you another link. This one is sort of worse."

"*Sort of worse?*" she asked with humor in her voice. That emotion evaporated the minute she opened the link. It was in the Overheard section of *The Weekly*, the gossip section. Austin read out loud. "It's ironic that a person so admired in the industry who couldn't solve her own financial crisis is now solving those of others." She shook her head. "Nice touch. How in the world did Clive Garrison dig up that information?"

"It has to be Leonard," said Darren, somewhat sympathetically. Now he, and the rest of the world, knew about her bankruptcy and the foreclosure on her home.

"It doesn't matter where it came from," she said, pragmatism reasserting itself. "The only good thing about the last recession is that it was the great equalizer. I wasn't the only one to hit the wall by losing my home. It's just unfortunate Clive had to bring my personal life into it."

Darren raised an eyebrow. "You know, I bet that man has so much dirt on all of us, if he spread it around he could fill a pit."

"If that's your way of making me feel better, thanks. I appreciate it. Going back to Leonard, we did take two clients from him in one week." The fact actually gave her a bit of pride. "He might be the source of Clive and Bernie's tips." She then shrugged. "It's America. We need forty-two brands of cold cereal. The world can certainly handle another crisis firm with a CEO who has an ax to grind."

When Darren left, Austin pulled up *The Weekly* site and read the article again, infinitely grateful Clive's reporting had ended with the bankruptcy. The story could have been worse. Much worse.

Garrison sat at Starbuck's nursing an ice tea. It tasted like thin, bitter water, reminding him of the blueish, nasty one percent milk when he was used to the creamy whole milk.

Being healthy sucks. Overnight, he'd gotten a headache. *Because I've kept myself going with so much caffeine my body is dependent on it.*

He opened a packet of sugar and poured until it was empty. His retreat from dependency on oral stimulants had to be gradual, but his weight loss wasn't. He'd lost three pounds in the last week, though it hadn't been intentional. It was a bi-product of following Austin around town, staying up late, watching her apartment and living on a liquid diet.

The article that came out today wasn't bad either. The fact that Jax over at the *News* had written a piece that also dinged Austin was simply good timing. A bit more heat under her seat.

He unconsciously shifted in his chair, adjusting his rump. Doing so caused him to look around. The same guy with the hat was in the corner, this time in a camel hair coat. The SoCal tourist-look was okay for a single day, but now it was just eccentric.

Garrison looked at his laptop. Leonard hadn't mentioned her name to him, but the man had called her out in his first sentence, using Marks Communications as the shining example of all that was wrong with the industry. Even so, Garrison wasn't going to be Campbell's puppet. He'd left that role to the idiot Bernie Jax.

"You have conflicts all over the place," Garrison had bluntly pointed out to Campbell. "What's the difference between your two firms, and why shouldn't I write about you?"

"Because Austin is bottom feeding on the troubles of others."

"And you just lowered yourself into this cesspool to clean it up? That's very magnanimous."

"Yes, it is."

Let Jax write about the war of agencies. At this point, Garrison was focused on one person. What bugged him was that Kell had taken out the juice of the piece.

"Why'd you take the suicide part out?" he demanded of his editor.

Kell pulled at his red facial hair. "Because you made absolutely no connection to the fact that the woman's boyfriend committed suicide, presumably to avoid paying a lot of debt, which he then dumped on her. If anything, the fact she paid the money back made her look like she's one of the few upright and ethical people in the city, not some irresponsible, grieving girlfriend. You can't have it both ways Garrison. Either you skewer the person you are writing about or you saint them. Make up your mind."

Garrison took another sip of ice tea, grimacing. He had returned to his original hypothesis that somewhere, there was a story with Dolphin, Austin and her sister and getting that eleven million-dollar contract. If she signed, and if he could prove collusion, it might result in the resignation of Royce Slade and the dissolution of the board.

And Garrison's promotion, or a new job with a different paper.

He swirled a bit of ice in his mouth. Dolphin employed about three thousand people around the world. They had families and lives. Royce may not come across great and Sydney was certainly a prick, but did he really want to write a story that might negatively affect a lot of people?

I'm getting morals, and that's a real problem in my line of work.

He adjusted his earpiece. Austin was on the phone with her friend Karen, admitting she was checking Midnight Blue, waiting for the photo of her anonymous suitor to appear.

Garrison made a decision. He accessed his back up photos on the cloud and went back as far as he could. His senior prom. He imported the picture of him in a tux and cropped out his date. His neck was tight, jawline a straight line, hair thick and dark and he was at least fifty pounds lighter. Nope, she'd never recognize him.

With a click and another drink, he pressed the upload button. A wave went down from Garrison's sternum to his belly. He couldn't tell if it was from nerves or excitement.

CHAPTER 25

GreatLife Insurance inspector Devann Boggard looked through the report a second time. The analysis of the concrete from the Met had come back from three, independent forensics firms. The flaw was in the concrete, with a product called betasydene, a small, white bead comprised of eco-friendly materials created and patented by the firm New Frontiers. He'd already had a conference call with the husband and wife who invented the product, along with Detective Snow and Lt. Nolebrow. The conversation did produce one piece of critical information: the composite strength was not what it should be. That meant the firm who had manufactured the product had erred.

Once off the phone, the three men reviewed what they knew.

"This could be a colossal product error at the site of the Metropolitan building by the mixers," Snow offered. "Human error. They didn't read the directions correctly."

"The second scenario is that the ingredients in the cement mixture were in fact wrong at the product facility," suggested Boggard.

"Which leaves two sources for error, neither are Interface."

"What's gnawing at you?" Nolebrow asked Boggard. "I would think this is good news for you, since you insure only Interface, not these other organizations."

Boggard ran his fingers through his thinning hair. "If this building collapsed because the concrete was defective, how can we be sure that all the other buildings already up, or going up, aren't at risk? This is only one of three manufacturers of the product. Do you tear down a half-finished structure because it might one day collapse? And gentleman, it's not just buildings. What about bridges or airport tarmacs? We have seven years of using this material across three continents. Forget what we insure. It's possibly much bigger than that."

Snow and Nolebrow shared a look and it needed no interpretation. "We must contain that theory, for now," Snow said.

"Not from Petrano," Nolebrow said. "I'd better talk to him myself. Once this is beyond San Francisco borders, I'm not touching it."

Boggard flipped a pen between his fingers, then tapped the end on the table. "Perhaps we should be thanking the Met for going down because it alerted us to a much bigger problem."

Nolebrow glanced at the clock. "I'll be sure to point that out to the AG."

While Nolebrow called Petrano, Boggard rang Austin.

"Devann," Austin said cautiously. "This is great news for our mutual client. But to your other point, when this first happened, one of my team members pulled a list of sites using this concrete. It's nearly sixty sites around the world, and that's just Interface."

"I know."

"I'm with you on keeping this quiet. It's a fine line between instilling panic or being complicit when you know a product is defective, you know?"

"Yes, I do."

Garrison watched and listened as Austin placed another call.

"Tom, for now, let's keep the circle of those who know what's happening to the three of you at Interface, myself and Asa here. I'd advise against telling your board members. One errant word on this and chaos could ensue in the general public."

You are absolutely right, thought Garrison. He crossed bridges on a regular basis and rode in buildings.

It was a bombshell. He could envision a Pulitzer, and a job at the *San Jose Mercury News*. While Austin went about her day as though nothing out of the ordinary had happened, he was re-reading his work of greatness. The shocking news was going to hit the world all at once. With visions of grandeur, he waited impatiently at his desk as Kell read his piece.

An hour later, Kell called him to his office.

"Beyond the fact that you have referred to multiple conversations that can't be used in court, I have to agree with Petrano and even the Marks woman. People running around in a panic don't buy papers or click on the ads in our online version of the paper. They are too concerned the building they live in is going to crumble on them or the bridge they are driving on will collapse. They, you, and now we, keep our mouths shut for the time being."

"But it's the scoop of the century!" Garrison argued.

"Not if you can't provide direct quotes, on the record from sources. I'll say it again. In-ad-miss-ible. The paper won't be standing here to pay the legal costs you will incur from just about everyone if I published this. Focus somewhere else and do it right."

Garrison went back to his desk, his mood dark. "Rejection jokes will get your hair cut off with these scissors, right here," he threatened Max, who had the temerity to laugh.

Max leaned over and handed him a photo. "Maybe this will brighten your day."

Garrison scanned the page. "Do I even want to know who you slept with to get this information?"

"It wasn't me that did the sleeping. My girlfriend's neighbor was around back then. She remembered the incident and I dug it up."

"That entire Carmichael family has a whole lotta big, fat, ugly baggage."

"Almost makes you feel sorry for her, doesn't it?"

Garrison put the photo in his briefcase. "Almost."

He pulled up his phone. By now, he was absolutely convinced Austin had zero social life. No party invites, girls activities or a date. Given his file on her background, it didn't come as a surprise. If he'd had the history of being betrayed the way she was, he'd never look at the opposite sex again.

And I certainly wouldn't ever talk to my sister again.

He returned home to eat and take a walk along the waterfront. His one bedroom in the Mission District was less than ten minutes from the ocean. Small, affordable and nearly as old as stone tablets. He checked his phone. Austin was at the dojo, her schedule as predictable as the tides.

Rummaging through his crammed closet, he found a pair of barely used running sneakers. Putting the collar up on his windbreaker, he kept his head down but his eyes focused on the path in front of him, as though the wind would bring along the inspiration he sought. What had made Austin hook up with a man who killed himself, left her on the hook for over a million dollars and wrote the suicide note not to his fiancé but to her sister? That was as cold as the wind he felt on his face.

He pulled out the folded photo Max had given him. Austin and her sister, standing side by side in front of a gravesite, sharing a moment of grief. In the dozens of hours he now had Austin on record, she'd not once brought up her sister. It was like she didn't exist.

People disowned family members over fallouts all the time, why not her?

He unconsciously increased his pace along with his line of thinking.

The woman was running. She clearly ran from her sister, who was sleeping with her fiancé. Then from the bankruptcy during which she lost everything. And before that, she was already running away from who-knows-what-else that had caused her to change her name in the first place back in New Jersey. He briefly thought about writing the anthology of Austin, because this story kept getting more and more interesting, up to and including the present situation with Dolphin Software.

Garrison pulled his turtleneck higher and zipped up his windbreaker. What if Royce's company went down the tubes and he could pin it on Austin? It might make his wife very happy. Now *that* was a diabolical scheme.

He had to admit, the picture of Austin Marks wasn't as black and white as he thought. Maybe shades of grey.

CHAPTER 26

Austin shoved her dirty uniform into the washer, grimacing. Three days of toxic build up had produced a nasty odor. No defensive movements tonight. This was a grueling form of chung-doe, low, squatting movements stretching the length of the room before a quick turn, then back again. Forty minutes of torture, pushing her legs to exhaustion and collapse followed by high kicks. The low to high had made a twenty-two year-old puke in the men's room and another female had passed out. No sympathy was expected or given. It was endurance, plain and simple.

She was glad. The excruciatingly focused activity kept her mind off the image she'd seen on Midnight Blue. Granted, the picture was probably three decades old, but he had been a good looking teen. Plus, he'd matched her humor by putting up an old photo.

"Baby steps," Austin said to herself as she put the machine on sanitary cycle. "I give a picture. You give a picture, and we'll see how far this progresses."

She was still in her bathrobe, hair up in a bun as she slathered Aquaphor on the bottoms of her feet, rubbing the hardened soles. Slipping on thick socks, she made herself soup and sat down at her desk.

Twirling her fork in the noodles, she opened Midnight Blue.

"Is it time to start chatting?" She explored the features for an on-line conversation. She saw three; one for text only, another for audio and a third for video. "Nope to those," she said, clicking off buttons. "But just in case," she continued. She took a small piece of paper, folded it in half and placed it on the top rim of her laptop, directly over the camera. "No peeking," she said as though someone were already watching.

She ran her tube of lip gloss on, laughing to herself. She felt as though she were getting ready for a first date, from the tentative smile to the tingling sensation moving down her arms. For good measure, she pulled a glass tube from her desk and dabbed the cold perfume on her neck.

"Please don't be a jerk," she said in an almost inaudible voice. With that, she clicked on the chat feature.

That's going to throw me. His phone was on and he had the mobile application open. It was a good thing too, because he'd had to keep driving around the block until someone left and another car immediately pulled in. It had cost him thirty bucks as a bribe, but he got the kid to give up his slot.

Garrison blocked the audio and visual as well. It was smart and safe.

"That's good timing," he heard Austin say. He wasn't imagining the excitement in her voice, and clearly saw her lean closer to the screen. "Oh man, I don't have a name," Austin said, laughing. Garrison smiled, a bit of panic setting in. Neither did he. At present, they were two anonymous people.

"Greetings," he wrote. Unlike his contemporaries, he wasn't versed in the protocol for on-line interactions. The safest play was to default to simplicity.

"Hi," she said out loud as the text appeared on his instant messenger. She included a wave that went back and forth. Nice. "I've never explored the underworld of Internet dating before. Have you?"

He could believe that, so she got points for honesty.

"Nope. I'm old school or have been until recently," he replied.

"Then what, your grandmother died and left you an inheritance which you decided to spend here?" Garrison worked to push down a smile.

"That's right. It's my one shot, so don't kill the dream for me. Let it last for at least one conversation, will you?"

Austin laughed and shook her head. "Are we going by real names or fake ones?" she wrote.

"Hmmm. I like real. I'm Grant." It was his middle name, so it counted.

"Austin. No last names though. We might be neighbors." He appreciated that she talked to him as though they were having a conversation. Two points in her favor. He wondered if it would last long. He had a few subjects he knew were going to get her.

"East coast or west?" he asked.

He watched her take off her towel turban, shaking out her hair. It was wavy when wet, the blond falling in loose curls around her face. "West. You?" He affirmed the west coast as well. "So, in seconds, we have moved past the names stage but aren't well enough acquainted to talk cities. At present, are you single?"

"Yes. In the last few days since joining, I've somehow managed to stay that way. Not a girlfriend in sight." Although Garrison knew she didn't have a boyfriend, it would be odd to not ask. "What about you?"

"No girlfriends either," she quipped.

"That's comforting. How is it a girl like you isn't with a guy?"

"Work. Life. I'm busy. I wouldn't even be on this site except that my uncle signed me up for it and I couldn't say no."

"Wanting to see if you are missing anything?"

"Yeah. I'm an Internet dating virgin."

"OK. If we were out on a first date, what would you expect? A fancy dinner or a dive bar?"

"Ooh, this is like speed dating," she replied. "Ok. I'm ready. The answer is somewhere in between. I'd want to dress up but not overdo it. The part where you could afford to take me out is a sign of gainful employment."

"Fair enough. On my typical first dates, I take them to a dive-like Taqueria. It weeds 'em out. But to be clear, I'm not stingy, I'm prudent. Why spend a fortune when the woman eats on my nickel and has no real interest in me?"

"Good strategy!" she applauded. Garrison watched the dot on his screen blink as she wrote. "What is it with women who think that an impressive dinner has anything to do with potential love?"

"Amen sister." That got Austin to laugh out loud. Garrison appreciated drawing a positive emotion from a female, even if that was from a woman he didn't like.

Refocus.

It was time for Garrison's next question. "Are you a woman who eats salads all the time or do you like real food?"

"Ah. Well, I am rather limited in what I eat, but that's not by choice. I like real food very much."

"How's that? I mean, who else is going to tell you what to eat?"

"Well, when I was young and visiting my grandfather, a relative gave me something to drink. It ruined my throat and esophagus, and eating has been an issue ever since."

"What could have done that?"

"Lye."

Garrison involuntarily swallowed. Lye was a product used in cleaning. "How did you not die?"

"The doctor attached a string from my ear, down my throat and intestines to keep the scar tissue from closing and suffocating."

Gee, that was pretty awful. "But you healed okay?"

"As well as I could. I can't eat tomatoes or anything acidic. I love meat, but too much burns. No citrus."

"Wow. Maybe I shouldn't be so quick to judge the next skinny girl I see."

"Don't be so hard on yourself," was her response. "I find myself making that judgment all the time, along with the associated attitude. And by the way, I'm not that skinny. My turn. What city do you live in?"

"Well, since you sufficiently passed the first-date dinner test, I will tell you San Francisco."

He watched her withdraw her hands and lean back, speaking to herself. "Crap. What if we know each other? What if you are Scott Petrano? No, he's married. Double crap."

"I'm also in the Bay Area, and now I regret telling you my first name."

Garrison felt her anxiety in addition to hearing it. "Don't regret telling me your name. There must be hundreds of Austins in the Bay Area. Besides, the real truth here is that you sound as desperate as I am to find a person of quality."

From his vantage point in his car and his binoculars, he watched Austin's face lose a bit of its sassiness, the lines of her eyes turning down slightly. It was an expression he'd never seen before, and it bothered him. "Sorry. Maybe desperate was the wrong word. Eager? Excited?" That resulted in her shoulders lowering.

"No, your first guess is closer to the truth. Being in a relationship hasn't been a priority. It represents the only really bad parts of my life that I've had."

"That sounds serious." He gnawed on the inside of his cheek.

"It is. And it still bothers me, or I wouldn't be on this site."

Garrison had an instantaneous moment of clarity. "If it were so easy for either of us to find compelling people who were good and upright, we'd have no need to spend our Friday night messaging one another, would we?"

"Correct."

Garrison began typing without thinking. "I'd like to continue talking. It's an even playing field as far as I can tell. Would you?"

"Yes."

CHAPTER 27

It was just past six p.m. but Elaine felt like it was much later. Her eyes burned and her fingers cracked as she stretched them out in front of her.

It's ten, William Cole's time.

"Lucky, look up and dial Bill's mobile number please." He had called her earlier in the day to tell her the problem was unlikely to lie with Dolphin, despite what the anonymous caller had said. She replayed the conversation in her mind, making sure she hadn't missed anything.

"The onus is on the three facilities who have licensed the betasydene," Bill had said.

"That word just rolled off your tongue you know, like a real scientist."

"I just play one on tv," he teased back. "But ideally the situation with Dolphin will end soon."

"It's not going to end *that* soon," she drawled. "I have some news and it's not so good. It also throws cold water on the notion that it's not Dolphin's issue." She told him the software had anomalies, deep in the code base, and it had numbers tied to it and specific client accounts as well. "Interface and Blendheim were tagged with the same number sequence."

"Wait—please. I'm no engineer, but of all the millions upon millions of lines of code in this software, how in the world were you able to spot an anomaly?"

"I took the grass roots approach and looked up the manufacturing date of the pills that had caused the deaths from Blendheim. Same date and same lot. And guess what else? That same date, but set in the European convention, was in the software."

Elaine heard Cole hum. "What are the odds of a coincidence?"

"Lower than you winning the lottery but probably higher than getting hit by a meteor." Cole chuckled. "But wait, there's more. Unfortunately, I'm not sure this is going to make you laugh. Dozens of other firms have numerical sequences similar to this one. Different industries, different product lines."

"So, the Dolphin Software is corrupted after all."

"And beyond that, the doomsday scenario we are looking at has future failures in several different entities."

"Are you kidding or serious? I can't tell."

"Well, my friend William, who insists I call him Bill, we are going to find out together. What are the names of the three licensing companies? I'm pretty sure we can do this on line."

"Hold on." He found the list and told her.

"All right," she began. "Behind door number one, we have a hit. It has here 31September2018. Door number two has come up empty, as in, no hits. Door number three, again, it's 31September2018."

A moment passed before he spoke. "I need to process this for a minute."

"I'm smarter, so let me do it for you," Elaine offered, without a bit of vanity. "This troubled me, so I went back into the system and put in the date sequence for the last two years, just to see what came up. I found four companies, smaller, what I consider regional with the same sequence, but the dates were different. I had nothing else to do," she paused, laughing. "And I looked each one up. Guess what? They all had their own version of a meltdown, not on that day exactly, but very close. Too close for it to be a coincidence."

"Can you give me an example?"

"Sure. A medical equipment device with a blood pressure product. The product shipped, it was faulty, it gave incorrect readings, doctors prescribed the wrong medicine, or no medicine, and enough patients ended up in the emergency room where they were tested with different equipment. The source was eventually discovered."

"And you can link this to Dolphin software?"

"The product was built on the software, as were the other three. This was different, because the Met went down because of a natural disaster, and the concrete was manufactured on site, using a prescribed recipe. Two of the licensed manufactures had the exact date insert into the line of code. That could have triggered an anomaly in the mixing process, which I know to be a very finicky, precise event. It's not just the amounts of the ingredients, but the order of creation that causes the compound to change."

"And these two licensors use Dolphin?"

"They're on Dolphin's list of clients right on their website."

"Elaine," Cole said, his voice subdued. "You have a hunch, don't you?"

"I do. Bill, I know every aspect of how this code and logic is ordered. This isn't a part of the construct."

"You're saying it was intentionally inserted."

"It had to be. All of them. First off, it was done in a way only someone intimately familiar with the system would understand. Second, this is at the operating system level. The vast majority of coders at the company can't even get to this."

"How many?"

"Have access? I'd have to call the CTO or Royce, but less than five probably. It's too valuable." They were both silent. "Once I found the four in the last twenty-four months, I bit the bullet and ran a query on Dolphin's entire customer list, looking for any instance of the sequence, not just the last two years."

Cole exhaled. "I wish I was there with you, having a drink, offering you moral support or something."

"That's two trips out here, you know, but who's counting?"

"Me, actually."

Elaine grinned. "Awesome, but until you come out here in person, the phone will have to do. I'll give you a call back when I'm finished checking on a few more things."

Now, more than three hours later, Cole answered the phone on the first ring.

"Are you sitting by the phone?"

"I didn't want to miss taking your call."

"I'd like to accept that as any self-absorbed and vain woman would, but I'm afraid my news has effectively killed my mojo. Have your pen handy? I found more."

"Go for it." Cole wrote down electronics, oil and gas and accessory companies. "What does accessories mean?"

"In one case, it's a company that makes car accessories."

"Sounds benign."

"I wouldn't know more unless I looked into their product list."

"Probably not a priority for right now. How many on the list in total?"

"Nearly thirty, in a half-dozen industries."

"US only?"

"No. They are global companies." For the second time that day, a moment of silence passed between them. "Bill, I have a theory. It started with smaller firms in specific areas of the company. Then the sequence was applied to larger firms, first national, which were another five, according to my count. Then—now, the firms with the sequences are much larger, and the dates are closer. It's like the person who has manipulated this software is working against a countdown."

"Like a global deadline."

"Exactly."

CHAPTER 28

For the next hour, Austin felt like she was speed dating with her new online friend. With the Internet as a barrier had come a certain reckless abandonment. She had the freedom to be more direct than she'd ever be in person.

"What's your favorite ice cream?" he asked.

"Chocolate. Plain. Yours?"

"Chocolate. Next topic: music. Country or retro British?"

"Retro British. No question," she replied.

"Agreed. Tabasco?"

"Love it, but only on tacos and eggs. It's a must have."

"In both green and red. Big bottles of each just in case the zombie apocalypse happens."

Each lived on top floor apartments: hers facing the street while his one-bedroom unit had a garden view. It was established they both preferred sushi and Mexican over Italian, loved the smell of cigars but neither smoked.

"I recently gave it up," he offered.

"Good decision," typed Austin. "Smokers look like the collagen has been sucked out of the skin. A walking shar-pei dog."

"Laughing here…"

"My turn," Austin wrote. "What's your profession?"

"I'm in the security business," he lied, unable to help himself. He couldn't rightly call himself a reporter. "Private mostly, corporate executives who need looking after. I dabble in publishing on the side," he added, feeling better that he'd told at least part of the truth.

"So, you get to fly around on cool planes and babysit wealthy executives, and want to write about all the juicy, behind-the-scenes-stories but can't? Sounds like my job."

"Wait, we work together? How did I not know this? Perhaps I'm guarding you."

"I'm not important or rich enough for you to be guarding me. But it's true. My job is in fact, similar. The only difference is that I usually deal with clients who are already in a bit of a fix, whereas you are trying to keep them out of it."

"Bit of a fix? That sounds like politicians getting caught in the wrong places with the wrong person."

"Thanks for the non-compliment. I do get the fringe benefit of flying in some planes though."

"Are you an attorney?"

Austin shook her head. "Your second non-compliment in a row. Do I sound like an attorney?"

"No. You answer my questions directly, and attorneys dodge and parry like Sylvester in the Bugs Bunny cartoons."

"So, you were insulting me to get a reaction? For shame."

"You're making me laugh again. BTW: non-compliments are called insults. Back to my turn. Are you fat?"

Austin burst out laughing. "RU kidding me? Awesome. Didn't I already tell you I had dietary restrictions? Besides, would it matter if I was?"

"Only if we were naked. But maybe not even then. I've had more mental stimulation during this conversation that I have in the last two years."

"Such a sad state of affairs, but it's tempered by knowing you are skin deep as far as looks are concerned."

"Well, I don't deserve what I can't give. What that means is this: I am presently packing an extra thirty pounds, mostly around my waist. I've started working out, but it's going to take some time. You aren't talking to Mr. Hardbody here."

"I'm more interested in the attitude of fitness and health than I am with the body itself," she wrote. "My turn. Have you ever had a relationship with a client?"

"No. That's the fastest way to lose your job. Besides, my clients are male and I've already established I'm straight. Wait. Did you ever answer if you are fat?"

"Stop making me laugh!! No. The worst of all physical sins? My second toe is longer than my big toe, which I'm so self-conscious about I won't wear open-toed shoes."

"It's your turn to stop cracking me up…no wait. Don't stop. It feels good, and I've forgotten what the vibration of the rolls on my belly feel like."

Austin almost spat up her water. This guy, whatever his size, was so delightfully funny and self-deprecating, she imagined sitting in a restaurant with him, laughing for hours.

I'd like that, very much.

Garrison stared at the words on the screen. He'd been laughing, happy even, comfortable enough to be his true self.

Genuine begets genuine, he thought, and this is who she is. No fronts. No disguises. It had disarmed him and he hadn't even known it.

"Next topic. Children. I'll go first," Garrison wrote. "She dumped me after I started drinking and spent all the money, but I contend I started drinking because she wanted children."

"The notion of kids drove you to drink?"

"The truth is," he began, "I was spoiled growing up, an only child from an old-money family in San Francisco. I had the honor of spending the legacy, at least my portion. By that time, I was married and drinking, unhappy with it all."

"You think it was because you weren't true to yourself?"

Was it the way she worded her questions or the fact she was genuinely interested, that made him want to respond honestly?

"Looking back," he wrote, "I'm not even sure I knew what that meant."

Garrison watched as Austin put a lock of wavy, blond hair behind her ear. "Though I didn't turn to alcohol in the face of heartache, my fiancé's drug of choice was heroin."

Garrison whistled. She was putting it out there. "Tell me." She's going to sugarcoat a story that I already know, he said, prepping himself for vindication. The words—his mantra—came back to him again. *No one is as good or pure as they seem.*

He read as the words appeared.

"I moved out west to get away from my family, and that included changing my name. I started a small firm in San Francisco, met a guy in the club scene and had no idea he was doing drugs until cash started missing from my purse. He came clean, went to rehab, and remained clean for almost two years.

"I met his family, he met mine, we got engaged and bought a house. We were remodeling it, and my sister, who has a good sense of design, helped out. What I didn't know was that they were sleeping together and his drug use had started up again. I was giving him money to spend on the home decorations and he was injecting it. One day, I came home and he's lying on the floor, the needle still in his arm." The words stopped appearing on the screen, and Garrison looked up to the window. Austin was staring out at the night sky, as though reliving the moment.

"I'm here," he wrote. "Was that the end?"

"For him, and me and my sister. The final page of this story ends with us at his gravesite, and only then do I learn he had left a suicide note, which the police had found, but had only told my sister, since it was addressed to her. Needless to say, I've not spoken with her since."

"Did your sister ever apologize? What happened to the rest of it?"

"No, she never apologized. She's very much like a man in the sense that sex to her is physical. It has no bearing or relation to romantic intimacy. Whereas I was devastated, thinking I would build a life with a man who had recovered from addition, she saw a body that was good in bed. Pretty pathetic, huh? As I write this, I wouldn't wish my baggage on anyone."

"Don't kid yourself. Everyone has baggage. Some people hide it deeper in their closets while others carry it around."

"For a security guy, your prose is awfully elegant."

Garrison pushed his lips out in thought. This is it. The critical moment. Up until this point, she'd been truthful about the entire story of the suicide, her career, and her name change. But what was the real truth here?

"Thanks. But back to your sister, you have never had contact with her again? Not once?"

"No. Not since the gravesite event. I have no idea where she is or what she's doing."

"Not at all?"

"No. Maybe one day we'll move on, but this wasn't the first issue in my family."

"Seriously? There's more?"

"Indeed. When I was about to enter college, my dad asked me to stay and take over the company business. Run it with him, really. That summer was the hottest on record, the building caught fire and the nearest well ran dry. There was nothing left. My father killed himself shortly after. I went home for the funeral, my mom and sister refused to speak to me, essentially threw me out. They blamed me for his death. Told me I killed him first. His suicide was only mechanics."

"Wow. That's harsh."

"Only my uncle still speaks to me."

"What if your sister was married to someone down the street, or is residing in a town nearby?" He saw Austin tip her head back and scoff.

"I don't know and I don't care."

"Do you have regrets?"

"You mean, do I wish I had a family I could love and trust? Sure, but no more or less than a man I could love and trust."

"So, your work is your love," Garrison typed. This time, Austin rolled her neck from side to side, as though stretching out her muscles.

Keep it business. Keep it impersonal.

"Is it wrong if we both like chocolate ice cream and sushi, and have messed up, addiction related backgrounds and are still interesting to one another?" she wrote.

"Are you implying you'd still give me a chance, knowing that I had an addiction in the past, and may still have the residual of smoker's breath?"

"Yes. You make me laugh. Do you think the reason you've stayed sober is because you don't have a trigger in your life?"

"A trigger being a woman?" Garrison asked in return. "Yeah. It's safer to be single. No hurt or loss."

"But no love or pain."

Garrison waited, wondering how an anonymous Internet connection had become so intimate. "So…." he wrote, feeling tentative. "Were you attracted to me because I'd written I'd drunk it all away?"

"If your deeper question is whether or not I wanted to save you, the answer is no. It took a hard lesson to learn I can't save anyone else. For once, I'd like someone to be there for me, to save me when I feel like I'm drowning. And hey, if you are in the same city, you might be available."

Garrison felt an unexpected wave of tenderness. *Something about this woman makes me want to be there for her. To protect her.* "I could definitely see myself wanting to be there for you."

For the next hour, Garrison raised every subject and fact he knew about her, and each time, she gave direct answers. No avoidance or hedging. No stretching of the truth.

I initially despised this woman and everything about her. Now he realized his bias was based on his experience with his ex-wife. Two beautiful, intelligent and strong women who had come from money.

That was where the similarity stopped.

Austin had worked for her place in this world, his ex hadn't. No woman he knew had been through the life of pain and injustice Austin had endured, and she hadn't only survived. She'd thrived.

Garrison realized he couldn't find a single, negative word to describe her.

He thought back to the week of following her and listening to her conversations. Analyzing her looks and her interactions with people. Professional, yes. Rude? No. Not even with him at the press conference. She'd matched tones when required but never displayed unjust emotions. She could have slammed Asa for being out of line at the meeting in the office, but not even then. She'd given him an impactful, but respectful admonition.

No. You are not falling for her, he told himself. You are simply intrigued with her and certainly respect her.

Garrison looked at the time. "You know we have effectively crammed two or potentially three lame dates into one really good on-line session?"

"Yikes. That's a lot."

"Who even says yikes?" he queried, smiling to himself. "You need to hang around in the gutter with me and learn some real swear words. But I'm starting to think you're up in the clouds, flying with the angels."

"Oh, now that was the first awful thing you have written so far."

"Awful? It's the truth. Don't go being the trigger for me taking a drink over this almost-relationship we are creating."

"That would make me feel bad," she said softly to herself, but typed nothing. After a few more moments, Garrison typed.

"Austin? I'm sorry if I went over the line, or...maybe I'm so out of it, I can't even flatter a woman properly anymore."

"No, no apologies necessary," came her reply. "Maybe you don't know how to give them and I don't know how to receive them."

"Chocolate ice cream," he wrote, reminding her of their shared, favorite flavor.

"Exactly."

He felt a bit of relief, guilt and tension. "Austin, I really was kidding about being triggered to drink."

A few seconds ticked by before words appeared. "No, I don't think you were. The truth is often said in jest. Relationships trigger stuff, good and bad. Agree?"

Garrison had never intended to use the word relationship with Austin, but it was too late. They had established one.

"Agree," he wrote back.

Garrison watched as Austin pushed her hair behind her ear. It hit just below her chin line, the individual lines touching points on her skin. No makeup or lip gloss.

She really was beautiful.

"Austin, do you want a serious relationship or just to play around and continue to flirt?"

"Haven't the last three hours proven we are already doing that?"

"I didn't want to presume."

"I can appreciate that. I also appreciate that you call me Austin just before you ask me a serious question. It makes me feel like you know me and care. It's nice."

Garrison thought carefully about his next words. He felt a roll of nerves go down the back of his legs, just as though he were a fourteen-year-old boy.

"Austin, would you like to do this again with me tomorrow night, say eight p.m.?" He saw her nod.

"Another date?"

"Yes. A virtual, Internet date, safe from within the confines of our own environments."

"Looking forward to it."

CHAPTER 29

Cole began tapping his pencil.

"Do you have any idea if the sequences are linked to certain products?"

"Not really. I put the first four together by doing the research on the companies that had issues and went public," Elaine answered. "Who knows how many things have occurred that didn't make it to the press. With the betasydene used with the Met, it was the manufacturers and you supplied those names. But the others, no idea. Also, I can't understand who would have the motivation to do this? To get into Dolphin, ruin companies and kill so many people."

Cole had a thought. "My boss tends to believe the root of all evil is money. In one way or another, that's what this is going to come down to."

"But for who?"

"Petrano always says one must think like the criminals in order to outsmart them."

This got a slight laugh from Elaine. "Okay man of the penal system, tell me how the criminal mind works. I'll play the judge."

"Okay, before I start giving my oral arguments, Your Honor, I want to give you a hypothesis," he said, employing his official deposition voice. "The investors win on the rise or fall of the stock, assuming they are public—"

"Most are, even though they are smaller, yes. Proceed."

"Then, as the criminal, I want the biggest payout possible while not completely napalming an entire industry."

"Which means you short-sell the smaller players and invest in the larger ones simultaneously."

"Thereby winning on both ends," he finished. "Further, you'd want to test this out on the smaller, regional players, and once proven, graduate to larger firms."

"Which increases the chance people are going to get hurt, or killed. Now you've got *me* thinking like a criminal," Elaine said thoughtfully. "Here's a strategy. Unless the person on the inside had lots of money to invest, wouldn't he or she be in league with a deep-pocketed person outside, so the hit is bigger?" Cole agreed it was possible. "So, we see who's buying up chunks of these firms along with their competitors. But then what? Do you put a stop order on all the products?"

"Possibly. I am stuck on something you said though. *We,* as in you and I?"

"Yes, we," Elaine affirmed. "As in, we are in this together now, aren't we?"

"We are."

Devann Boggard woke Saturday morning to the ringing of his phone. It was William Cole, who had spoken with his boss and received approval to provide Boggard with an update on what Elaine had found and their strategy. Boggard agreed with Cole that the profiteers were either fraud experts, stockholders or both. He also confirmed Cole's fears that the insurance companies would crater under the weight of so many liabilities. Above and beyond all of that, someone was going to have to go out and support or build up the bridges, buildings and roadways using betasydene.

His head started hurting with the sheer scope of the effort. Governments would have to support it, contract and pay all the workers—keeping the entire effort a secret from the consumer.

"We'd be forced to use our re-insurers, and even that wouldn't be enough," Devann explained to Cole. "The government would have to step in to keep us solvent, just as they did with AIG years back." Without insurance, consumer spending would grind to a halt.

"Does this mean I need to get Petrano on line with someone in D.C.?"

"I've actually never been involved in a catastrophe so large it's required the government, so I can't say for sure. What were the dates Elaine gave you again?" Cole told him. The first was a week away. "And you are sure Petrano wants to wait it out because we have no proof?"

"Correct. Elaine and I were hypothesizing that the cars will start stalling out or something like that."

"What's the next after that?"

"Telecommunications in the southeast part of the country. Then banks."

"Notice a trend?" Devann asked. "The intensity of the potential impact. First, you can't drive your car, then you can't call anyone, and finally, you can't get to your money."

"There's another category on the list. The manufacturing of car accessories."

"Like what? Seat belts?"

"Could be, but we don't know exactly. It could be exotic rims for all we know. What's your protocol?"

"I'm going to start modeling different scenarios of catastrophes. But if this proceeds according to your theory, we may go directly to the White House."

Boggard ended the call, took a shower and went back to his desk. He ordered room service and looked through the list Cole sent over. At the bottom, Cole had mentioned the four regional companies who had the same sequential number pattern.

"Oh, boy," he muttered. He recognized each one. He opened his computer and ran a search on the names. "This is no happenstance." He methodically looked up the cases, and the payouts made. It was over half a billion dollars. Now they were looking at multiples of that amount.

He picked up his phone and waited. These were the phone calls he hated placing. The ones that told his boss, the second-generation leader and CEO of GreatLife, that his company was going to be on the hook for another payout.

"Stenson here."

"Sir, you asked for the update, and I have it for you." Boggard went through the findings of Cole, their plan moving forward, and the tremendous liabilities.

"I'll call the White House when it gets to that point. But son, tell me the names of those first four companies again." Boggard did so, appreciative that Stenson Black treated him just the same no matter how good or bad the news he delivered; more family member than employee.

"Continue to work with all the other groups as necessary, but I'd like immediate updates when you receive them. I'll keep the information Cole shares confidential until our attorneys need to get involved at the AG's request."

"I don't think that will be necessary, but of course, sir. You'll be the first to know."

Stenson Black took a moment to find the number he needed, poured himself a brandy and made another phone call.

"Hello."

"Where are you now?" Stenson asked, taking a sip.

"San Francisco. Visiting friends."

"The visit is officially over. I may have a job for you to do." Stenson Black related all he knew about Dolphin Software, the payouts and GreatLife's liability. "See what else you can find. I want to know what our options are."

"Are you suggesting we are going to change the way we handle these situations after twenty years?"

Stenson lifted the brandy to his lips. "Not at all. The options I was suggesting were for you."

"My methods are unlikely to change, regardless of the circumstances."

"Someone is intentionally doing us harm, you know what that means," Stenson said, feeling as calm as his brandy was smooth.

"I do."

CHAPTER 30

Austin lay in bed, wondering how long it would be until she could feel the morning sun hit her face.

When I decide to get a place with an east facing window, that's when.

A place in the city would be painfully expensive, and her rental situation was ideal: low rent, convenient and totally anonymous. Visitors always thought she lived in Russian Hill or the Presidio, and she took enjoyment from bursting their prejudicial bubble.

That was one topic which hadn't come up last night during the marathon messaging session with her new Internet friend. Grant didn't ask where she lived, and she didn't want to know his whereabouts either. This way, he could be right next door or on the other side of the bay in Oakland or up in Sausalito, the inability to pinpoint his demographic a relief.

Austin looked up at the overcast sky. She and Grant went into a deep dive on each other's background but it hadn't been uncomfortable. In fact, it was liberating. It would all come out eventually, and this way, they both had full disclosure right up front. The cautious, prudent part of her nature spent some time telling herself not to get her hopes up for anything more than a one-off conversation. He might have dater's remorse and not show up tonight as they'd planned.

But even if that happened, it was validating to know others had issues and were still out there, trying to find happiness.

And thinking of men, she owed her uncle a call. He answered on the second ring.

"Good morning to you," he answered, sounding very relaxed. She imagined him lifting a mimosa to his lips.

"I'm calling to thank you for taking matters into your own hands, you sneaky, match-making man." She glossed over the specific details, only admitting that she'd gone ahead with submitting an old photo and had a few interested parties.

"Are they worthy?"

Austin laughed, sitting up, looking down on the street below. The cars were still in place, save for an empty space directly across from her room.

"Worthy of who? Me or you?" she teased. "Only one so far."

"Balance, Austin. That's the key."

"Right. You have been such an example of that, haven't you?"

Another laugh dismissed her question. "When are you going on a date?"

"Well, as a matter of fact," she began, standing and stretching. "We've got a call scheduled for this evening. Does that count?"

"No. If you can't see the person you are conversing with, it doesn't." He chuckled. "I was most concerned there was a filtering mechanism to weed out those who'd only want you for your money."

"Which I'm not counting quite yet," she added. Austin made her way into the kitchen, seeing what fresh fruits she had. None. "It wasn't until the Blendheim account, then Interface the same week that any kind of major profit was made."

"And that's millions."

"How do you know that?"

"*The Weekly.*"

"Ah," she said, peeling the overripe banana and putting it into the mixer. She added frozen blueberries and ice. "They do seem to have a pulse on the goings on as of late." And probably half of it could be traced back to Garrison.

"For a person who has so effectively avoided the spotlight, more than a little bit seems to be shining down on you now."

"I could do without it, I assure you."

"But as you always say, bad news can turn into good business."

Austin stopped, her hands on the mixer. "Did you just use one of my own lines against me?"

He chuckled and wished her a good day. "Let me know when wedding bells start to jingle."

"Yeah, I'll do that."

For the first time in months, Garrison wanted to get out on his bike. It was a cool, crisp, sunny fall day. He put on his all-weather gear and slowly pulled his ten-year old BMW touring bike out of the small garage. It saw the light of day on special occasions, like when he'd gotten the job at *The Weekly*.

He rode down Sunset, reaching Golden Gate park in less than five minutes. He took Park Presidio through the former base, then onto the Golden Gate Bridge. Riding on the red structure always gave him a sense of power, like it was the road to a new land, heading toward a horizon that was always bright, never dark.

Unless it crumbles, he thought, then immediately corrected himself. This was constructed decades prior, of all steel. No concrete.

Thank God.

Garrison turned off all negative feelings. He was riding his favorite toy on a wonderful day. He felt lighter inside, as though twenty pounds had been removed just by waking up. It was joyous.

Off the bridge he rode, into the hills above Sausalito. Up and around the windy road, until he reached the top of the bay view. Pulling his bike to a stop, he looked back to the city now across the bay. It was so idyllic; calm and peaceful.

He didn't stay long, just enough time to acknowledge what he'd been studiously avoiding thinking about all morning; the next interaction with Austin. At eight p.m., he was going to virtually go out with a woman for the first time since his last stint in rehab, and it wasn't a "sympathy" date. It was a legitimate woman of high intelligence and natural beauty. Tonight, he'd decided he was going to forget he was a reporter and that she was a person of interest. Tonight was about two people spending time together and enjoying each other's company.

Garrison leaned into the curve as he rode down the hill, making his way back to the city. He visualized his running shoes, putting them on and getting out on the beach, an activity he loved before alcoholism had taken over his life. It might knock him flat, but he was going to do something for himself.

Or is it really for me?

He didn't have to think of the answer; he already knew it.

Off the call with her uncle, Austin glanced at her watch. She put on comfortable jeans and walking shoes, grabbed her windbreaker and a light hat and was out the door in ten minutes.

Austin parked the car at the northern end of Ocean Beach, near the Cliff House and Seal Rocks. She looked to the three large landmarks that seemed to hover in the ocean, but saw no seals today. Only pedestrians enjoying the bright morning.

Austin tucked her hands into the comfort of the grey and blue jacket, listening to the crashing waves. No music or phone to distract her. She made her way down the concrete path, admiring the surfers who braved the coastline, known for both its beauty and danger. Every year, one to a half-dozen lost their lives in the currents, but that didn't stop the surfing championships from being held there. She'd just missed the last one, when Kelly Slater won his first and only US Championships in the US.

It took her an hour to walk to Balboa and by then she was starving. Three blocks up and to her left, she entered Kawik's Ocean deli, craving a turkey sandwich.

"Smothered with mayonnaise and cranberry please," she told the young man with a nose piercing. Taking her soda and the to-go bag, she unwrapped her sandwich as she walked toward the beach. It was just now warm enough to sit in the sun and not feel a chill when the wind whipped by.

She found an empty bench and watched the joggers and families with strollers. A man had just slowed to a jog, putting his hands on his hips the way runners do when a cramp hits right under the lungs. He didn't stop entirely, but he did look up at the sky, in one of those why-oh-why-did-I-put-myself-through-this looks.

She took another bite, watching him. His legs were lean and white, not uncommon in this area of little sun. He wore a long-sleeve t-shirt that didn't hide the paunch on his belly.

Good for him, she thought, admiring his effort. *I'm not out there running on a cold beach. I'm eating my wonderful turkey sandwich, warm and cozy while sitting in the sun.*

Austin looked the other direction, catching sight of a surfer cresting on the top of the wave. Now that was a crazy sport, and one that she had no desire to ever learn.

Half-way through her sandwich the man started up again, closing the distance between them. She could see the outline of his face, which was ruggedly handsome. He had a five o'clock shadow and his hair was unkempt, the windswept look that couldn't be helped unless one had a crew cut. His Oakley sunglasses cut along the top of his cheekbones, and she guessed he was in his late thirties or early forties.

She looked back at the ocean. In her peripheral vision, she saw the man had stopped again, chest heaving. She had to hand it to him. He was really trying.

Taking another bite, she thought about her company. She was conservative with the money she had earned so far, saving all the revenue from her clients which would serve as a cushion in case of a downturn.

"You feel like sharing that?"

Austin looked up, startled, her mouth half-full. "Excuse me?"

"It looks pretty good, actually."

"It is," she half-laughed. "Do I know you?"

The man gave a crooked smile and lifted his glasses.

"You probably wish you didn't, but you do. Clive Garrison. *The Weekly*." It was a good thing that Austin had already swallowed, because choking on food was never a graceful beginning to a conversation.

"Actually, I was admiring the fact that you seemed to be working hard out there, long before I knew it was you."

"And then what?" he asked, pulling an arm above and over his head, stretching out his elbow. "The admiration left?"

Austin squinted. "You may not know or like me Mr. Garrison for whatever reason, but believe it or not, I can admire people I don't necessarily respect."

"Ouch, that hurt," he said, dropping one arm and pulling up the other.

"I doubt it, but in my momentary lapse of judgement, I have to retract that comment about not having respect. For the record, I do respect two things about you. One, you have come a long way journalistically speaking. And two, you caught what no one else did at the Blendheim press conference, which says something. Those are very seasoned journalists. For both, you deserve credit."

His other arm dropped and he twisted one ankle on the ground, as though trying to loosen the tendons. "Well, thank you."

"You're welcome," she said, wrapping up the last part of her sandwich and standing. "Enjoy the rest of your run."

"That's it? You don't want to berate me?"

She cocked her head. "What for?"

"For getting after you in the follow up articles."

"Why would I do that? You're just doing your job, though I have to imagine those issues with me in them aren't selling as well."

"You'd be surprised. That said, I'd love to get on your list of beat reporters for stories."

"Okay. I'll give you an opportunity. Call me Monday and I'll provide you the details. The short version is that the error has been found in the manufacturing process, as we hypothesized in the press conference."

At this, Garrison moved his neck around, stretching. "That doesn't sound like it will sell many papers."

Austin observed him for a moment. "Honesty rarely does," she replied, unable to hide the disappointment she felt. "What's worse, is that you openly admit it. Have a nice run."

"Hey, I was just kidding," he said a bit too quickly. "Seriously. I'd like to talk Monday. I'll take you up on that offer of a conversation."

"Have you ever heard the phrase 'the truth is often said in jest'? You weren't kidding, and we both know it. I gave you an opportunity and you blew it."

Austin went in the direction of her car. She'd have the next hour of walking to think about her interaction with Clive Garrison.

CHAPTER 31

Garrison wasn't going to run past Austin on his way back to his home, so he continued in the opposite direction, cursing himself the entire time, periodically stopping to catch his breath.

I just had to make the comment about selling papers. I just couldn't keep my mouth shut.

Words unprintable in any self-respecting publication flowed through his mind at pace with his running. The only positive outcome of that short dialogue was his heart rate and pumping feet, as though running faster could stamp the utter stupidity out of his body.

She had paid him a genuine compliment. Two, in fact. Real, not fabricated, off-the-cuff platitudes. *And like a snake, I had struck out at her at the first hint of my own insecurity.*

He cursed himself again. Austin was perfectly justified in rejecting him, but she did so in a fashion where he couldn't even be offended. She'd taken him down in the most effective, yet polite way humanly possible.

It's what she does. She's a PR flack for heaven's sakes, he argued with himself. *Bull crap. She's not one person when "she's on," and another when she's herself. This is her, all the time, day in and day out.*

On he ran, mulling the conversation over until he had shredded himself, just as he'd done with his feet, which were starting to blister. And just like the physical wounds he'd created for himself, he couldn't avoid similar damage to his emotions.

Once in the car, he wanted to follow her and listen to her follow up conversation but remained firm. *No more eavesdropping.* Somewhere, in the field of his amorality, a seed of decency had been planted and he thought it would now be invading her privacy.

Yet, wasn't following her around an invasion as well? No, not really. He just knew her location. Spouses tracked spouses. Parents tracked children. *In the digital age, it was normal.*

Garrison pulled up his phone and watched the car move along the streets. Once he was sure of her destination, he went to her apartment. He sat and watched, and finally, couldn't help himself. By the time he had set up his listening device, Austin was recapping their brief meeting.

"He was an idiot," Austin was saying. "Yes, you are correct. I did think he was rather handsome from afar, and yes, I did admire his ability to try. Heaven knows I wasn't out there jogging in the cold wind. I was walking and eating." Moments went by before she spoke again. "I *do* respect the man," she emphasized. "I would never give anyone false compliments to get my way, let alone a man like Clive Garrison, who could probably smell a person shining him on from a mile away."

That's right. I can read them good.

"I don't sound defensive," she was arguing. "Why in the world would you say I come across that way? One can admire certain aspects of a person, both physically and mentally without being attracted to them. You know that better than anyone." Silence, then an abrupt: "You think I should give him the first shot with the Blendheim update? No way. He'd then believe he could get away with talking to me like crap. Nope. I can't do it."

Garrison was nodding his head. She had him nailed. That's exactly what he'd think of her.

"Oh. I didn't see it from that perspective."

"What perspective?" Garrison asked out loud, willing the universe to compel Karen to explain. His earbud practically vibrated as Austin let out an exasperated exhale.

"Look, the man dislikes me for some unexplainable reason, but bitterness and making up for lost time is probably why he's proven to be so good at his job. But no one even wants to be in the same room with Garrison, me included."

Garrison was fixed in his seat. The sweat on his body was cooling now, blanketing him with a chill of his own doing.

"Can we please change the subject? Yes, but now I'm so unhappy I don't even want to talk about tonight. Just another opportunity to be rejected."

"No, it's not," said Garrison quietly. "I'm sorry," he continued, hoping the universal forces of karma could take his words and put them on the wind, carrying them to Austin. *Please don't do that to me.*

"I'll see," Austin said reluctantly. "If I'm not feeling it, I'm going to bail and let the cards fall where they will. I'm not invested enough to care." Garrison felt gut-punched. "Okay, fine. I'm lying, but I still don't promise to make the call."

When Austin ended the phone call, Garrison went back to the house, took a shower and lay down on the couch. He had potentially screwed up the best thing he had going in a long time.

CHAPTER 32

"I was wondering if you were going to show," Garrison wrote. After what he'd heard, he turned off the listening device and headed home. He'd been a jerk, and was compounding the problem by verging into stalker territory. The downside was that now, he was operating blind.

Just like every other guy. But then again, if she likes me, it will be legitimate, not because I can see her face and anticipate or manipulate her reaction. There had to be honor in that.

"Standing up a date is bad form, be it virtual or real. Besides, you haven't given me a reason to do so," came her reply.

Garrison felt a spread of relief move from the center of his chest outward. His demon of worry had made him think she might have figured out the duality of his on-line and off-line identity. This proved otherwise.

"Sorry. I didn't mean to insult you. Those are my own issues cropping up," he wrote back.

"We all have them. Trust me. What'd you do today?"

Garrison smiled an answer as he typed. "I went for a ride across the Golden Gate bridge and up into Sausalito. It was cold but beautiful."

"I would have liked to be on a bike with you."

"Really? You like riding?"

"I like the notion of riding but have never been."

"It wouldn't freak you out to ride in the city?"

"I'm adventurous."

"I'll let you prove that sometime," he typed, pressing the send button the same moment he realized he just asked her out, *again*.

He felt like a teenager, awkward and unsettled, trying to be cool and completely missing the mark. "It's a great night out this evening. The stars are amazing, don't you think?"

"Yes, it is a gorgeous night. Thanks for pointing that out."

He took a deep breath. "Austin, I have a confession to make. Grant isn't my first name. It's my middle name. It feels strange being called a name used by my mother and grandmother, and only then when I'd done something wrong. I just wanted you to know."

She gave him a smiley emoticon. "You think I'm already trying to uncover your identity? Nope. I don't have the luxury of that kind of time in my life, but I will say I'm not surprised."

"Why's that?"

"Grant didn't seem to match your personality. Still, let's keep using it, since I can tell you aren't ok with me knowing your real name. yet."

"Got me."

She asked about his taste in music and shared her own preferences. Other than his love of heavy metal music and her tendency towards Latin rap, they listened to the same genres, both wanting to, but never going to the San Francisco Opera.

"Have you thought about the fact that we both come from privileged backgrounds but have left that world behind? You did it proactively and on purpose, whereas I rebelled and got kicked out."

"Yes, I did think about that today while I was walking along the beach. Both fighting against our family legacy."

Garrison nodded in agreement. "It's not easy for a grown man to admit that he is and was so weak as to make a mess of his life."

"Why do you keep saying that? It's as if you think you are a total loser and you're not."

"You are a severely blunt woman, you know that, right?"

"Yes. Am I wrong?"

"No. But consider this. I'm not the owner of a company. I don't have the CEO title or a million dollars in my bank account. And since it's all coming out, you might as well know this as well: I didn't pay for this subscription. I happen to know one of the executives and said I'd spread the word on the site in return for testing it out."

"Seriously? Good job!"

"Wow. I figured you'd think I was a deadbeat."

"There you go again. Boy (and yes, that word is intentional), you have to pull your man-panties up and start valuing who you are to yourself and the world. You are funny, and I imagine handsome, even thirty years after that picture you gave me. And if I may continue my thread of bluntness: humility is hot. Insecurity is not."

"Issuing challenges for my manhood now?"

"Absolutely. I already said I can handle a person with a past. I also said I can't fix anyone else's problems and don't want a project."

"Okay, Miss Supposed Secure, you must be awfully insecure yourself if you are so attracted to me."

Garrison waited for a quick response, but he saw nothing. The instant messenger light was still green, so she was still on line. Her comment had gotten a rise out of him, even if it was spot on.

"Did that offend you?" he typed.

"No. I'm in denial and thinking about the fact that you called me out."

"While you're in denial, I'll tell you something. Tonight, for the first time, I put on a tie. I even shaved. I figured, if we are going to go on a virtual date, I'd do it properly."

"Does it make you feel better or less insecure to know that I have on a skirt and heels, full on hair and makeup done while I sit here as well?"

"Yes, Austin. It does. It's been a while since a woman dressed up for me." He didn't even want to think about what it would be like for the woman to dress down.

CHAPTER 33

Elaine checked the clock. It was 10 p.m. west coast time. She knew Bill would be awake.

"Lucky, please call William Cole's cell number."

"Hi, Elaine."

"How are you this evening, Bill?"

"I wish I could say good, but as Your Honor is calling, I'll leave that conclusion up in the air for now."

"Good judgement, Counselor." They both laughed.

"I came across something rather odd," she began. "I have run and re-run the company names and found one thing which is completely and utterly random, yet consistent."

"You're killing me with anticipation."

"The link is down in South America. SanJo Holdings is based in Costa Rica and owns stock in all these firms, the amount large enough to be noted on the list of shareholders. I also found that SanJo has short orders for all of them. As in, to sell."

"All?" he repeated.

"Every last one. Conversely, SanJo has stock in their competitors, the smaller ones. I also triple checked what's been done. There is no way an outsider used the back door I created. I found no tracks or traces."

"You're positive?"

"On my life. But to track and catch the bad guy, I can put in code that tracks every activity and ties it back to a person."

"Which means I have to get you a court order okaying your work."

"Or I speak with Royce and he authorizes, it. Or," she paused, "I do it on my own and nobody knows."

Elaine heard the tapping of a pencil and wished she could smile but instead felt the oppressive weight of fear against her back, almost pushing her into the task before her.

"How long would it take to install this software and get it operational?"

"Only a few hours, because I'd be rolling it out to only a handful of developers."

"What's your gut on Royce?"

Elaine thought about the pros and cons. "The optimist in me says he'd want to know if he had a saboteur in his company and ensure that person was caught immediately. The pessimist says he'll tell me I'm crazy."

"Is there room for a pragmatist at this party?"

That got her to laugh. "Sure. He's going to be pissed that I did the work and didn't tell him. Alternately, he refuses the request and you have me do it anyway, with the full support of the court. We find out who it is, and before Royce has time to get mad, the bad guy is escorted out of the building in handcuffs."

"You sound like you'd enjoy that scenario."

"Yes, I would very much like the satisfaction of someone sitting at their desk, working away to destroy people's lives and the Feds show up. Personally, the part I won't enjoy is the stock price diving…hey, could you arrest the individual while he or she is at home? To prevent the whole world from witnessing it and word getting out?"

An image of Petrano's desire to use the event for all the publicity it was worth flashed through his mind. "How about you give Royce a courtesy call. See how he responds and acts. Then let your instincts be your guide."

"Bill, do you think he might be involved?"

"Elaine, if there's one thing that being in the law profession has taught me, it's that people's actions are indelibly tied to their motivation. Sometimes this means very good, honest people are put in situations where they make poor decisions, either forced or unforced."

"As in, someone has dirty pictures of him somewhere?"

"Or worse. I'm not saying it's a fact, it's just one more possibility we have to consider."

"But if he's receptive, and I'm basically positioning myself as giving him insider information to prevent a lot of blood being spilled, I'm pretty sure he'll tell me to go for it."

"The downside is if he's in on it, and you reveal too much, we'll be screwed because he wouldn't want to be found out."

"Bill, I hate to be the one to bring up the obvious, but you haven't mentioned me. I mean, I could be the person doing all of this."

"I did think of that already, for about two seconds. For you to design and destroy the company that you helped create, then concoct something else as amazingly brilliant as a countdown for all heck to break loose, then tell me about it? There are far easier ways to lose all your money and end up in jail."

"Or dead."

CHAPTER 34

"It's positively buoyant in here, like a helium-filled balloon being released from its tether."

Austin laughed, feeling the warmth of the morning sun through the window. "That was positively eloquent," she complimented Jackie, using the same inflection and words. If such a thing as a corporate honeymoon existed, then the entire office staff was wallowing in the glow of the morning after.

It's what a few hundred thousand dollars being spread around like pixie dust can do.

The floor was quiet, as though everyone understood that an awesome amount of money came with equal amounts of expectations.

At the staff meeting, she revealed the contents of her call with Devann Boggard. "We rarely receive the news our client isn't the true culprit in the matter, but this is it. So, enjoy the experience."

"How in the world did the manufacturing firms get it wrong at the same time?" asked Asa. "That's mathematically impossible, like lightening hitting the same place twice."

"Boggard said it had to do with the underlying manufacturing processes."

Asa pushed out his lips. "Not sure the press is going to buy that."

"You could sit on the news," Darren suggested. "Wait until the crisis is technically over."

"Thanks for the advice, Darren, but I got this."

"Still pissed I got the Dolphin account I see," muttered Darren, causing the group to rumble in laughter.

"Seriously," said Asa, leaning forward. "Is this going to happen again? Somewhere else?"

"If it does, make sure to have the company in crisis call us, and you can jockey for the lead," added Nichele. Asa glared at her, then turned to Austin.

"We have no more information and the underlying manufacturing process isn't our issue," Austin said, pulling her papers together. "I suspect Boggard has already called Montegue and they are cracking a bottle of champagne."

"On that really nice jet," Asa added, sounding slightly less pissy. Nichele was right. Soon enough, he would be on the hunt for another main account to keep him busy.

That afternoon, Austin got a reminder notice for her evening session at the dojo. She looked up the calendar and smiled to herself. Her motivation level to work out had always been high, but the notion of strong legs not being a turnoff to a man had increased her contentment factor. Grant was right about her insecurity, she had some to be sure.

Rain pelted the window to Cole's right, the beats out of time with his bouncing foot. In front of him sat his boss, whose only movement were his eyes, scanning the report Cole had written.

"It's no longer a question where the fault lies," read Petrano out loud. "It's with the manufacturers, not Interface, the subcontractors or anyone else on site. Those entities have verified the data entered was accurate." Cole watched Petrano skip down. "On page two, paragraph three: the date within the software itself corresponds with the batch of faulty drugs."

He put the paper down.

"Your theory, agreed to by Boggard, is that a technology terrorist planted the dates within Dolphin. Blendheim was the first targeted attack. Upcoming will be a series of high profile product failures. Is that about right?"

"Yes, noting that the cement error could have gone months or years without being noticed, but nature helped us out. It turned us on to this, otherwise, we never would have known."

"And now you are asking me to allow your contact to go through the backdoor, remove the dates, and ensure that none of these activities ever occur?" Cole nodded. "A reasonable request, but at present, I have a bigger problem on my hands. You."

Cole felt slightly nauseous as his boss stared at him with eyes usually reserved for criminals on the stand. "Me?"

"Yes. As in, do I fire you now and claim complete ignorance of your actions, or do you resign, leaving this information behind, ironically resulting in great things for the country?"

"Cole," Petrano continued, now leaning back in his chair. "You have known about, and encouraged, breaking and entering. In case you have forgotten, being an accomplice still gets you jail time. You have been so blind in your zeal to follow this lead through, none of the legal ramifications occurred to you. And this same focus made you think I'd go along with this plan because saving lives matters, correct?"

Cole nodded.

Petrano pulled both his lips in, an almost sympathetic look which transformed the man.

"Look, I get it. You firmly believe something big is going down here, but let's go through what I know." Cole hated that Petrano was talking to him like a junior attorney fresh out of law school. He also knew that at the end of this conversation, he would be out of a job. Petrano was now simply clarifying the reasons why.

"Elaine could have sent the tip to you and that reporter Garrison. She knew you were going to call her because she was, in fact, the one who gave you the tip to do so. She then comes in and saves the day. A hero by any name. But," he put up a hand, forestalling Cole's interruption, "I can already tell you are completely blinded by this woman and don't believe it's her."

"No, I don't," said Cole without hesitation. He didn't have twenty years under his belt like his boss, but he wasn't stupid. "She's already rich. Why would she bother driving the stock up and down? Why kill people?"

Petrano's expression was the one he wore when a client was guilty. "Alone and bored? Munchhausen complex? People do crazy things all the time.

"But let's pretend I went with your recommendation. You rightly hypothesized that Royce might slap criminal charges on both of you if she tells him what she's done. Alternatively, he believes you, the bad guy on the inside changes the code, the events don't happen, and for his time and trouble, he sues you for damages to his business and reputation."

"I thought…" Cole trailed off.

"You thought like a moral, logical person, not a criminal. Don't do that. In an unjust, amoral world, you will lose every time, just like now."

"I believe I'd done a pretty good job of thinking like a criminal."

"No. A real criminal wouldn't have told me any of this. He would have just gone and done it. Don't you see? You, an assistant to the A.G., have been set up nicely and will face the consequences. The whole office could be shaded over this affair."

Cole leaned over his knees, his fingers running through his hair. "What now?" he asked, subdued.

"I'm verbally giving you your two-week notice. I want to make it clear that during that time, you will continue work as usual. Understood?" Cole moved his head imperceptibly. He and Elaine had already broken the law multiple times. Doing it again over the next two weeks wasn't going to change a thing. This time, he just wouldn't tell Petrano.

"During the next two weeks you have one other task, and this you'll need to do behind closed doors with Boggard. With the proof that the product inside the concrete is faulty, we need a solution, and as you hypothesized, it's going to be a colossal task to address, keeping quiet the entire time."

"You think it will reach the White House?"

Petrano nodded. "It's going to be necessary. A gag order on everyone, the structures addressed in stages. And all the other stuff about a company called SanJo being linked through investments, let it lie for now."

"Cole," Petrano said, his voice slightly lower. "You have four dates on this list, each one corresponding with a supposed event. If those dates come and go without an incident, we will know this is nothing more than a coincidence. If that's the case, I'll print that letter and you'll be done."

"And if not?"

"Then you better have a strategy worked out with Dolphin and Boggard because it's going to get ugly."

CHAPTER 35

Garrison woke with a start at seven-forty. He reached over to grab his phone, missed, and it fell on the floor. Rolling over, he groaned in pain. This new lifestyle was sucking the life out of him, one atom of energy at a time. That morning, he put in a run by the beach and returned forty-five minutes later, collapsing on the couch. After years of culinary and toxic abuse, his body was paying the price, and it hurt.

"It will come around," he said with a groan, sitting up and rolling off his shirt as he went into the bathroom. It would catch Austin completely off guard to know that her sister was married to Royce Slade, but he had no doubt she'd keep the account, and her man Darren would complete his work. He had to write this one last article.

Under the shower, he recalled the inflection in Austin's voice when she told her friend he wasn't bad looking. That had felt good. Later, as he pulled his neck side to side as he shaved, drawing up his chin, carefully moving the blade along the skin, he thought of her smile as they communicated on-line. That was also nice, and unexpected.

He slapped his skin. It felt tighter than it had even a few days ago.

Cutting out carbs, soda and sugar will do that.

He opened a new bottle of gel, taking a small amount within his palm, evenly rubbing it through his hair, pushing back flat above his ears. The technique was transformative. He turned his head in either direction, approving. He definitely needed to carry this look to the office, although Max was sure to give him crap.

I'm starting to look more wall street financier than disheveled journalist.

"Look the part, before you play the part," he said out loud, adding a spray of cologne.

As he ironed his shirt, his thoughts naturally moved from Austin to his job. Senior reporter? Managing editor? A corner office on the top floor? Why stop there? Why was he content to be a reporter when he knew enough about the process, margins and readership to start his own entity?

A growing sense of impatience welled up inside him. One step and story at a time, he mentally repeated. He just had to be methodical about his approach. The tawdry and sensational stories that had been his entire focus until the press conference for Blendheim were going to keep him employed as he concentrated on the career enhancing pieces; those that garnered the attention of editors and publishers.

And Austin.

He pulled up his pants, drawing in the belt buckle tight. Then he rummaged through the first drawer in his dresser, finding two pairs of cashmere socks, choosing the navy blue. A good impression could hide a lifetime's worth of misdeeds.

He selected a pair of dark brown wingtips, applying the right amount of the dark lotion to the leather, pushing it into the creases. He turned on the buffing machine, the red and black material whirring as the rapidly rotating ends transformed the dull exterior to a high gloss. In sixty seconds, his shoes looked like new. He slipped them on, tying the ends, his thoughts back on Austin.

At some point, she may uncover this whole charade and I'll be back to where I was before, alone.

The quiet voice of optimism whispered that Austin wasn't that shallow.

Can she really ignore all she knows about me and fall in love with the man I am inside? The one I want to be all the time, but can't?

He looked himself up and down in the mirror and was impressed. He appeared to be the kind of person you felt was implicitly trustworthy, with whom you could have a conversation and leave comfortable in his ability to keep the details of your life secret. Yes, he looked to be a man with integrity, morals and values. Exactly what he had not been in the past.

It's never too late.

CHAPTER 36

Austin spotted Karen inside the Wildflower Café and walked past the line, nodding to the host.

"How in the world did you manage to get the deep dish quiche when the breakfast menu is closed to the rest of us?" Her friend grinned, happily smug. Austin took a seat and ordered a glass of sparking water with lime.

"The chef plays bass and I got to know him playing gigs."

"Every musician in this town needs two jobs, retired software saleswomen notwithstanding. How's Petra?"

"Teething and fitful, but Dirk packs her up in the stroller or gets out of the city for the few hours."

"Did you break down and buy another car in anticipation of daughter number two?"

"Doing that this weekend, and thanks very much for encouraging more money out the door."

"It's just a car, Karen, and it's not like you can't afford it."

"It's the accessories that will kill us, like car seats."

"And as much as I love you, that's exactly why I got you a diaper warmer instead."

"Which was still spendy!" agreed Karen.

Austin's world did not include anything baby, and thought the best things ever were gift registries.

"Your turn will come," predicted Karen.

Garrison saw that Austin was at a café, but he had to attend the editorial meeting. After that was an hour spent honing his line editing skills. A co-worker was out with a broken jaw, the unfortunate recipient of a fist that had connected with him at a bar fight.

"Only in San Francisco," Garrison muttered to himself.

"What or who are you defaming now?" asked Max.

"Joe. Only former muckraking reporters like myself should feel the brunt of a fist, not the line editor."

Max barked a laugh. "Did you say former? You turned legit all of sudden?"

"Give him three stories in a row and he thinks he's Woodward working at the *Journal*." Kell had happened to walk by at that moment, his Irish burr making the insult come off as a compliment. Max waited until Kell was back in his office before he continued to talk.

"Speaking of which, are you going to steer a wide path away from a certain woman on Thursday?"

"Why should I do that?"

"Because the paper runs on Thursday, and you're on a one-man jihad to ruin a perfectly fine woman's life, and from what I can tell, for no good reason."

"I'm not ruining," Garrison emphasized. "I'm reporting. There's a difference."

"Whatever you say," Max replied, turning back to his desk.

Garrison cranked his chair back, hands off the computer and laced on his belly. "What does that mean?" Getting no reaction, he continued, still staring at the back of Max's head. "You're telling me you disagree with putting out the fact she took eleven mil from Dolphin and that her sister is married to the company's CEO?"

Max, in an uncharacteristically firm move, swirled his own chair and faced down the much bigger and imposing Garrison.

"You didn't prove the sisters were in collusion. You don't have any quotes from anyone, other than Campbell, who essentially already told Bernie Jax and yourself that he started a competing firm and wants her clientele. You're not even bothering to call Austin herself for a quote. Even the most junior reporters do that."

"You pretending to be my editor now?" Garrison asked, in disbelief. "You wet nosed kid."

"Yeah, I'd rather be wet-nosed than brown-nosed."

"I think you just called me an ass-kisser."

"Aren't you? You do any more for Campbell and I'll start to think he's the one you're working for."

Garrison and Max stared at one another. "When did you turn righteous in your indignation?"

"About the time you decided to make it personal and destroy a person's life who already had it destroyed once."

"Are we talking about morals, all of a sudden?" said Kell, who had stepped out of his office. "You've taken a liking to the Marks woman, Garrison?" Max started to dispute the comment, but stopped as the red-haired editor pulled on his beard. "Max, you haven't been here long enough to know this, but Garrison always goes after the person who has cut him down in some way. You still pissed she nailed you at the press conference?"

"Yes," said Max firmly.

"Oh, shut up," grumbled Garrison.

"No, you shut up," Kell told Garrison, his brows furrowing. "Finish the line editing and keep delivering me stories. And you," he said, turning to Max. "For the record, insinuation of nepotism does in fact, qualify as a reportable story. The role of an investigative reporter is to search for the truth and report what is known. It's only defamation—and this is according to supreme court law—if a reporter knowing and maliciously reports an item known to be untrue.

"Garrison," Kell continued, looking down at him. "These two women are sisters, yes? And Tracy is married to Royce, and Royce is the CEO of Dolphin, the firm which just wired millions into the Marks Communications account. True? Then Max, it's a verifiable fact and we are running with it."

Garrison felt vindicated and was already wearing his I-love-being-right smile when Kell turned back to him.

"But I will agree with Max on one thing. Of all the people you could be focusing on, you are purposefully choosing this woman. I'm only going to ask you this once, and your journalistic integrity is at stake—however loosely we use that phrase in this organization. Do you have any kind of relationship with this woman, wherein you are trying to get back at her through the paper?"

"No," Garrison replied, his voice flat. "I have no reason to *get back at her*," he put in air quotes.

"And you have no relationship?"

"If, by relationship, you mean spending time with her, I have seen her twice in person, once at the press conference and the other day we accidently ran into one another at the beach. She was none too pleased to see me."

"Good," Kell replied. "Because the minute that changes, you are bound by the journalistic code of ethics to not write about her. It's a conflict of interest, and for that, we could get sued. You for writing about her, and me for publishing your work."

Only after Garrison nodded his agreement did Kell leave. He caught Max looking at him before the kid turned around again.

Garrison read the words on the screen, trying to concentrate. *Relationship*, as far as he knew, meant a romantic connection. He and Austin had been sharing the standard getting-to-know-you-stuff. Simple conversations didn't qualify as a relationship, right?

He'd look up the definition later, just to be sure.

CHAPTER 37

Lucky alerted Elaine to her voice messages, both from Cole. He'd called once in the morning, then in the afternoon. In the midst of the pressure cooker that held the mystery of Dolphin Software, she was glad for the break, even if that meant a trip to the dentist.

"Good teeth prevent a root canal," she told Lucky, knowing the electronic bird could do nothing with the information. While she was in town, she had her hair trimmed and got groceries. "Play back the voice messages please." Cole said he'd spoken with Petrano and would she please call him back. She asked Lucky to dial Cole.

"Why do you have a delay when you pick up?" he asked her.

"That's my assistant passing me the phone."

"Really? You didn't strike me as the type who would employ an assistant."

Elaine laughed. "*I'm the type*," she said with emphasis, "who creates an electronic bird named Lucky as my assistant. Depending on my mood, Lucky is male or female, but always sassy. Changing subjects, is it an attorney thing not to leave important subjects in a voicemail, or a Bill thing?"

"It's a legal thing."

Elaine poured and drank mango juice as she listened to Cole's summary of his discussion with his boss. "We're on our own," she said when he was finished.

"Yes, and I have no right to further involve you in this. Just because I'm gone in two weeks doesn't mean I want you to stick your neck out. Certainly not to Royce, because as it was identified, two of the three possible scenarios could mean lawsuits for you and I. Elaine? Are you there?"

"Yes. You have done your job. What I do now, you don't need to know."

"I can't let you do that," said Cole.

"Does that mean you have to make yet another trip to stop me?"

He briefly joined in her laughter before turning serious. "I'm being serious Elaine. Petrano is right about this. Royce could turn on you."

"That's right. On me. No one else."

"You're going to do what you want, I see."

"Answer me this, Counselor. If the roles were reversed, and you were in my shoes, what would you do?" She heard him sigh. "Exactly. You would be unwavering in your conviction and doing what's right. Now, if I do nothing more than inform you of what I learn, is that bad?"

"I don't think it can get much worse. Just talk to me in person. Nothing on my computer unless people are dying."

"You got it."

"Elaine? It's good to be unwavering, isn't it?"

This time, her smile was broad, and she was nodding as she spoke. "It's the best."

That afternoon, Garrison took up a new spot at Starbuck's, hoping that at least one of Austin's people would make a run down. He was in luck. Asa came in with a woman and they took a far table. Garrison waited for an open seat and snagged one on a couch. He overheard Asa talking about the city officials. He was speaking in an undertone, but Garrison still caught every bit. Word on the street was neither Petrano nor the city were going to go after the manufacturing firms, and the payouts for those killed or injured would be completed within thirty days, if not sooner. GreatLife was already preparing the settlements. All done quietly and discretely. No one had a clue about the betasydene being faulty. It would all look legit.

When they left, Garrison headed back to the office. Blendheim was practically old news now. The stock was back at pre-crisis levels, and as far as Garrison could tell, Austin's team was looking forward to the next client engagement.

After work, he went to the Occidental Cigar bar, waiting for Austin to finish at the dojo. He ordered soda water, sipping it as he watched the room. As sun set, the crowd and the cigar smoke thickened. He was here for a single reason: to watch, wait and listen.

First one hour passed, then another. Garrison moved seats, ordered dinner, and chatted up those he knew and many he didn't. Being an investigative journalist was like being in sales; it was a numbers game. At some point, someone would talk, especially when filled with liquor and ego.

At eleven, Garrison left the Occidental with an entire conversation recorded on his pen that he fiddled with as others drank. He wasn't going to print it. He was going to use it for a future favor, one that he hadn't even yet thought of, like the cop who had loaned him the high-end recording equipment.

It wasn't his fault the CEO of a large software company was telling his tablemate a board member wanted him to fudge the quarterly report. The other guy, whom Garrison guessed to be the head of sales, said he could move up bookings and push around the numbers so more were on the spreadsheet. The sales guy was convinced the products would be shipped, the figures realized and then by the end of the next quarter, the numbers would jibe. No one would ever know.

Lying is lying, thought Garrison as he drove home. It was only when presented with the evidence did people come clean, and by then it was too late. The bill was due.

He parked his car, slipping off his shoes the minute he entered his flat. An image of Kell appeared in his mind's eye, the red beard, squinted eyes bearing down on him. It caused him to think of Austin.

Yes, I'm walking a very fine line with that woman, my journalistic integrity, and my job.

Garrison rationalized that an emotional or "other" connection was going to be a non-issue if Kell asked, because after his upcoming article, there was no more dirt on Austin for him to dredge up. He'd move on to covering other topics. With luck, the bitter taste left in her mouth might fade, he'd eventually redeem himself in her eyes, and perhaps after a period of months, they could start a real relationship. She'd never know he was the person on-line, at least initially. By then, if they were lucky enough to last, they'd be so tied to one another it wouldn't matter. It would be one more story to tell their grandkids.

"Wow. You have gone seriously delusional," he muttered to himself, making his way to the bedroom. He put away his clothes, still scoffing at his vision. The outlandish scenario he'd played out morphed into a dream like fantasy, one that he could admit was pure fiction, never to be reality.

Still, it didn't hurt him to dream. He checked his watch. Another hour before their next conversation. Again, his thoughts turned back to Kell and the journalistic code of ethics he was supposed to be following.

Exactly where did a conversation end and a relationship begin, he wondered.

CHAPTER 38

Austin stopped by the seafood market and made crab fettuccini for dinner, using a simple recipe she'd taken from the Fog City Diner cookbook, but adding her own flair by sautéing the onions and colored peppers before mixing. The flavor was richer, as was the calorie content.

Anything sautéed in butter was better.

She showered, reviewed her email and had music playing in the background, mildly scared at the notion she was creating a romantic environment for one. Her.

In a state of insecurity, she called Karen, who laughed.

"Why don't you just meet this man in person for heaven's sake?"

"We're not there yet," she answered. "Maybe another week or two and we'll grab coffee."

"You like this guy more than anyone you have talked about since the funeral. When do you think it will go to the next level? Please don't tell me you're going to be intimate on the internet first."

Austin squealed. "Karen, that is *so wrong*."

"On the other hand, you could figure out if you guys are physically compatible before you get more emotionally attached."

"Stop it!" Austin laughed. "I'm NOT going to test him out virtually. I'm not taking advice from a woman who got married for the sake of sharing medical coverage. Now if you don't mind, I'm going to finish getting ready for my virtual date."

When she logged into Midnight Blue, she saw he was there and waiting.

She wrote a greeting, noting he was early. "Is that that equivalent of holding open the digital door for me?" she questioned.

"Gallantry never goes out of style."

"OOO," she cooed out loud as she wrote the same words, already smiling. In fact, she'd been smiling since her call with Karen. "That and chivalry are both very medieval."

"You didn't really want me to write something about being your knight in shining armor, did you?"

Austin's smile widened to a full grin. "Got me. But you have proven to be eloquent with the keyboard. I couldn't help myself."

"Enough to schedule another date?"

"Definitely."

CHAPTER 39

Austin woke to the ringing of her phone at five-thirty a.m.

"Check your local paper," her uncle said abruptly, not bothering with a greeting.

"What are you talking about?" groaned Austin.

"*The Weekly*. That reporter Garrison. He linked you and Lacy and that software company." Austin pushed herself up, reaching over to the nightstand. She had her phone in both hands, looking down. She couldn't believe what she was reading.

Her sister Tracy Carmichael was married to Royce Slade. Incestuous relationships within the valley were thriving, moving millions of dollars between known entities.

"I can't believe this," Austin said to herself. "There's no way Royce knew. If he had, I think he would have acted differently or not given me the account." Royce seemed as opportunistic and greedy as the next CEO, but he was a fiscal and operational hawk. He wouldn't do anything to jeopardize his business or his standing in the community.

"Who knows, Austin. Perhaps Tracy was the one who suggested hiring you. Her way of making amends for past mistakes?"

Austin scoffed, rising. "She doesn't rectify mistakes. She compounds them. I have to go. This is going to cause me some major problems."

"Sure, honey. You take care."

Austin read the article again and practically threw her phone on the bed. Of all the things Clive could find, he had dug up the one family member who was right under her nose the entire time. Had she attended galas or auctions, or even read the vanity pages of the papers instead of the business section, she would have known, but no. She took a quick shower and got dressed, pulling her hair back in twist. Was it possible her uncle was right? That Tracy had encouraged Royce to hire her? Only one way to find out, and that was to have the conversation with the man.

Austin was still thinking about what she was going to say as she entered the lobby two hours later. Jackie was at her desk, wearing the look of a person ready for battle.

"You saw it?" Austin asked. Jackie nodded, pointing at her screen. "I love these little surprises, don't you?"

"Are you being serious? I can't tell."

"I'm being sarcastic," Austin replied, going straight into her office.

She shut the door, left Royce a message, then looked up the phone number for *The Weekly*, requesting Clive Garrison. As the receptionist transferred her call, she told herself to be calm, to act the way she did with all journalists, regardless of their organization.

Except that no other journalist had it out for her the way this one did.

"Garrison here."

"Clive, it's Austin Marks. How are you today?"

"Fantastic," he answered, thinking about their most recent virtual conversation. "And you?"

"Not so great, to be honest. The article on me was…well, it was good reporting. It revealed things I didn't know."

"Are you serious?"

"As serious as I was when we saw one another at the café. This is the third time that I've tried giving you a compliment, none of which were received very well."

"Sorry," he said, meaning it, still trying to get his head in the conversation. "I'm unaccustomed to being on the receiving end of compliments."

"I can guarantee if you keep unearthing facts like this, the compliments will continue. The part I didn't like were the insinuations about familial relationships and incestuous patterns among companies. It would have been a courtesy for you to call and ask me about either."

"I checked the facts and they were accurate."

"So, you could have called but chose not to?"

Garrison pushed his fingers into his temples. Max had said as much. "I won't do that again. I promise. I'll be fair."

"You're talking about being fair now? After the fact?"

"Hmm. That's an interesting comment for you to make. Did fair apply when you blamed another company for the mistake with Blendheim?"

"That was a business strategy which was perfectly legal."

"And what I used was a journalistic strategy that was also perfectly legal. Were any of my facts I wrote about you wrong?"

"Facts? No. You got them correct, as I said."

"So, you are unhappy about the inferences I included, correct? To be *fair*," he continued, emphasizing the word, "you inferred the entire responsibility the manufacturing malfunction by Blendheim was on the software used. How were our approaches different? Why can't you just admit that I'm doing the exact same thing you are doing, but somehow, when you are on the receiving end, it's not okay?"

"It's not welcome, no."

"Here again, you don't give me a straight answer," he chided. "Maybe it's not right of me to say this Austin, but perhaps you may want to consider that what comes around goes around, and that this is the universal karma coming back to you."

"Are you actually saying that your motivation for writing about me is to give me a taste of my own medicine?"

"It didn't start out that way, but I will acknowledge the more I saw you stepping out of the spotlight, the more it encouraged me." Garrison wished for a piece of gum. He wanted to chew away his nervousness.

"Fine," she answered. "As a journalist, I'll pitch you a story. How about one that focuses on how I'm helping companies preserve a lot of jobs and saving shareholder value?"

Garrison watched Max enter the kitchen, wishing he still had the place to himself. "Not sure how that would go down with the editor."

"It wouldn't, because all *The Weekly* focuses on is negative situations and insinuations. My next question is if you are best friends with Leonard Campbell, because it appears he's using you to hit at my reputation."

"Campbell is a source, like anyone else," he answered evenly. He had no wish to talk about that helpful, but self-serving man. "You are a public figure, someone of interest who has a great deal of influence in this town and nationally. That makes you interesting. *I* find you interesting." He was putting it out there, as clear as diamonds on the road and she wasn't seeing a single one. Still, it gave him a high to say the words.

"Why do you even care about anything to do with me?" She sounded exasperated.

"Because you are a king-maker. You have devoted your professional life to helping firms or people in crisis resurrect themselves, and your personal life reflects it. No marriage, no kids. No life that I can see."

"Then why didn't you write that in the first place?" she asked, her voice higher. "It would have been far better than focusing on my sister, who I haven't spoken with in years. In fact, you don't even sound like the individual who wrote the article." Austin was talking so loudly he wouldn't be surprised if Max had heard half her comments.

"Information and context changes things," he conceded.

"That's a start," Austin said, sounding appreciative. "Will you do one other thing? If Campbell or anyone else feeds you more information, would you do me the courtesy of calling me for a comment?"

"I already promised I would. I'll do my best. Can I take you up on that offer for more details?"

"Sure. I have a few calls to make, one to Royce Slade." Garrison heard her voice lose its luster.

"Hey, I'm not…I hope that didn't cause problems."

"It won't put me out of business, if that's what you were wondering."

"I hope not. Eleven million is a big chunk of change."

"Speaking of which, how did you learn that information? It's confidential, known only to a handful of people."

Garrison's buoyant mood fled, replaced with the hollow feeling of deceit. "Confidential sources," he said, then quickly added, "you'll call me back in a few hours?"

"Around lunchtime, if that's okay."

"That would be perfect."

CHAPTER 40

Royce was sitting in his office when the call came through from Austin. He'd spoken with the company's attorney who confirmed the relationship between the sisters didn't constitute a breach of contract. When asked, Royce confirmed he no idea Tracy had a sister, let alone that she was Austin Marks. Sam wisely kept his mouth shut on the matter of marital communication, which had made Royce's humiliation greater.

"What kind of woman hides the fact she has a sister from her husband?" Royce had demanded of Tracy.

"The kind who recommended Dolphin hire Marks Communications as the scapegoat in case they needed one," she had replied calmly. "A strategy you thought was fantastic, and your board supported."

"But with me, you couldn't be honest?" he'd said, still in disbelief. "Lying by omission is still a lie."

"It's all about protection," Tracy said firmly.

Royce shook his head and picked up the phone.

"Hi, Austin," Royce greeted.

"Hi, Royce. You can guess why I'm calling. To start, I had no idea Tracy was your wife. We haven't spoken for years, and honestly, I'm out of it from a social perspective in this town. Did you know?"

"No."

"Then it came as a shock to both of us."

"You could say that," Royce admitted. "My attorney said the relationship doesn't constitute a breach of contract, even if either of us had known, because it wouldn't materially affect the program."

"What's legally right doesn't always mean what's ethically or morally right," Austin replied. "I would have stated it right up front, so there was no concern you were getting unduly charged."

"It's a moot point. I came to you with a pre-determined amount."

"All true, but I don't want people thinking or even talking about the possibility that money went from your company to me, based on a familial relationship."

It was exactly the issue Royce had raised with his wife. Tracy was adamant that her intentions were designed to protect his company not to enrich her sister.

"What happened between you and Tracy that caused the falling out?"

"She didn't tell you?"

"I asked, but she said it was a family matter."

"I'd tell you, if it weren't for two issues. One, it doesn't put my sister in a flattering light. Second, it doesn't reflect well on my own personal decisions. If you need more information than that, it's going to have to come from her. For now, would you like us to continue our contract or cancel? I'm sure the opinion of your shareholders has got to be loud about now."

"No. Let's continue," he said with finality. "I'm pretty good at ignoring shareholders when I'm doing what's best for the company. I've got just one last question, and I want a direct answer. Can I trust you?"

"If you have to ask the question, it means you're not sure you can. I'm certain you agree it's not a great idea to be in a contractual relationship where the foundation isn't one of trust. My saying yes, I can be trusted, doesn't mean much, regardless of my track record, successes or reputation. That said, I'm going to have my attorney write up a letter, cancel the contract and send the money back."

"Hold up," he said. "I'm not sure I want you to do that. I know the board doesn't."

"Royce, we don't want people questioning our motives. I know I don't. Actions are remembered only for a short time, but a tarnished reputation is eternal."

Royce felt as though he'd been outflanked, and by the very woman he had called the smartest one in the room.

"Are you positive?"

"Yes. It's early in the day yet, so you'll get the money back in your account by two. On a final note, I'll give you what Darren has created so far."

Royce was impressed by her offer but then second guessed it. He knew crisis communication plans normally were at least a quarter of a million.

"How much do you want to deduct for it?"

"I just said we'd give it to you."

"Austin, as much as I appreciate that, too good a deal could be associated as the in-law discount."

"Oh, right. I've never had to think about that before. Wow," she said, laughing a little. "We're related."

"Wow is one word for it," Royce said. He suddenly felt morally corrupt for trying to set her up for a fall by outlining the strategy to the board.

"Charge me one-fifty and we can get it done. Before we get off, I just want to say I'm appreciative and impressed with how you've handled this situation."

When the conversation ended, Royce swiveled his chair to face the Woodland Hills, holding off calling Sam back with the outcome of the call. He watched two bikers on the path, both no doubt training for an upcoming race.

He thought back to that time in his life, when he was invigorated with the idea of creating a product, full of passion and the blind desire to succeed. Elaine had been there for the ride, the two of them, just like those cyclists, drafting off one another, pushing and pulling to make it over the tough, uphill battles, coasting and high-fiving on the fun, exhilarating curves of the business.

Unlike Tracy. She'd entered after he'd made it big. She never encountered any struggles. No challenges. Just the windfall.

The thought that his wife had lied, even if it was for his own protection was unnerving, and for the first time in their marriage, the foundation of trust had been cracked.

He got up and shut the door, looked at the time and decided to wait a few more hours until Elaine would be up. Right now, he didn't want to be the CEO of a software company. He wanted to be the person he wasn't to Elaine: a friend.

CHAPTER 41

Austin called Darren into her office and gave him the news. He wasn't entirely surprised. He, along with the rest of the team, had already read Garrison's story. Austin pointed out to Darren the commission associated with the cost of the plan would still be his, reiterating that she hoped his professionalism would carry over to the rest of the team.

Jackie assembled the group who grew quiet when Austin and Darren entered and took their seats. She told them the news: she'd withdrawn the account and the money was being returned, save the cost for the plan.

"Royce thanked us for the work and reiterated the board had wanted to keep us on. We couldn't, although I appreciated his support."

"It's just unreal Garrison put it together," Susan said with grudging respect.

"And I was lucky he either didn't know about, or purposefully omitted, the more lurid details," added Austin, still relieved.

"Seriously? There's more we're going to read about?" asked Asa, incredulous. He leaned back with force, causing his peers to glance at him, their facial expressions reflecting her own annoyance. "You want to give us a heads-up now, or just wait, until we're all blindsided again?"

"As though it's Austin's fault," said Darren, eyes narrowed at his peer. "Everyone has a past, especially you. You want the press to go cataloging everyone you have slept with in this town and write about it? Women would require you to take a blood test before getting in bed."

"Austin wasn't sleeping with her sister," Asa shot back.

Austin waited for their undivided attention. "Darren, Asa does have a point. None of you deserve to be blindsided, and because this involves me, I'll give you the full story.

"I've not spoken to my sister in four years, since the funeral of my then-fiancé, who left a suicide note addressed to her. It was only then that I learned the two had been carrying on an affair. He was a heroin addict who got clean, but then she started funding his habit again. As you can imagine, this isn't information I'd proactively share with anyone, but some of the information is public. Anyone could have found it. What my sister has done, and who she's done it with, has not been something I choose to think about."

"Holy crap, Austin," Susan remarked.

"Yes. It was, and still is, crap." Now that the information was out there, Austin wanted the subject changed and the meeting finished. "At the very least, I imagine it's only a matter of time before Leonard takes over Dolphin's crisis communications, using the plan we created."

"And then blaming us if it fails," noted Asa with some bitterness.

Austin shrugged. "Not our problem. In fact, nothing to do with Dolphin is our problem any longer, and given the circumstances, I'm rather grateful." Her directors, save Asa, echoed that sentiment.

Back in her office, she didn't look up when Asa entered. She was as fatigued of him as he was likely mad at her.

"Is there anything I can do?" he asked her.

She looked up, her forward-thinking, mentoring attitude replaced with his own dismissiveness. "Yes. Go to your peers and offer them assistance. Better yet, get on the phone with your past clients and see if they need updated plans. Perhaps the abundance of time on your hands is the reason for your increasingly bad attitude."

"You think?"

"You tell me, Asa. Your demeanor and comments suggest you believe you are being poorly treated here. If that's what you think, you can give your two weeks' notice and start looking."

Asa's eyes broadened slightly. "I don't have the interest."

"Really? You don't seem to have an interest in being a team player either. Ironically, the more success you have the less desirable you are to have around."

Asa put a hand on his chest, thinking through her words. "Are you firing me?"

"I don't need to do that. You keep going the way you are, and you will end up firing yourself."

"So, it's an ultimatum?"

Austin chose her words as if being recorded, because in today's environment, just about every interaction with one's peers or bosses could be. Nothing was sacred any longer.

"My request is for you to do your job, be supportive and respectful of your peers and manager. It's a requirement where you are a professional making a quarter million a year without bonuses. If that's too much to ask, then please, go right back to Campbell's door. His standards are far lower than ours. What will it be?"

Watching Asa's palm tap his chest, she felt at peace with her words. She believed Asa and Leonard deserved one another. Both were solely focused on their individual objectives, not the good of the whole, unless it served their own ambitions.

"I'll stay."

"Under what circumstances?"

"That you accept my apology for me being a jerk." He removed his hand, placing it to his hip and walking to the window. "Call it a six sense or whatever, but I didn't want Dolphin as an account. We did blame the Blendheim crisis on them after all."

"Then I paid the price and we are moving on." She waited a moment. "Are we?"

"Moving on? Yes. I've moved on."

"Good. Because the rest of the business hasn't stopped, nor should it."

CHAPTER 42

"Squawk! The freaking phone!" cried Lucky.

"Caller number identification?" requested Elaine. A breeze was kicking up late morning as it always did, increasing the waves and pushing at the large palms outside her white shutters.

"Main number, Dolphin Corporation." In response, she pulled down the center lever, closing off the view.

"Answer please."

"Hello, Elaine."

"Hi, Royce. Nice of you to return my phone call."

"You called?" he asked.

"Yesterday afternoon. Isn't that why you're calling me?"

"No, not at all. I was, uh, just saying hi."

Elaine glanced at Lucky, who flapped and raised its short feathers above its ears.

"Royce, have you changed so much that you can't just come out and tell me what's on your mind?"

"Well, being the CEO of a public company does cause me to watch my words a bit."

"Self-censorship is not you. It's not believable."

"Fine," he said. "The board is concerned about anyone selling large chunks of stock."

"I'm still one of the largest shareholders and I haven't sold any stock, nor do I plan to. But I still don't believe it."

"Don't believe what? I'm being serious."

"No. I get that. But it's not why you're calling. What else is going on?"

Royce sighed again, this time louder. "Do you think it's possible Dolphin's software could be responsible for issues such as Blendheim, even if they said their software was customized."

"Absolutely. Very easily so."

"What do you mean?"

"I was contacted several days ago by a member of the California attorney general's office. They were tipped off on Dolphin Software before the Blendheim issue arose." As Royce started to swear, Elaine spoke over him. "I took it upon myself to look into it."

"How?"

"I will tell you," she said firmly, "if you promise to be rational. Can you do that?" He affirmed he could. "Someone has corroded the software from the inside. A person with source code access. I found patterns in the software attached to both Blendheim and Interface and several others. I ran a scan on every customer in your database to ensure this wasn't an anomaly. Royce, the same code is there for other major companies, all triggered by one thing."

"What?"

"Dates. Royce, and they are sequential."

"You're absolutely positive?"

"I wouldn't be telling you otherwise. I called yesterday to feel you out and determine if you were going to sue me for looking into this on my own or help me try and determine how the code was inserted, and by who."

"Come on, Elaine. I would never sue you for trying to do the right thing."

"Rational reactions aren't always bedfellows with bad news. Can I put the code tracking software on the system?"

"Absolutely. I want to get this son of a B who is trying to mess with my company—our company, and I want to nail him hard."

"How do you know it's a he?" she asked.

"We only have five engineers who have access to the source code, all male."

"I need it in writing that you are giving me authorization, in case anything happens."

"What you're really saying is that the person might sabotage you?"

"Royce, anyone who is smart enough to get into the system and create code that kills will have no hesitation doing the same to me, or you."

CHAPTER 43

Garrison waited until four o'clock then left work. After what he'd heard today, only one fix existed for his moral dilemma, and that was to be found at the Cigar Bar & Grill.

It's because people smoke and talk more, and right now, he didn't want to talk. Just listen.

When Austin didn't call by two, he rang her. She'd been brief, providing him with details on Blendheim, much of which he already knew. He thanked her for giving him a second chance.

"Everyone deserves at least one second chance," she'd said, although some of the kindness she'd used earlier was gone. It was to be expected. She'd lost the Dolphin account, given back the money, was dealing with an ego-filled employee and being hounded by Leonard Campbell.

His guilt would have been alleviated had Austin been angry with him, but she was the inverse: professional and polite throughout, all that she'd been with Asa and anyone else who had screwed her.

Including me.

Garrison found a seat at the bar, taking the stool closest to the wall, glad it wasn't a Saturday night. He wasn't interested in a salsa lesson, or the long legs and sensual dancing that came along with it. The Latin music was nicely distracting though, the sounds blending with the water pouring down the fountain in the center of the Tuscan-styled restaurant.

"Tequila," he ordered. "Double." The bartended poured him a glass. He'd been on the wagon for two and a half years, and if he was going to fall off, he might as well do a backflip to the ground.

Following the call, he received an email from Asa's distribution list that was clearly sent to the reporters in the valley.

Well, at least I've made the cut regarding my peers. He should have been gratified. Instead, he ordered another double.

At five, the lights dimmed, the level of music increased, and occupancy was standing-room only. The couple next to him were engaged in a quiet and intense conversation.

When he ordered a third double, the bartender eyed him. "You driving?"

"Nope. Taxi."

He subtly dipped his tongue in the tequila, feeling the burn less than he had two hours before, his mouth having gone numb, which wasn't the point. He wanted other things to deaden, the pain in his chest being one. Instead, it was rising to the surface, his body and soul out of sync, splitting further apart.

Austin's legs and arms felt heavy as she worked through the multi-step tai chi chung sequence. In four years, she'd made it up to fifty-seven movements, the starting motions of strength and breath control flowing into mid-air spins. This session, Instructor Sean had noticed her focus and given her a reward: three new movements. She dropped low, spun on her back left foot, then sprang up with a side kick, hitting her opponent's chest. She bowed and said her thanks.

"You are ready," was his reply.

Ready for what? she wondered. To be able to duck and defend against an attacker with a knife, then knock it out and crush his lungs? Too bad the business coaches didn't offer the equivalent verbal maneuvers.

As she changed, another thought struck her. Advisors, like herself and her nemesis Campbell, did just that. They spun the storyline, ducked the bullets from the media and then attacked, but in such a way as to hurt the inside of the company without leaving a bruise. Both were powerful skills and equally as deadly.

Austin drove along the Embarcadero until road work stopped her progress. Annoyed, she hung a right on Broadway, then up to Montgomery, not far from her office. Seeing a motorcycle cop, she took it slow as she approached Pacific. A man was on the corner, swaying slightly, his hand in the air.

Not the best spot for a cab. He swayed again, nearly hitting a pole.

The light turned red, and she stopped, watching the man. This time, he did lean over, then fell right into the metal.

"Ouch," she said to herself. She watched one cab, then another, pass right in front of the man, who just had the sense to raise his hand again as he lurched forward. "He might get hit," she mumbled. Rejected again, he turned to Montgomery.

"Just my luck," Austin muttered, recognizing Clive. As she drove forward, she couldn't help but look in her left mirror. Clive was still trying to hail a cab.

He's going to kill himself and I'm going to get the wrong end of the karma train for not helping.

She turned left on Jackson, then another left on Sansome, then back on Pacific. She put on her hazard lights and pulled up to him calling his name. He turned, squinting.

"Clive," she called to him as she neared. She put her hand out, keeping it low and not aggressive. "It's me, Austin. Looks like you need a ride."

He slurred something unintelligible, and leaned over again, narrowly missing a fall off the curb. He overcorrected, and she jumped forward, bracing his fall into the metal pole.

"Here, hold on." She firmly placed his left hand on her forearm, holding his lower back with her right. "Lean in to me." She didn't need to encourage him. He practically collapsed on her.

"Here you go," she said, easing him into the passenger seat. "At least you smell good," she said to herself. The brushed wool of his jacket was soft, not unlike the skin of his face that accidentally brushed hers when his head fell

205

forward. "And you didn't crack my lip, which is also a bonus. Okay, there you go. Keep your hand here."

Austin placed both hands in his lap, shutting the door quickly. Once in the driver's seat, she turned to him and stared.

"My, how the world turns." She shook her head once. Then she realized she had a dilemma: no address. "Easy enough to solve." She pulled open his jacket and found his wallet on the upper inside pocket. Clive G. Garrison was engraved on the ostrich hide. Inside was his address.

"Interesting," she remarked.

"We're practically neighbors, did you know that?" She glanced to her right. He faced her, eyes closed, his lower lip hanging ajar. Not super flattering, but then, for a drunk person, not completely unsightly either.

Austin drove down Montgomery, hung a right on Market and then left into the Mission district, then to Sunset. She pulled onto Guerrero, quickly finding the three-story, taupe colored building. According to the address, Clive lived on the third floor, facing the garden.

"Clive, do you have a parking spot?" He groaned in response. "What about a code?" She pulled into the driveway, choosing the one on the left.

She unbuckled him, searching his coat pocket for the second time. The heavy, silk lined jacket had three, the set of keys in the lower left. "Try and help me here," she muttered to herself.

Maneuvering the man out of her car was awfully intimate, she thought. She ran her hand behind his back, leaning him forward, then wrapping her left and right arms around his chest. Her chest touched his shoulder and arm, her face against his more than once as the weight of his neck gave. He was lighter than she expected but still required effort. Unable to dislodge him, she gripped his left hip with her right hand, pulling towards her. His body fell into her, and she barely braced herself in time.

Austin started laughing. She hadn't had this much physical contact in years.

And all it took was a drunk man who essentially hates me.

CHAPTER 44

It took a few minutes before a person answered their buzzer. She described the situation through the intercom, relieved when a man in boxers came out with his girlfriend and together the three of them helped Garrison up the three flights of stairs. Once she got the key in the door, they helped him inside, and left after lowering him to the couch.

Austin relaxed, momentarily closed her eyes, experiencing a surreal moment. *Helping the very man who had been the thorn in my side, costing me a ton of a money, and ripping the scab off an old, dry wound.*

He breathed loudly, and she turned to him. He was completely gone.

What to do now?

She heard Instructor Sean patiently counseling her to find her inner calm. Her center. Closing her eyes, she visualized peace. His leg twitched, and she opened her eyes. The fireplace in front of her was lovely, a patterned carved wood, with etchings along the mantel and down the sides. The ivory tone set off the mint color of the walls.

Which matched the stripes on the couch, she thought. For a recovering alcoholic of a reporter who had lost everything, Clive G. Garrison had pretty good taste.

Austin stopped cold.

Recovering alcoholic. Both him and Grant. Coincidence?

Very quietly, she rose and went into the kitchen. One by one, she opened the cupboards. Right above the stove and were two big bottles of Tabasco, a green and a red.

"Big bottles of each, just in case the zombie apocalypse happens," she whispered to herself, recalling "Grants" words in their first on-line encounter.

She looked back to the living room, feeling queasy. Clive's head hadn't moved. With her heart pounding, she walked through the kitchen, searching for open letters or mail. Finding nothing, she explored the one-bedroom apartment. The bathroom, a small closet, then the bedroom. She walked in, turning on the light. The bed was a king with inlaid mahogany wood. She glanced through an open door to a closet. It was packed full of tailored clothing, the shoes as old but as luxurious as the clothes he wore, but she kept walking towards the window. Her heart pounded louder as she neared.

Her fingers shook as she gently moved aside the drapes and lifted the blinds. The moonlight bounced off the leaves, the reflection of the city lamps revealing a small garden.

"Okay, that doesn't prove his identity beyond a shadow of a doubt." Austin needed one more definitive piece of evidence.

Retracing her steps to the kitchen, she began opening kitchen drawers. Closest to the refrigerator, she found letters and old business cards but nothing with Clive's name.

Luggage. She went to the hallway closet, turning on the light. Under the bottom shelf, she found two suitcases, each with tags.

Clive Grant Garrison.

Austin retrieved her phone, sitting on the edge of the couch. She typed his name and instantly, her worst fears were realized. A photo of Clive Grant Garrison appeared, alongside pictures of his former wife, the details of their divorce, his decline and then later, his rejuvenation as a reporter at *The Weekly*. Seconds later, she was looking at a mirror image of him. It was the photo from high school "Grant" had sent.

Austin quietly put away her device before she acted on the compulsion to hit him. How could he??

She closed her eyes. *Find your center.* Rebalance the spirit and the mind. Words of peace and being non-judgmental came forth, but they didn't give her an immediate calm. Ironically, that came from hearing Clive's easy breathing.

Looking back at his face, she imagined all she knew of him. His own choices, his decline and hitting rock bottom, the changes he had to make to pull himself up from the depths of ruin. Even convincing an editor to take a chance, finding and writing the stories no one else would deign to cover. Then this.

This being me. If his life were the major leagues, then he'd made it to the big game by even being at the Blendheim press conference. He'd hit a homer when he'd heard what no one else did. Could she really blame him for focusing on her, the person who stopped his run around the bases?

No.

She closed her eyes again, reflecting on what else happened.

Each subsequent conversation had gone deeper, he'd been funny and blunt. He'd called her out just as she did him, and they'd both been right and justified. It had been real and honest.

Then did it matter he clearly knew it was her on Midnight Blue? He couldn't read her mind and make up answers. He revealed portions of himself before she had, there again, proving they were more alike than she ever could imagine.

Chocolate ice cream.

Austin thought about yesterday. The article he'd written had been a massive hit to her business, but it was in no way a mortal blow. She sighed, sinking deeper into the couch. He'd felt bad about the article. It was in his tone and words when she'd called him. And although no amount of remorse would make up for the lost money, she'd told Asa last week that he had his job to do just as she had hers.

As she sat in the man's apartment, she felt a different emotion.

"I'm sorry you got drunk," she whispered. "It wasn't your fault that my sister and I aren't friends. You just happened to be the guy that reported it. But you certainly know the whole story, and I'm grateful you didn't publish my dad's suicide. That was good."

Sympathy merged with a strong physical desire, one that included the colors of compassion and empathy.

Careful not to move the back cushion of the couch, she placed her elbow on the top, draping her hand down. She felt the soft wave of his hair, turning her finger over, gliding it down along his cheek.

"I think I was falling in love with you," she said quietly. "And now, I don't know what to do with you or any of those emotions."

She was leaning closer to him when his phone beeped. Once, then again. She wanted to turn it off before he woke, which would be seriously awkward. She found it in his coat pocket, intending to turn it over and put it down, but her name on the screen caught her up short.

Austin's location.

What the....? She held it, staring. Her location was pinpointed on a road in Guerrero. The address his own.

She moved the screen around, pressing the menu which showed past locations. The dojo on Friday nights, the Wildflower Café with Karen, her movements to and from the office.

Austin felt the sick, rise of fury growing from her core.

How could he? But…how *did* he? Had he really been following her all around town, at all hours of the day and night.

Furious, she put his keys on the coffee table, leaving as quickly as she could. She knew too many ways to seriously hurt someone.

CHAPTER 45

"No news of oil or gas issues from the mainland," Cole told Elaine.

"Nada on this side, either."

It was almost three p.m., Friday afternoon, Pacific Standard Time, and the presumed deadline for the first trigger in the oil and gas business. Elaine had debated with Cole about the timing.

She took a sip of the guava-mango smoothie she'd made for herself. "If this doesn't pan out, do you think Petrano will change his mind about your job?"

"Don't worry about me. Former junior attorneys with the AG's office don't usually have a problem finding a high-paying, soul-sucking job at a large firm. Devann is already working with his CEO and the government about covering the faulty concrete. It's requiring a lot of confidential meetings, but it's happening round the clock."

"And your boss is getting all the credit?"

"Haven't I already said I'll get a well-paid job somewhere else?"

Elaine grunted, disgusted. "You deserve the top job for uncovering this Bill. If you hadn't read the original tip, it would still be in the round file."

"I've never heard you get mad. You are mad, right?"

"You bet I'm mad! And protective. And wanting to push pins in your boss's voo-doo doll."

Her mood was lifted by Cole's laugh.

She took a big swallow before making another call. Royce was eager to learn the latest. He picked up on the first ring.

"The good news is the date has come, and so far, nothing has happened."

"Trust me, I've been watching the clock along with you."

"Royce, as much as I want to think this was one, big, random, coincidence, I'm having a hard time with it."

"Likewise."

She sighed. "We have nothing new, and even though my gut tells me different, it looks like I've gotten you spun up over nothing."

"Maybe, maybe not. Remind me again, though. What was it that was going to be triggered today?"

"Oil refinery."

"Come again?" he asked.

"An oil refinery. It would have been bad if something went awry, but like I told Cole, it might be nothing."

Royce swore. "Elaine, think about it. Processing oil takes time. Hours or days. Then it gets put in transport containers and is shipped around the country. An error of any size wouldn't be caught until you and I put gas in our cars and they sputter. Which firm had this trigger?"

"Loron Corporation. I looked them up. They have refineries on both coasts. What are you thinking?"

"Too late now is my guess. If this theory of yours holds true, whatever was triggered within the process is already done. The gas is already corrupted." Elaine thought of thousands of gallons of gas being deposited in big, underground barrels.

"And you can't call them up and say- 'hey- we think your gas has been corrupted, you need to recall it all, reprocess it and then reship it,' can you?"

"Not unless we are going to pay the millions required to fix the problem, then prepare for lawsuits because it was our software that created it."

For a few moments, the line was silent. "What's the next account on your trigger list?"

"A company called Trimade."

"That's telecom. They have more cellular posts than anyone else in the country. When is the date?"

"This coming Tuesday." Elaine heard Royce curse again under his breath. "But Royce, we are in the same predicament. We can't send out a software fix because we don't know where the problem lies, again, assuming one exists."

"Like you said, we have to wait it out."

It might have been the ensuing silence, but her thoughts turned elsewhere. "How are things in your personal life?"

"Let's just say I am waiting that out as well."

CHAPTER 46

Cole headed straight to the SFPD, where he found Boggard behind his computer. Cole shut the door behind him. He brought the insurance man up to date, then intertwined his fingers behind his head. "You still going to be here until Wednesday?"

"All these discussions with Petrano, the White House and everyone else can be made behind any closed door, not just this one. I'll call headquarters and see how much longer they want me to be here."

Cole leaned over and picked up a rock. "Odd momento."

"Those are samples of concrete from the Met," Boggard explained. "That's how we tracked down the faulty ingredient in the first place. Austin Marks is coming by shortly to pick them up, and get them back to Interface."

Cole thought about Dolphin and was reminded of what Petrano had taught him: when things fit together too perfectly, something's wrong.

"She never had an idea of the problems that might have awaited her had she kept the account," Boggard reflected. "In fact, speak of the devil…"

Devann Boggard stood, with Cole following. Austin Marks was led into the room by an officer and Devann greeted her with a handshake. Cole said hello, remaining where he was.

"Here you go, ready and waiting," Boggard told her.

"Thanks so much Devann." They made small talk about the Interface project, and how quickly the city had removed much of the rubble, doing so twenty-four hours a day. As they were talking, Cole noticed Austin looking at the whiteboard behind him.

"Good group of companies," he remarked, watching her.

"Yes. What do the yellow circles around these businesses represent?"

Cole glanced at Boggard, who barely moved his head. "Special companies that we isolated as having close relationships with Dolphin. Does anything unique pop out to you?"

"Sure. They have been, or are, clients of ours. There are a few others…" she continued. Without being asked, Austin picked up a pen and wrote a star beside a half-dozen others.

"Impressive," said Cole.

"Thanks. Well, gentleman. Have a good weekend."

The two men said their goodbyes, waiting until she'd stepped into the elevator before speaking.

"Are you thinking what I'm thinking?" asked Boggard.

"Yes. You want to do it or me?"

"Do what?" It was Detective Snow, who had come in the room as Austin left.

Cole caught Boggard's look of approval. "Snow, we have a theory which involves insider trading and wonder if you'd like to help us look into it."

The stocky man put one hand on his hip and used the other to wipe his mouth, as though he were removing a bad taste.

"It's a Friday night and I ain't got nobody," he said, lyrically in tune with the ancient pop song. "Give it to me." Cole took the man through the companies on the whiteboard and gave him the name of SanJo Holdings. Before Cole left, the detective was already pulling up every shareholder in the companies circled in yellow.

Boggard excused himself to have a conversation with his boss, and Cole walked back to his office, calling Elaine on the way. She agreed to work on any ties the targeted companies had to Marks Communications in parallel with Snow.

"Are you doing this as a ploy for me to call you back in the middle of the night?" she asked.

"Now that's a good strategy, your honor. I'd like nothing better than to have your voice be the one I hear late at night."

"Well then, I'm all ears."

CHAPTER 47

Garrison drank coffee, made multiple trips to the bathroom and exercised deep breathing to make it through the morning. He barely kept his eyes open during the short editorial meeting, then after lunch, he slumped over his computer, hanging on for dear life.

"The forthcoming article better be worth it," Kell had intoned, slapping the back of Garrison's head with a folded newspaper. "Go home. You're not doing any good here."

Garrison nodded, shutting off his screen. His eyes ached from the glare. The pounding was made worse by the knowledge Austin had taken him home and what he was going to do now.

Do I send her flowers or a sympathy card for having to smell my tequila-soaked breath? He said a prayer that she'd not snooped around his home, relying upon the notion she was far classier than he and would rise above such an urge.

At home, he sat on his couch, trying to clarify the blurry images from the night before. One or two other people helping him up the stairs, Austin saying something to him as he moved in and out of consciousness, and that was it.

He called the florist, paying an extra twenty bucks for immediate delivery. He asked for a recommendation on 'apology flowers,' and took the woman's advice for the Star of Bethlehem.

"It's pure white and stands for reconciliation," the clerk explained. He thanked her and gave her the text for the note.

"It should read: Thanks for last night. I owe you one. Clive."

Short, to the point and truthful. She'd receive it before the day was out.

He kept down soup and a dry piece of toast, then took a nap, followed by a shower, not bothering to check the GPS for Austin's whereabouts. He knew she'd be at the dojo, then go straight home. It was Friday night. That meant they'd meet up online.

Unless she discovered who I am.

He dismissed the thought. Throughout all his years of alcoholism, talking while drunk was one side effect he'd resisted.

He buttoned up his shirt, slipped on his slacks and socks, only suffering from queasiness when he bent over to tie his shoes. He thanked the Lord above it had dissipated by the time he notched his belt, gratified to find he was a size smaller.

He hoped his efforts would pay off, and if she'd had any feelings for him whatsoever, she could forgive him.

Austin ended her Friday by giving the flowers Clive had sent her to Jackie.

"My mother-in-law will love these," Jackie said, happily accepting the arrangement.

The mood at the office was sullen, the team still not quite over the loss of the Dolphin account. By five thirty, the space was quiet. She did a walk-through of the floor, turning off lights, then going into the computer room where the servers were located.

These weren't really necessary any longer, she thought, thinking of Asa's last change. He'd moved the email from local to hosted in the cloud. If a fire broke out or who-knew-what natural disaster, the team would have access to emails from any device. He'd also moved the client folders and documentation to the cloud, ensuring a back-up plan. These physical computers were more for redundancy instead of need.

She left at six, making it to class a half-hour early. It was fortuitous, since Instructor Sean announced he was changing the self-defense session to one on deep breathing and meditation.

He assigned groups of eight to form a circle, indicated the pattern and level they were to use. It was a complex series of movements, inside kicks and turns, moving inward, then outward, switching back one way, then turning the other direction, all done while in the circle. It left her slightly dizzy and unbalanced.

Like my emotional state.

By the time she turned the lock on her door at home, she'd made a decision.

No more Midnight Blue for me. She went to the computer with the intent of closing down her account. That would let Clive know she knew something was up. That he'd been found out.

Austin tapped her fingers in sequence, from her index to her pinky.

Then he might pursue me more. What if…

She stood up and went to the bathroom to shower, thinking about the best way to play this. Feed him stories that were incorrect, so he would get fired? No, she'd only feel guilty. Play with his emotions, pretend that she was in love with him and then break his heart? Ugh. That was emotional terrorism and she wasn't a fanatic.

The word fanatic triggered alarms. If he knew where she was at all times, he knew where she lived….he could be anywhere.

Austin walked to the window and casually peeked down to the street. None of the cars were occupied, but what if he was there, watching her?

She returned to the bedroom and changed into sweats. She applied a black, charcoal mask and put her hair in a bun. She was going to make her life appear so boring and unattractive, he would regret ever wasting his time on her.

CHAPTER 48

Garrison pulled into a spot directly under Austin's third story window. He was very close this time, so much so it worried him. He moved to the passenger side of the vehicle and still had a view.

"Whoa, that's a new look," he said to himself.

He'd seen her at her professional best and natural worst, but this was pure…spa. Her hair was slick and up in a tight bun, her face black with a mask and she had glasses on. It was rather comical.

"You have to work at it, like the rest of us."

He logged into Midnight Blue and waited. And waited. After an hour, he watched her leave her desk. The lights turned off, and she made no phone calls before she went to bed. He gave it another hour, checking his cell phone to pass the time. Finally, he started the car and left.

Austin was determined to change the roles. He'd been watching her, and now it was her turn. She remained at her desk, pretending to watch her screen, when in fact, her attention was on the cars below. Nothing struck her as out of the ordinary, until the faint blue of a screen appeared in one of the parked vehicles. It was on the opposite side of the street, an older model Acura. She couldn't see much else, other than the color of the screen.

The color of Midnight Blue.

She logged on, and sure enough, "Grant" was there, ready and waiting. She ignored him, already feeling in charge. She checked out the other men who had been looking at her profile; an investment banker in Silicon Valley was interesting, as was a rancher in Montana, but her heart wasn't strong enough to respond. What if they were fake profiles created by Clive to rope her in to revealing more of herself? She'd look like a serial on-line dater, a digital philanderer.

When she'd made him wait long enough, she left her desk and turned off the light, retracing her steps, peering out the window, just enough to observe the Acura. She took a leisurely bath, ate a snack, and after an hour, the blue screen within the car shut off. The car pulled out of the spot and she grinned. She had no doubt it was Clive, watching her every move, and that she'd effectively wasted two hours of his time.

The following day, she stayed at home, leaving her apartment only to pick up groceries. It gave her time to plot. While she suspected Garrison didn't know she'd found him out, she decided to test his alter-identity using one last conversation.

She opened up the dating site. He was on-line.

"We missed our conversation last night," she typed. "What have you been up to?" The cursor blinked in response.

"Work. Nothing exciting." *I bet*, she thought, nodding. "You?"

"Getting ready to go for a walk. It's good for my complexion and clears my head."

"It is a great day for that. Will you be back this afternoon?"

"Is that code for you will be waiting around for me to get on line?"

"Perhaps." *Uh-huh,* thought Austin. *To get more information about my life and use it against me.* "I enjoyed the other night," appeared the words on the screen. "Talking to you as though I were with you in person."

She tempered her thoughts, trying to give him the empathy she'd had the other night when he'd been drunk.

"The timing had been right," she wrote.

"It's not now?"

"No, my head is elsewhere."

"I wish it were on my chest, your arm wrapped around my neck."

Never. "And with that image, I'm going to say goodnight."

Austin logged off before she saw his response, already determined not to check in with the site before she went for her walk by the ocean. His presence at her exact location was going to confirm what she suspected. The only question was how she'd deal with it, and him.

CHAPTER 49

Elaine heard the phone ring and didn't need to ask Lucky for the caller ID. She knew the ringtone for Royce's mobile phone and direct line. He was calling on a Sunday morning, eleven his time, seven a.m. hers.

"You're making a gross assumption I'm not otherwise occupied," she said, skipping the greeting.

"Actually, I'm giving you the compliment that you've already had your morning run, and if anyone was in your bed when you left, they would have gone by now."

"Or are still sleeping."

"Nice try." They shared a brief laugh, one created in the memories of knowing the habits of the other. "What's up? Do you have news that I don't?"

"No, and that's what worries me. I just want to make sure I'm not missing anything."

"Royce, if I or Cole had anything, we'd have told you. Cars are still running, the lights are on, and no one is evening mentioning Blendheim or Interface. Go have yourself a nice Sunday. Go to the club or something. Take up tennis."

Her former love laughed. "I eat at the club. I don't swing the racquet. That would be my wife's job, and where she is as we speak."

"Hmmm. You do the deals inside while she spins around in a skirt. Is that still working for you?"

"Not so much."

"Then you take the concept of change management and apply it to your personal life, knowing that it's going to be difficult and ugly, but the end result will be worth it."

"Spoken like a true engineer."

"No, Royce. Spoken like a true friend."

Austin called Karen on the way to the ocean to tell her what was going on with Midnight Blue. The update was accompanied by a renewed desire for retribution against Clive, but Karen advised against it.

"You have more to lose than he does," her friend counseled. "Restraining orders are public, and it would look like you are angry a reporter communicated the facts. Your journalist contacts would run for the hills."

"Fine. No retribution, but you agree with what I'm going to do today?"

"Absolutely. Might as well know if that GPS tracker is working. Are you going to call him out?"

"Unsure. I'll see how it goes."

"Austin, can I point out one thing?"

"Here it comes," Austin intoned.

"Anger is a second emotion to hurt. You are hurt, and therefore angry. Working backwards, you wouldn't be hurt if you didn't care. You care. A lot. I told you that much when he was just the anonymous Internet guy."

"Does that invalidate my feelings of invasion?"

"No, but I am counseling you to consider this: nothing was forced or staged before you found out his identity. You can't make up the comments he made because that's all personal to you. The chocolate ice cream. The broken relationships. Just like you said."

"And so, you are saying…"

"Maybe you go in the opposite direction of what you are thinking."

"You're kidding me?"

"Nope. Look beyond the fact that he was deceitful and has been following you around," Karen said with a laugh. "He's reformed, employed, smart and handsome. With your certain brand of baggage, you need a man who has the depth to handle you, not some never-married, thirty-five-year-old who's never faced loss."

Karen's words caused her to go silent. "Is he all I can expect in this life?"

"A man who makes you laugh, calls you out and stimulates you intellectually and hopefully physically? What else do you expect? The millionaire part, too?"

"Slightly unrealistic," she said glumly.

"Sor-ta," she drawled. "Look, Austin, you can't ignore men for the rest of your life. Those that understand you are the ones with scars. Touch the bumps and appreciate what they mean."

Austin thanked her and hung up, finding a place to park a mile down from the Cliff House. She started her walk along the waterfront, thankful she brought a hat. The glare off the water was intense today. She wondered if it was a sign of things to come.

CHAPTER 50

Garrison watched his phone, knowing where Austin had parked. As the GPS stayed in the same location, he knew she was on foot. He ran along the waterfront, moving in her direction, hoping to see her in the distance. With any luck, she'd stop at the café again, and their second meeting would appear to be another one of chance.

And then I'm deleting the tracking application off my phone. No more listening. No more following. From here on out, it's one hundred percent authentic. The resolve encouraged him, giving a lightness to his being he associated with pure intentions.

Not a normal feeling for me, that was sure.

It wasn't long before he saw her walking toward him, and for a second, he slowed, then regained his pace.

It's what I want. What I need.

"Hey, look who it is." One corner of her mouth raised slightly. His insecurity rose as his pace slowed, then stopped all together. "I guess we both use this strip of water for exercise."

"Quite a coincidence," she said, adjusting her sunglasses.

It was encouraging she hadn't completely blown him off, so he continued. "Look, I'm really glad you're here. I can express in person what I tried to do in the card with the flowers. Thanks for…rescuing me from certain death at the hands of a San Francisco cabbie. It would be a great write-up but an awful way to meet my demise."

"Sure. Dead people don't help the tourist population, and without them we'd all be paying higher taxes."

"You going far?' he asked.

"Unsure. But you look like you were heading in the opposite direction."

"S'okay. The view is beautiful both ways."

He took her silent nod as an agreement to join her. "I took a look around at my apartment the morning after you helped me. I was glad it wasn't a complete mess."

"Nope. You keep a very clean house."

"Did you expect otherwise?"

"I can honestly say I'd never spent a single moment thinking where Clive G. Garrison lived."

His heart was already pumping from the run, so he couldn't discern if it gave an extra hard beat at her words.

"I'm sure you didn't," he joked.

Suddenly, she faced him. "Clive, stop. I know."

"Know what?"

"All of it. Your name. Midnight Blue. The fact that you've been following me around, tracking me with your GPS device. God knows what else you've been doing." She looked out to the ocean, willing her disbelief to flow out with the tide, to be replaced with serenity from the continual waves.

"Can I explain?"

"No. I can do that. You didn't like me. You got me on line. You made me vulnerable, and now I'm the sucker. How's that?"

"It's accurate except for the last part. You aren't a sucker. I was the idiot." She turned and started walking in the opposite direction. He caught up with her and continued in a rush, keeping up with her increasing pace.

"I admit, I saw you on that stage, so in control of the client and the journalists. I was impressed and prejudiced. You sidelined the entire crowd, and it was brilliant and infuriating. It an injustice for everyone, myself included."

"And that's when this campaign of yours started? To personally pick apart my business and me?"

"Yes, and I'm completely and utterly sorry for the initial articles and following you around. I just…"

"Just what?"

He touched her arm and she pulled away, barely slowing. "I learned I was wrong."

"You could have learned that if you would have been like any other reporter and created a business relationship with me. Who knows where that could have led? But as you said twice over, that wouldn't have sold papers."

"Please, Austin," he plead, still walking alongside her. "You were direct and fair, interesting and funny. Your very attitude impressed me to better myself, to think higher of myself. It's been real…and wonderful."

"Glad you were able to benefit."

He stopped, hands on his hips. "Fine. Walk away then. But I know you were into me, when it was just us on-line." Austin stopped but didn't turn around immediately. "That was real, Austin, and I liked it. I think you did too."

Garrison's heart felt like it was moving from his chest up into his throat when she turned to him, taking a step closer.

"You called me out on honesty before, so I will be blunt," she began. "Yes, my feelings and response were genuine. What wasn't genuine was you. How could you ever expect me to trust you after starting a relationship like this on such false pretenses?"

"I could earn it back, Austin. Give me a chance."

"Why should I?"

"Because you said that everyone deserves a second chance. If you believe it for others, then why not me?"

He saw the fluttering of eyelashes behind the lens. His own hope teetered on the edge of faith, praying to all that was holy she'd find it in her heart to take just one step closer to him.

"Please forgive me, Austin. I've never asked that of anyone in my life, because I've never cared like I do now, and believe me, I do care, deeply. Please?"

Her chin moved up and down, reluctantly at first, then the second time with more energy. He felt like a mountain climber reaching the peak of Everest. It gave him the courage to smile.

"Thank you. I was hoping this would happen. Someone who can go for two straight weeks and never say an unkind word about a soul is a special person."

Austin removed her glasses, her eyes narrow. "How would you know if I ever said an unkind word about anyone?"

Her voice was quiet and dangerous. He instinctively took a step back. He had promised he wasn't going to lie to this woman.

"I, uh, I did listen in on a few conversations. Not many--"

The slap was instant, his head cracking back. He saw spots in his left eye as she spoke.

"Don't ever contact me again. And if I see you outside my apartment or anywhere in my vicinity, I will file charges against you."

CHAPTER 51

Monday morning, Devann sat in the lobby of the SFPD, observing all the activity around him. The day after a weekend was never a good time to be at the police department, he concluded.

He saw Detective Snow cut through the lobby like Moses and the Red Sea, cops and perps parting on either side.

"Let's get Cole on the phone," he said, the minute he got to his room. "You should hear this at the same time."

Boggard was already dialing. "Victorious?"

"Better believe it." Once Cole answered, Snow began.

"I looked into SanJo over the weekend. The owner is an individual who just happens to have two nieces: Tracy and Austin Carmichael, otherwise known as Tracy Slade and Austin Marks who are wife and sister-in-law to Royce Slade respectively. SanJo had to be receiving insider information through one or both of those two women."

He pointed to a photo he placed on the table.

"Asa Crey and Tracy Slade?" asked Boggard.

Snow explained to Cole it was a photo of the two in a romantic embrace.

"Saturday afternoon, we trailed Tracy Slade. Turns out she met up with Asa Crey on the tennis courts and got lost in the clubhouse for a few hours."

"Snow," interrupted Cole, his voice booming through the speaker phone, "I'm assuming you want me to get search warrants for both Asa Crey, Tracy Slade and SanJo?" The detective affirmed his request.

"Also warrants for the computers of Austin Marks and her company. It could be the devilish trifecta of insider trading."

"Royce is going to go ballistic," predicted Boggard.

"As he should," agreed Snow. "Two women screwing him on either side. Not really sure I want to be the one to say his wife is having an affair and trading information for profit. But there is one more bit he's not going to want to hear. We checked into the board members of Dolphin, to see if they were clean. Turns out Sharon McKenzie is dirty as well. She's made one too many timely trades in competing companies."

"That makes three women. The man is going to flip," said Boggard.

Once Cole was off the phone and Snow had left, Boggard placed an update phone call to his boss. Stenson asked about Austin Carmichael Marks.

"You know," his boss began. "The name Carmichael rings a bell. Do you have any other data on her, like where she's from? Her family?" Boggard didn't, but brought up the four other firms who had been affected by the software problems.

"I looked them up. All four were ours."

He complimented Boggard on his work. "It's why you rose so quickly in this company," Stenson told him. "You can get the details fast, it's always accurate and meaningful to the business. I knew it when I hired you."

Boggard welcomed the words, and the unique relationship he had with his boss. Not many senior investigators had a direct line to the CEO.

"Now, son, while we've been on the line, I looked up Ms. Marks myself. Turns out her father was a client about twenty years ago, or rather, his company was. That didn't end well either."

"Really?" asked Boggard, surprised.

"He was one of our first clients outside the United States. Put quite a strain on our young firm back then, but we covered him. Unfortunately, he didn't last long enough to spend the money. Poor guy died not long after his lumber mill burned down."

"No kidding," responded Boggard, his shock replaced with somberness. That put Austin in her late teens or early twenties, he guessed. "Tough road for his girls."

"Don't kid yourself, son. He was no gem of a person. And if history is any guide, a person related to, or employing unethical, immoral persons, is one herself," said Stenson Black. "Mark my words. Evidence will be found on those computers in Austin's office that confirms she's a part of this."

Another thought struck Devann. "You think her father was unscrupulous, or had something to do with his lumber mill?"

"We were positive. The evidence was crystal clear."

"Then why pay out?"

"It was Costa Rica. That family was prominent. We had more to lose in terms of customers and revenue than one lumber mill. It was fate that came around and got him for us, that's what his death was."

"I guess," said Devann, shaking his head to himself, a visual of Austin Marks dying an untimely death coming to mind. He dismissed it, hoping that wasn't the case. Austin hadn't seemed the type to construct such an elaborate insider scheme, dragging down relatives and employees while using clients for profit.

"We have a few more days to see if Dolphin or these other firms have issues. Should I hold tight and remain here?"

"Yes. I need you on the ground until this is cleared up. No matter what goes down, this firm has been through three wars, two recessions and far too many presidents to count. We will make it through this."

Devann agreed and said goodnight to his boss, his thoughts on Austin. He knew exactly what Black meant to do to Austin's firm if she, or anyone in her circle, were benefitting. She might not end up in jail, but she would be a pariah. GreatLife's public relations agency was three hundred and fifty strong, twenty-three countries, multiple languages. He knew Black's course of action. He wouldn't stop until Austin Marks was on the street, without a way to earn a living and with nothing to show for a decade's worth of work.

CHAPTER 52

By 3:45 p.m. Monday afternoon, Austin was antsy to finish up and leave the office. She'd studiously avoided speaking with Uncle Ramon, who'd called her for an update on her business and romantic life. She'd thrown away another bouquet of flowers from Clive who begged her forgiveness. In response, she'd shot off an email to him reiterating he never contact her again, copying her attorney. The office was returning to some level of normalcy, the stain of the Dolphin Software account washed away somewhere in the recreational activities of the weekend.

She checked her bank accounts. She had one for monthly expenses and another for savings, which held the bulk of the money. It was fat now, as the Blendheim and Interface fees were untouched, although each were half the full amount, per the contract. The monthly fees didn't kick in until next month.

"The group needs the pick-me-up after last week," she'd told her accountant, requesting the bonus money be distributed now, instead of at the end of the year. It was noble, but not financially smart, dropping her cash flow to sixty days. But more clients would come. They always did.

Austin informed the team when the distribution posted. It certainly lifted the mood from a depressed blue to a happier yellow. She was glad of it, because hers remained variations of black. She'd not gotten over Clive and their interaction. Just as she'd forgiven him and made herself vulnerable, he'd opened his mouth, revealing yet another deceit.

"Where does it end?" she'd asked Karen. Her friend had no answer and only provided a listening ear as Austin had held back tears of anger.

"Things will settle down," her friend finally said. And they would, Austin told herself, finishing up her review of a program summary document from Darren.

She tried to ignore unfamiliar, male voices in the lobby, until Jackie's tone made her look up. Three men in dark suits were showing their identification. Austin rose, filled with an unsettling sense of foreboding that she'd had only one other time. It was when she was told Justin, her fiancé, was dead.

"Austin, these men have…" said Jackie, glancing around, biting her lip.

"I'm Detective Grant Snow. We are here for two things." He handed her a document. "Take a look. When you're done, tell me where can I find Asa Crey."

Austin scanned the first page, then the second. What she had thought was a bad situation with Clive Garrison was nothing compared to this.

"Jackie, show them his office." It was better they cuff him there than in the lobby. Heaven forbid a client or prospect walked through the door as it happened.

"Asa was responsible for our technology here at the firm, software and hardware," she explained, referencing a question in the document. "Who is going to be taking the computers?" Snow gestured to an associate. "I'll show you the server room first," she said, leading the way while Detective Snow followed Jackie.

The man asked about the protocol for shutting down the computers. "You'd have to ask Asa," Austin explained.

"I'll just shut it all down manually, then."

"Do you want me to stay or can I go back to my office?"

"Your choice. I'll make an inventory of everything we take, including the employee laptops. If you want to be helpful, you could ask your staff to shut down their systems and have their computers ready for me to take. The sooner we get through the forensics, the faster you'll have your computers back."

"Sure."

Austin pulled out her phone and typed a group text as she walked. It was short and to the point. Asa had been indicted on insider trading charges and all the computers at the company were being confiscated for evidence. Work would continue using phones or tablets.

As she reached the offices of her directors, she told them to check their phones, leaving before they could ask any questions. Back in the lobby, Asa had both hands behind his back, held in place by Snow on one side and his associate on the other.

"Earning it legitimately wasn't enough?" she asked. "You had to do this?"

He broke eye contact, the non-verbal admittance the worst moment of her professional career.

Austin went to her office, shutting down her laptop. One by one, her employees came to the front, silently giving up their machines. She joined them, surrendering hers. Within thirty minutes, the third officer was gone, their systems along with him. Austin called everyone in to the conference room.

"I've never been in this situation," she began, "and I don't even know what to say."

"Do you think it's true?" asked Darren somberly. He hated Asa and the feeling was mutual, but that didn't mean he wasn't shocked.

"Darren," answered Susan. "Police don't get to arrest people or seize computers unless they have rock solid evidence."

Austin nodded. "The document said it was insider trading. He was shorting our clients, starting not long after he arrived, while buying up the competitors. It escalated in the last year."

"Do you think he had it planned the whole time?" asked Nichele, her tone clearly indicating she thought it was purposeful.

"We'll never know. With the computers at his disposal and the ability to create dummy accounts for trading transactions in the name of family members, who knows. Anything's possible."

Nichele glanced around. "At least it was limited to him."

"Um, no," Austin said, placing her chin in her fingers. She closed her eyes for a moment, centering herself. "He was having an affair with Royce Slade's wife. My sister. The cops think they might have been sharing information, thereby, both benefitting."

"Oh, Lord," said Susan, putting her hand to her mouth.

"I know you all want to make a quip about him having no standards, but for once, I have to agree with you." The news was so bad, the room echoed with soft laughter.

"But Austin. You know what that means?" Austin nodded to Darren, who had spoken.

"It's already begun," Austin acknowledged. "They are crawling up my personal fanny right now, wondering if I am, or was, colluding with my sister and Asa for insider trading. Snow didn't come out and say it, but I could see from the way the document was worded that I was implicated. It's only a matter of time until my files get subpoenaed, along with bank accounts in my name. They will be searching for anything on the computers that might implicate me. The good news is they won't find anything, but it's going to cost money and take time as we go through the process."

Austin laid her hands out in front of her, wishing she were a person with magical powers to calm the storm on the sea.

"We don't have our own crisis communications plan, but I think we need to embrace a strategy identical to what we do for our own clients. Reporters are going to start calling if they get word about Asa, we'll need to answer. You are welcome to respond to your personal contacts, replaying the exact words on the indictment." Austin nodded to Jackie.

"I'll photocopy it for everyone right after the meeting."

"Until then, I'd like to say it's business as usual, but we know it won't be the case."

Nichele glanced at her two remaining peers. "Clients are going to bail."

Austin agreed. "And others will sue us if it appears Asa had conflicts of interest in dragging out their programs for his own gain." Once again, she put her head in her hands. "I've got to get on the phone with our attorney."

"We don't have the money to settle with them?" asked Darren.

"If our clients demand their money back and then sue us for damages, the doors of the business will be closed within the week. If the account runs dry, they'll come after me personally."

The air in the room was hot, Austin feeling warmer by the moment, the walls of the room closing in around her.

"I will personally track down that POS if I can get my hands on him," threatened Darren.

"Not sure a visit to the jailhouse is on your bucket list," quipped Nichele as she winked at Austin. It lifted her spirits slightly.

"If fortune is on our side, the press won't be proactively looking to publish this information," she continued. "I'll place calls to Mackelby and Montegue. Let's allow the others to ride and not bring it up until they do. They are out of the state and this might not make the national news." It was a single employee after all, having an affair with a client's wife. It wasn't like it was a political party leader or CEO of a publicly traded firm.

Nichele agreed. "One person with no morals who went rogue."

The team supported the plan and Austin went back to her desk. At five, the offices were empty. Feeling sick, she went for a walk along the Embarcadero. The wind off the bay became progressively colder, distracting her, but failed to make the fear of losing all she'd created go away.

CHAPTER 53

"That woman!" roared Royce, slamming down the phone. His corner office on the South Bay of San Francisco had a rare view of both the old candlestick baseball stadium and the bridge that crossed from the city to Oakland. Both were lit up thanks to the afternoon game, which was continuing despite his immediate corporate and personal crisis.

"Who? Austin?" asked Sydney as he walked through the door.

"Not quite, but close. My soon to be ex-wife."

"Women. Why marry them if you can just pay a small hourly fee?" Royce ignored him. In truth, Royce had never liked Sydney all that much. A stuck up Brit who had done a tremendous job establishing Dolphin everywhere in Europe but always offered up grating comments that were now like the edge of a glass shard.

"I can't tell you just how much those words are a comfort at a time like this. I'll ask you to refrain from crap-remarks at the board meeting."

"You've already called one?"

"It's in an hour." He told Sydney about Sharon. It was a cruel twist of fate that every woman in his life was betraying him. But by God, he was going to exact penance from each one.

A quick rap on the door was followed by his assistant. "I'm sorry to interrupt I've got a call from a William Cole. He says it's urgent."

Royce nodded his head, dismissing Sydney at the same time.

"Cole," he said.

"Hi Royce. I just heard from Elaine, who told me the code tracker software caught an anomaly. She said the triggers had been changed. They've been moved up a day."

Royce let off a string of curse words then apologized. "Sorry Cole. I'm a little pissed at quite a few people right now, mainly women, but certainly not Elaine."

"Royce, do you have a fix or a plan in place just in case this goes off the rails?"

"How could I?" he yelled. "I can't tell anyone for fear that the person responsible will change things around or make them worse."

"I see your point. Okay, then. We're going to hope for the best."

Royce hung up, angry, humiliated and vengeful. He thought of Austin. If her employee and his wife were sleeping together, she had to be involved.

And if I lose everything in this debacle, I'm going to make sure she's lost it all as well.

A soft buzzer rang on the thick, mahogany credenza next to Stenson Black. He'd just finished a particularly rewarding experience with a local beauty pageant queen, a young gal of nineteen he'd subtly pointed out to the judges was a favorite of the sponsors. GreatLife had to do its part in the community and placing the crown on this lovely little brunette's head had shown just how much Stenson and his firm took care of the next generation.

Mrs. Black didn't mind Stenson's civic duties. *All those she was aware of,* Stenson thought with a smile on his face, his fingertips tracing the dip of Miss North Carolina's lower back. At the moment, Mrs. Black was at their home in the Bahamas, vacation with his daughter and grandchildren, giving Stenson plenty of time to give back to the community.

His cell phone rang and Stenson rose, took his phone and stepped outside his room.

"News," was all the man said. "I've just sent you a copy of the indictment for Austin Marks' employee."

Stenson scanned the document. He didn't think a little dilly dallying on the side of marital confines hurt anyone. But Lord Almighty, business was the foundation of this great country, and sorry was the person who could not act with business ethics when it came to the customer.

"I told Boggard she was involved somehow. She's the bad apple, just like her father was before her," said Stenson.

"Yes sir," replied the man.

"One other thing. The woman in Hawaii, the co-founder of Dolphin, has traced the source of the bad code within Dolphin. The person who has cost this firm millions so far, and is putting us on the brink. Boggard says Cole doesn't think she's involved, but she could be another bad apple that's rotting out the barrel. You know what I believe we should do about bad apples, don't you?"

"Yes, sir. Take the worms outs."

Stenson smiled. "That's right, son. Proximity breeds more worms. You got someone over there who can take care of the software developer? The woman?" The man affirmed he did. "You stay in San Francisco, close to the source. Who knows where these two women lay down at night, or sit next to at lunch, which have been wormed."

"Yes, sir. And to clarify, when you say two women, that includes her sister?"

"Absolutely. I thought we were done with this family when we took out the father and made it look like a suicide, but it clearly hasn't ended. The two daughters need to be dealt with before they have a chance to propagate."

"Yes, sir."

Stenson re-entered his room and quietly slid into bed. *Do what you will in your own bedroom, but leave business alone,* was his motto.

His hand followed his thought.

The world had enough problems without unscrupulous people such as that woman and now her sister, and would be a better place with them gone.

CHAPTER 54

Austin went straight home where she sat on her couch, staring at the fire. She replayed Asa's words, the fact that he didn't want to take on Dolphin as a client. Perhaps he'd known that the house of cards he was living within would come crashing down and he'd be found out.

Her appetite gone, she went to bed, feeling more alone and betrayed than she had when Justin died. The next morning, Austin arrived at the office dreading what the day would bring.

"Did you see *The Weekly*?" asked Jackie.

"No."

"You might want to open your phone and check it out."

Austin meant to, right after she opened her email. Once she read the cease and desist orders from the attorneys representing Blendheim and Interface, she forgot all about the article.

A lot of good my calls did yesterday. Both Mackelby and Montegue had been dismayed but understanding. What company hadn't endured a morally-bankrupt employee? Yet those words were clearly meaningless. In addition to stopping work on their behalf, the funds already paid were demanded back, less expenses. Evidently, both CEO's had spoken with their attorneys and had a change of heart.

She didn't really blame them. What CEO wouldn't try and get money back when the opportunity was right?

Those who knew we'd done a good job, saved their stock prices and their jobs. Too bad profit outweighed values.

She called her attorney, who promised to negotiate a deal. "Do you have operating capital?" he asked.

"About sixty days."

"Then I'd recommend you look at downsizing before the next pay period. You don't know what else will happen."

She soon found out. The news of Asa's arrest was having a devastating effect. Past clients were contacting her, all demanding refunds, even those that pre-dated his hiring. She calmly explained that fact and was met with threats from their legal department. If this wasn't enough, a savvy reporter from the *Seattle Times* had picked up the story in *The Weekly* and written a piece including the names of even more clients. Those firms were also seeing a dip in their stock as word spread up and down Wall Street of insider trading and pumped up public relations campaigns. In all her years of crisis communications, Austin had never seen anything like it. Each company called her, demanding a return of funds or a threat of a lawsuit. Austin's thick layer of armor served her well as she replied they could contact her attorney, which she did herself that afternoon.

"You did the work, they agreed on the outcome. Continue to send them my way. The ones we will have to negotiate are the accounts Asa touched while he was there."

At the front desk, Jackie had been forced to wearing her headset. And, for the first time in the history of the business, she'd locked the front door to prevent reporters from just walking through unannounced, leaving a few of the junior assistants to ring in from the corridor on their cell phones. Austin finally read the article Jackie had given her that morning, glad she hadn't done so earlier.

At four thirty, her attorney called with his recommendation. "It's going to cost you all of what you have in the bank, save thirty days," he said. "Agreeing to give money back is a lot less costly than being sued and it protects you personally. You need to layoff everyone who's not critical to getting new business."

Five minutes later, she called in her directors.

"I'm going to have to lay people off," she said bluntly. "I'd like to keep you three, but you need to know up front I only have one month of cash."

"I may join you in the effort to hurt Asa," Nichele muttered to Darren.

Darren nodded. "Austin, do you want us to return our bonus money? I'll do it."

Austin smiled gratefully at Darren. "A generous offer, but no. You earned it and you all get to keep it. That might be the severance you receive if the doors shut." They nodded, and she felt their relief. The money she'd paid out should hold them over for six months, a reasonable amount of time to find a job.

Austin then spoke with her accountant, deciding upon a small severance fee in addition to their next pay check for the other employees who would be given pink slips. At five, she called her final staff meeting and delivered the news. As the employees exited the conference room, one by one, they gave her hugs, several shedding tears of anger and regret.

"I hope he rots," said Darren after the last employee left.

At five-thirty, Austin pulled out her phone and called up Clive. She'd shut and locked her door, just in case someone came back into the office. She told herself to be calm, to not jump to conclusions, to remember how he'd begged for her to forgive him. The mounting flow of emotional lava that had been trapped within her was still simmering, and she feared it was going to blow.

"Garrison here," he said.

"I have one question," Austin began, her voice even. "Were you so upset that I couldn't look past your deceit with me, you decided to tank my company by ghost-writing the article that appeared to day?"

"Austin, calm down—"

"Why? I have lost every client. My bank accounts are empty and all but three of my employees had to be let go." She briefly closed her eyes, popping them open with resolve. "What do you have to say that I will trust?"

"Austin, I didn't write that article."

"After your pattern of dishonesty, and the morally corrupt behavior I've witnessed, why would I believe you now?"

"Austin," he said firmly, "that was written by my publisher without my input or knowledge. He took a call from Leonard Campbell who told him everything. Somehow, Campbell called within minutes of Asa being handcuffed at your offices. He had the indictment in his hands. I tried to convince my publisher not to run it, and he accused me of having a conflict of interest with you."

"Bull—"

"Austin!" he broke in. "Kell told me I'm no longer allowed to write about you because he's convinced we have a relationship."

"Well I can tell him where to put this supposed relationship." She slammed the phone down, bursting into angry tears as she did so. She didn't bother try to find her center. That had collapsed into the vortex that was her life.

It wasn't long before she was speeding home along the Embarcadero. Rounding the corner, her car lurched, almost causing her to hit the vehicle in front of her. It snapped her into the present, forcing her to concentrate on what she was doing. *Please. Please just let me get home.* The car barely made it into the Mission District. She was drenched in sweat when she pulled into her parking spot, grateful no one saw her, or her car. *The Weekly* had used her photo from the Blendheim press conference in the article, making her feel like the world was watching.

She glanced around. She had naturally believed Clive was lying about Campbell, but now she was unsure. How had he known the moment Asa was arrested? Was someone else in the office feeding information to the press? When the first leak to the press had occurred, she'd suspected it was Asa, but perhaps she was wrong about that as well.

Austin entered her apartment, knowing that she was doubting her decisions, her intuition and ability to read people.

And I thought I'd learned so much after Justin's death.

Maybe she'd learned nothing at all.

CHAPTER 55

"Good morning Elaine, I know it's early and I'm hoping you are still sleeping. Just wanted you to know what's going on here. Cars are having issues all over northern California, starting last night. No fatalities but lots of crashes. The Attorney General has already been in contact with Royce, and together, they spoke with the CEO of Loron and their attorney. We are keeping it under wraps. The official explanation is bad gas. Call me if and when you find anything on the code tracker."

After Cole left Elaine the voice message, he got Boggard on the phone. Initially, Boggard said the car insurance companies would fight Loron to determine who paid for the accident coverage. Boggard told Cole he'd call him back, and after speaking with Stenson Black, Boggard told Cole that in the end, both GreatLife and the car insurance companies would go after Dolphin.

"Why not....about...Dolphin?" asked Cole.

"What...you're breaking up, Cole. Say that again."

Cole repeated his question but heard only silence. His phone had cut out. He went to his desk, heaping praise on the landlines that had largely gone out of fashion. Then he realized he had a problem. He only had Boggard's cell number and had never asked where Boggard was staying. Finally, he sent Boggard an email.

"Bad gas started last night. Phone lines down," Cole wrote. "Next on the list are banks. I'd suggest you get cash out while you can, and keep that hotline to the White House open."

"Got it," Boggard wrote back.

Cole's next call was to Elaine. Busy signal. Trimade, the telecommunications company, was officially off-line. Without thinking, Cole pulled out his wallet. He had twenty bucks. His mom always said to keep a hundred dollars in small change around for emergencies. This definitely counted as one.

It was six-thirty a.m. Tuesday morning, but Garrison was already in the office, shaved, and dressed as though he were attending a press conference. Kell accused Garrison of having a lovers spat with Austin, then concluded that Garrison's aversion to writing "a real piece" on her was because he was trying to win her back. Garrison threatened to quit over the unjustified accusations, and Kell told him to shut up and get back to reporting, and keep his love life out of the office.

Campbell was the one who had it out for Austin, not him. And how could the man have known when Asa was arrested? Anyone looking for a new court filing had to proactively look it up. Those didn't make the paper unless the name was a big-time CEO or investor. No, something else was going on with Campbell, and Garrison wanted to know what it was.

He thought of Asa, the insider trading and the affair with Royce's wife. That was some dirt alright, and the way Kell had written the article was exactly the piece Garrison would have done, before he'd gotten to know Austin. By its very wording, the piece implied the sisters were in league trying to reap rewards from stock purchases. Kell had even suggested that perhaps Asa was intimate with them both.

Clive ran searches on Campbell, using the exact same process he'd done with Austin. He quickly found that the man owned a home in Presidio Heights, a condo in Sun Valley, Idaho and was three million in debt, this according to the divorce papers filed by wife number two. His alimony payments were running nearly twenty grand a month, his firm employed twelve, and he had recently become the champion of the people, by claiming that other, unscrupulous practitioners in his industry were taking advantage of their clients.

What about taking advantage of your competitor?

He quietly looked over his shoulder, his eye on Max's screen. The kid hadn't spoken to him much since their last conversation, where Max accused him of going down too hard on Austin. He was right, but now wasn't the time to give him compliments.

Garrison kept to his task, waiting until he saw Kell enter the office to pay him a visit. He made small talk about the potential stories of the day, and when Kell was interrupted by the receptionist, glanced at his screen. Sure enough, Kell had more emails from Campbell. Austin's name was in the headline.

Austin to be arrested. Uncle implicated. The first paragraph of the email was displayed on the screen. He couldn't believe what he was reading. It was another indictment. They had to have something concrete to get that in place, but what could it possibly be? He was now convinced she was the only honest person in this entire mess.

"I've got the runs," Garrison said, gripping his belly. "Going out for some medicine. I'll be back."

"Don't be making a mess of my offices," grumbled Kell.

Garrison walked out of the office and went to his car. He hoped Austin would be at her home and not at the office, but he couldn't take the chance.

I know I promised not to do this, and you would file charges, but by then it will be too late.

He opened up the GPS tracker and saw she was on her way to the office. He took the side streets to her parking lot, waiting on the opposite side of the road until she handed her keys to the attendant.

Once she was on the sidewalk, Garrison watched for traffic and cut across the road, calling her name. She saw him and kept walking.

"Austin, I know you don't trust me or want to talk to me but you have to listen. I learned something this morning and we have to talk."

"You had a come to Jesus moment and learned you can no longer live a life of deceit?"

"Yeah, sort of," he said and walked beside her. "Austin, I'm serious. I told you Kell wrote the last piece, but what I didn't know was where he was getting the information. Today, I saw it with my own eyes. It's Campbell. This morning, he sent Kell an email saying that you are going to be indicted for insider trading. For fraud, Austin. Do you understand what that means? And they don't do that without evidence. Austin, someone is setting you up. I'm sure of it."

Clive was grateful Austin's steps slowed, but she continued to stare straight ahead. "My question is still the same from yesterday. Why would I believe you?"

"Because I've changed, and I'm trying to make the wrong things right."

"Not good enough."

"You're going to take your chances, going to the office and being arrested? Austin, it will ruin you."

"What if I'm already ruined anyway?"

"You aren't," he said emphatically. "I can help you. We can work together to figure out what is going on, so you still have something when this mess is all over."

She stopped, facing him. She looked worn down, fatigued from keeping her nose above the water when the seas were becoming increasingly dangerous.

"Why? Why do you even care? Your mission in life was to destroy me."

"Because I…I do care, Austin. Pure and simple."

They stood in silence on the corner of Sansome and Clay. "Please, Austin. I'm begging you, don't go to your office. Come with me and we'll figure this out together. What I read involves your uncle and your sister."

"My uncle? How could it possibly…?"

"Austin," he said, tentatively touching her arm. "Come with me. I'll tell you in the car. For once, trust your instinct that I'm not lying. I'm being honest, and I want to help you."

Austin glanced in the direction of her office, then nodded, following him. He opened the door for her and she slid in.

"An hour, is all I ask," he said. "Then I'll take you back to your office or wherever you want, okay? But at least then you'll know what's going on."

"An hour."

CHAPTER 56

Royce woke in the guest bedroom and saw he'd missed a call from Cole. He tried him back, but his cell wasn't working, and he didn't have a land line hooked up in the home. He had to drive to the office to get an operational phone.

Once he got there and called Cole, he learned about the gas situation, and of course he'd experienced the downed phones first hand. The two discussed the potential banking crisis, and Royce confided he had a few thousand at home in the safe. Cole then told him about the four, smaller, regional companies who had the same sequence of codes that had been affected months prior.

"I'm so sorry I didn't tell you earlier. I honestly thought it might have been a fluke, banking on the fact it was irrelevant."

"It's irrelevant now," grumbled Royce. He found himself in a strange position. How was he going to modify the software without including the five individuals who were under suspicion? He'd have to let his senior technology officer know and the attorney. In reality, the entire executive team and board should be aware of what was happening. But Cole had counseled against it.

"Only a few should be clued in," Cole had said. "Your chief technology officer and that's it. You can't trust anyone."

"Then I should probably shut the entire software system down if the banks go, don't you think?"

"It's a high probability."

"I need to call Elaine," he said. "Now."

"You can't. Cell phones aren't working and she doesn't use land lines."

"She uses email," said Royce.

"It's four in the morning."

"I know."

Royce thanked Cole for calling him and hung up. Two women were going to be arrested today, he thought to himself. Problem was, he couldn't determine who deserved it more.

Garrison had told Austin what he saw on Kell's email twice now, but she wasn't getting it.

"Let me play this back in very factual terms one more time," he started again. "The cops tracked down the Dolphin board member, Tracy and Asa, all on insider trading charges. Then literally overnight, your company is shut down. To be honest Austin, they've made a compelling case why you should be questioned hard and at length. It all makes sense that somehow you're also involved."

"Yes, but it's wrong," she cried. "I don't even have a stock trading account in my name!"

"What they found on the computer syncs with what Asa told the cops. He was making trades for you, with your knowledge. That's what Campbell related to Kell and what's in the indictment."

"There's no way that could have happened, unless....Asa was responsible for all the office technology," she whispered. "He was the one who set up the systems, put the emails in the cloud, along with all our documents."

"Did he have administrative privileges?" She nodded, her face pale. "Then he could have manipulated emails and read everything you were sending and receiving."

"And claim he was doing it all on my behalf."

He reached over and touched her cold hand. "I want you to listen very carefully to me, Austin Marks. I'm going to help you because I need to make up for starting this mess in the first place." Austin's eyes teared up. Clive took a chance and threaded his fingers between hers. "And just think, all good and strong relationships have something really horrid to indelibly tie them together."

He felt a squeeze. As he drove, he felt her fingers gripping his tighter.

"You know, whoever is going after you already has details of your life in hand."

"I know."

"Austin, think hard. Who could possibly know this much about your life?"

"Only one individual fits that description. It's my Uncle Ramon."

"Then we go see him," concluded Garrison.

Austin shook her head, despondent. "He's in another country. Costa Rica, to be specific."

Garrison downshifted to stop at the light, facing her when he came to a stop. "Then we will be paying that man a visit."

"How are you going to pull that off? By now, my name might already be at the security check points to get out of the country."

Garrison smiled. "Then it's a good thing I've spent a lot of time in the sewer chasing stories. I'm owed a few favors, and I know just the person to see on this one."

CHAPTER 57

Elaine had narrowed the list of five persons down to one who had access to the source code: Greg Kale. According to his human resources profile, he was twenty-eight, graduated from MIT and the lead program developer responsible for integration with third-party software. That meant he was in a unique position to determine what software worked best with each company.

Out of the corner of her eye, Elaine caught a flash, but it was gone when she turned her head. Maybe a bird with a streak of yellow in the wing. She'd never had a visitor up here, and the possibility of receiving one now was less than remote. All this interaction with people and the threats of having to go back to California had made her paranoid.

"Collect all data from the last three hours and send it to Cole marked urgent. Every company using Dolphin software must cease their operations."

She placed her elbow on the window and accidentally hit her funny bone, the odd twinge occurring the moment a searing pain tore through her shoulder. The velocity of the bullet pushed the left side of her body forward and to her right, the motion saving her spine from taking the second bullet. Instead, it tore through her right shoulder, and a third bullet ripped through her right bicep and grazed her chest.

Lucky squawked and flew off the screen, an instant before a series of bullets shattered Elaine's desktop. In another second, the room was quiet. Papers floated to the floor, a low wheezing from Elaine rising with the humidity in the room.

Blood ran from Elaine's body. Her body plummeting into shock, her useless right arm pinned beneath her. Pain induced double vision made it hard to see her left hand, but it was intact. She couldn't lift her arm, let alone her hands. Instead, she twitched her fingers. "Lucky," she whispered, pushing out the words with her ragged, shallow breaths. "Cole. Send it all to Cole." Lucky's visual eyes had been knocked out, but Elaine heard a squawk.

"Done! What happened?" The bird had been written to ask her 'what happened' when the screen went dead. In the early days, Elaine had momentary lapses where she'd scramble to figure out what cord she'd left unplugged when it was nothing more than the on-button. This triggered the basic question.

She heard sounds coming up the steps. Cole…Cole might be able to stop whatever was happening. Stop it before anything else happened. No matter what, Lucky could continue to record everything, the camera moving with the motion as it always did. Sight and sound.

"Lucky, don't talk. Intruder. Don't talk anymore. Continue recording and send to Cole. Intruder. Lucky…"

"Lucky you are not, young lady," said a voice, in a neutral tone. "Let me see here." Elaine's eyes were now just slits, and the right side of her face was covered with blood. Pain shot through her entire body as he gripped her left shoulder and turned her on her back. "Two useless arms, two holes through the chest. The pain you are enduring now is not going to last very long. Soon enough you'll be slipping away into unconsciousness, so I don't see the point in inflicting further damage."

Blood dripped from her nose into her mouth, causing her to choke. He ignored her and turned to the computer.

"Nicely damaged, but the hard drive. Hmmm," he murmured, and Elaine, drowsing in and out of pain induced consciousness, fought to keep breathing. She knew his inspection of the computer including determining how to destroy it. It wouldn't matter if he did. Paranoia caused from losing a hard drive in college had made her religious about keeping a back-up tape drive, which she stored in a fireproof safe. She hoped his expertise was with killing people as opposed to finding hidden files.

"Drive is intact and not one that can be pulled out I see. Cables of all types, but who knows what they are hooked to and where. We'll just make certain you don't send any information out and no one can send to you, okay?"

As if that concluded his one-sided conversation, he pulled out his gun and shot a number of rounds into the computer. A silencer did little to muffle the sound of metal flying in all directions.

Elaine opened her eyes to see him take another glance around the room before leaving. She prayed he would meet the local police on his way down the mountain.

Her thoughts slowed as warmth embraced her body. She had slipped into unconsciousness by the time the intruder left.

CHAPTER 58

William Cole pushed through the morning crowds which clogged the uneven sidewalks of the Embarcadero Plaza. The time stamp on the email from Elaine's assistant Lucky was exactly one minute forty-nine seconds before it was received on his system. Approximately two minutes after Elaine was shot, he'd gotten in touch with the emergency rescue team in Kuai. Lucky had attached a series of photos of Elaine standing by the window, hit multiple times and falling. Through the text summary and the voice recording, Cole had listened to the entire incident, seeing the video of the man right up until he shot the hard drive to pieces.

Cole's lanky athletic frame carried him easily past the motionless cars on Battery Street. Crossing through the pillars of the Federal Reserve building, he continued his sprint to the police department, up the steps and straight through to the detective's floor. Nolebrow was waiting for him, waved him in, and without getting off the phone gave him an update.

"They just arrived. Life Flight says she has a faint heartbeat. It will be another three minutes before they get her to the hospital where a team is standing by. The images of the man were clear, and the local and state police are already on it."

Cole nodded, his concentration on breathing as the lieutenant finished his call.

"Snow and our team have been with the Slade woman this morning. Royce insisted on being here. He's with the attorney over in the conference room."

"Get Royce out now."

"You got it." Nolebrow left and returned with Royce.

Royce stood at the door, and Cole motioned him into the room as Nolebrow followed and shut the door behind him.

"I'm sorry to be the one to tell you we are out of time," Cole began as he pointed to the whiteboard. "Elaine identified the source of the problem. I'm now telling you to take your product off the market or put a freeze so the customers can't use it."

"Hold up," interrupted Royce. "I'll want to verify the information with Elaine myself before I do anything."

"You will take the product off in fifteen minutes or I will have a warrant for the entire corporate campus to be shut down, and anyone who gets in our way will be arrested on the spot. Petrano will issue the press release and the entire world will stop using the software without your input. What will it be?"

This was not the polite but firm attorney general's understudy Royce had encountered before. Even Nolebrow arched an eye at the young attorney's tone.

"We'll see exactly what you can and cannot make my company do."

"Be my guest. But I can promise you this," he said, leaning towards Royce with his hands on the table. "I'll make sure that Petrano tells the world that it was your former employee who not only discovered the scheme within your organization, but was the target of an attempted murder as she tried to solve the mystery. Elaine has just been riddled with bullets and was Life flighted to the hospital. Just who do you think the media is going to blame for the attack? How about the arrogant president of the company who doesn't want it shut down, who's in denial about his wife screwing someone else for illegal trading and who, at all costs, wants his pocketbook to remain thick?"

Nolebrow stepped in. "Easy, Cole."

"Do it. Now," Cole commanded Royce.

The man was reeling from the news, but nodded. "Give me a land line." He was pressing the buttons as Nolebrow turned to Cole.

"We have something else for you," Nolebrow said to the attorney. "We found a link between the companies on the list. They all share the same holding company as a primary investor."

"The holding company is out of Costa Rica," said Cole. "We've known that since Saturday."

"What are you talking about?" interjected Royce, the phone at his ear. He paused to request his executive team get on the phone.

"SanJo Holdings owned by Tracy and Austin's uncle," said Nolebrow. "A man named Ramon Carmichael."

He saw that Snow had stepped out of the interview with Tracy Slade and her attorney. Nolebrow motioned his senior detective into the room.

"Do you have any idea why someone would want to harm Elaine?" Cole asked Royce.

Royce shook his head. "Everyone likes Elaine. Everyone. And their uncle? Unbelievable. Yes, Royce here…" he turned. He provided the details of the situation and the request. "That's right. The entire systems. All two thousand clients, now."

When Royce was finished, Cole spoke. "The person inside the company was close to getting caught. How could the person possibly have known that? It's the only link to Elaine. How many people at your offices knew Elaine was working on the project?"

Royce grimaced, his face blending fury, anger and pain. "No one. She made me promise. But…" Royce closed his eyes hard, and ran his fingers through is hair. He turned his back to the door, facing the men. "I'd told Tracy when Elaine first started working on it."

"Did you mention the code tracking software?"

Royce grit his teeth and nodded.

"Do you want me to state the obvious?" Cole asked coldly.

"I'll spare you. Tracy had to be sleeping with one of my five engineers, or paying him, or both."

"Yes. According to Elaine's last message, it's a guy by the name of Greg Kale. As if using Asa wasn't enough, your wife was literally and figuratively screwing you and your company," Cole said. "What in the world did you do to that woman to make her hate you so much?"

With his hands on both hips, he stared Cole straight in the eye. "I never fell out of love with Elaine."

Snow explained the banking transactions he'd found. "No one was making money from the stock transactions with the exception of Crey, SanJo and your wife. No ties, no paper trail to Austin. She simply isn't in the picture, other than being related to Tracy."

"So why are we going after Austin?" asked Royce angrily.

Snow raised a sheet of paper. "Because a public record search found that the named beneficiary of SanJo Holdings is both sisters. The money is to be split, unless one of them dies or is convicted of a felony. She'd inherit all of it if her sister's in jail. That would be a salve on that emotional wound."

"Wait, wait," broke in Royce. "These entities are a part of insider trading, which I can buy, but your suggesting that Austin was, or is, prepared to murder to cover up the scheme?" he asked. "That's a stretch, even for me."

Cole agreed. "Let's see what your wife has to say. Snow?"

His lips curled wickedly. "I'm ready."

CHAPTER 59

"Do I really have to answer this question?" Tracy asked her attorney, ignoring Detective Snow. He nodded his head. At four hundred and fifty dollars an hour, he figured it was twenty-five bucks a nod.

Had Tracy Slade given him the opportunity to speak, he would have had her back at home by now. As it was, every time he opened his mouth, the imperious woman in the couture form fitting outfit did his job for him.

The attorney's well-honed eye for troublesome clients had told him early on this woman would incriminate herself, which she had done within minutes. His natural inclination to fight like a dog in heat had given way to disgust, then boredom, with the realization she had no intention of listening to him no matter what he said. He regretted not asking for a larger retainer and a significantly higher hourly rate.

"Who cares if I was sleeping with someone who worked at my sister's company? It's not against the law."

"Asa made trades based upon information he received from you," Snow pointed out. She rolled her eyes.

"I talk in my sleep and can hardly be blamed."

"And you maintain that you had no knowledge whatsoever that Asa Crey was working for your sister?"

"It wouldn't matter if he'd been working for you. He was good at tennis, where we met, and in bed. The end."

The attorney heard a cough, and glanced at the mirror. He figured it was Lt. Nolebrow or Royce Slade, both who were likely watching the interview. His client was a witch alright, but a funny one.

"You know," began Snow. "We had a little debate going on in the office earlier about how injustice is served to some members of the family. We see it all the time."

Come in from the side and see if a trap could be set, thought the attorney.

"I'm sure you do," she answered, inspecting the length of her nails.

"Tracy," the attorney said into her ear, unable to help himself. He was getting paid, after all. "Don't respond to comments or answer questions. They could be setting you up for something that we can't defend later."

"Thank you so much, George," she said sweetly and loud enough for the room to hear. "But I can handle this. It's all better out in the open."

"But—" he leaned into her again.

She raised a hand to him. "I'll ask if I'm unclear about something, thank you."

Snow continued, pleased. "I'm sort of surprised you and she don't get along. I mean, according to all the financial records that we've gotten so far, the money she made, and the money you made, were all going to the same place. SanJo Holdings, owned by your uncle, Ramon Carmichael."

Tracy twirled a pencil absently. "We are family, at least technically."

The attorney was watching this drama play out with placid interest. As he continued to look at her, he realized he wasn't even sure he wanted to stop the process and miss her self destruction.

"Your uncle will contend this was you and your sister's doing, the funds going into his account not his problem. We might be able to claw back the funds we can tie to insider trading, but honestly," he stopped to smirk, "that's mice nuts when compared to the inheritance." Tracy just stared at the man. "Ah, yes, I thought that would get you. It's a bit more complex than insider trading, but the motivation is basic."

Here it comes. The grand finale.

"I'm sorry, what's so basic?" she asked.

"The money you will inherit if your sister is in jail, or dead," deadpanned the detective.

That was news. When he glanced at his client, Tracy shuffled in her chair, the first indication of discomfort he'd witnessed.

"So, you think Austin is doing everything in her power to incriminate me so she can get at whatever money my uncle has?"

"Actually," Snow said, leaning in, his voice light, as though he were discussing a case over a beer. "I think it's the other way around. I think you saw money in Royce Slade, a relationship which conveniently started when he was still dating his co-founder, Elaine Sylvies. He was swayed by you, she left, and you married him. But that money wasn't enough. You began sleeping with Greg Kale in order to make money, the good, old-fashioned way, by stealing it. You worked him, he worked the code at Dolphin, and you both tested out the insider trading scheme on a handful of smaller companies. Not big enough to be noticed, but the trades made you a few million. Your uncle was happy, as both of you were benefitting.

"In the process of these firms pulling out of their crisis, you discovered that your sister, Austin Marks, had the accounts for the crisis communications. You saw it, and did some research. You found that Asa Crey worked for her, was single, and just so happened to play tennis at your club. One thing leads to another. He agrees to create an electronic paper trail that makes it look like she's doing what we found: trading on her inside knowledge. A cut and dried felony. You know what that means?"

When the woman flicked her nails and kept her mouth shut, the attorney knew it was over.

"It means that she'd be a felon, and you'd get the inheritance named in the SanJo Holdings paperwork," Snow concluded.

"I already have enough money, detective."

"But not the intelligence to go along with it. At some point, we figure you got greedy. You had to have more, so you got Greg Kale to up the stakes. To corrupt the software of larger companies. That, combined with your sister being in jail, means you keep the money you've earned through insider trading, and you get the inheritance."

In a last ditch effort, the woman flitted her head back. "What could induce me to such a scheme?"

"Forty-five million dollars."

Royce was momentarily paralyzed. The notion of going in and strangling his wife strong, but fleeting. Only one of them was going to be spending time in jail.

"You still think Austin's involved?" Royce asked Nolebrow.

"No. I think she's ignorant and has had her company essentially shut down and destroyed by Asa Crey. Snow's guy did find a few other things on Crey's laptop giving motivation. He has sent multiple emails to none other than Leonard Campbell."

"You're kidding me?"

"Truth is always stranger than fiction. The computer forensics are black and white. Asa had a plan for going to Austin's business, and it was self-serving. Even if he hadn't hooked up with your wife—sorry—Asa's intention was to bring her down in some fashion. He was the one feeding Campbell information the entire time. It looks like he was going to start his own firm and take the clients, or if Austin went down in flames, he'd run the organization himself. Tracy provided an accelerant for his plans."

"Unbelievable. It also succeeded. Austin has no clients. No company or reputation. She also has no money. I feel worse for her than I do myself. My company and ego will recover."

Nolebrow tapped the window and Snow came out.

"Snow, would you like to accompany Royce to his offices? I believe you have an arrest to make."

Royce grimaced, tasting blood. At least he'd have the satisfaction of throwing one person out of his life.

CHAPTER 60

The nose of the plane lifted, the pressure pushing Austin's chest back against the leather seats. Clive sat next to her, silently looking out the other window. They were riding in the return favor he'd redeemed from the CEO who was cooking the books with his vice president of sales.

One hand shakes another, thought Austin. It's the way of the world. She shouldn't be complaining. If what Clive saw on Kell's computer was accurate, Kell was going to publish an article that told the entire world she was sleeping with Asa, and that they were both now indicted on insider trading charges. What few clients hadn't already asked for money back would do so, and finding the money was already gone, would sue her personally. On top of that, officers from the SFPD would come looking for her at the office, then her home to arrest her.

Garrison had stopped by her apartment where she found her passport, and he wasn't worried about her being arrested. He anticipated the local cops would think she was still in the city, not thousands of miles away. But if they were detained, Garrison had a wad of cash with him as a bribe.

"My little stash," he had explained.

Once they were up in the air, she'd asked him again about the information Kell had received, piecing it together what they both knew.

"I just want the truth," she said, feeling angry and defeated. Clive nodded. The lying and deceit had occurred on multiple levels.

He asked the pilot if the plane had internet, and learning it did, he turned on the flat screen, switching to the local news. "It's official Austin. You are now on the lam." Her employees would be wondering where she was and if she had abandoned the company.

When the segment changed, Clive turned it off. He took her hand, sandwiching it between his. It was all so unbelievable. She closed her eyes, wanting to pretend the world as she knew it didn't exist.

Yet, she couldn't find solace even in the dark. The image of William Cole came to mind, a young man doing his best to prevent more problems within the city he loved. He was honest, she was sure, and wanted to do the right thing, regardless of his boss's agenda.

She turned to Clive. "I need to speak with Nolebrow and Cole."

"Are you crazy? One or both will track down the phone line and be on the next flight to find us."

"Clive," she said wearily. "What am I going to do? Be on the run forever? I don't have the money or the inclination. And despite all the duplicity I've seen in people and the judicial system, I believe in justice for all. I want that man to know what I'm doing and why."

"Petrano won't care, and you know it."

"I do, and neither will Nolebrow, but perhaps Cole will, and I have to trust in that."

Garrison nodded and received instructions from the pilot on placing a call. Austin got the number and took the phone.

CHAPTER 61

"It's in poor taste to be calling for any reason at this point, don't you think, unless you are calling to give yourself up?" Lieutenant Nolebrow began. The line clicked several times and she realized the conversation was being taped in addition to being tracked. Garrison leaned close.

"I want to tell you I'm innocent of the charges being made against me."

"We were thinking that, actually, right up until the time that Tracy Carmichael Slade was killed in an accident just outside our offices following her interview. And now you are on the run. It will be hard to spend what you just inherited from jail."

What? How...?

"What happened?" she asked, her voice shaking.

"After wrapping up our interrogation, she was on Market Street when a car sped around the corner, ignored the cross walk signal and hit both her and the attorney. Her death was instant. Her attorney has a punctured lung and is in critical condition but will likely pull through."

"I can't believe it."

"You, of all people, have the motivation to get rid of her."

Austin's shock turned to disgust. "How can you even say such a thing?"

"Because it's a large inheritance. Plain and simple."

Clive shook his head. It was news to him.

"Lieutenant, I have no inheritance."

"Wrong. Your uncle designated you and your sister as equal beneficiaries of his assets, unless one dies or is convicted of a felony. At first, we thought Tracy was going to pin you with being a felon, thereby getting the money. But you beat her at her own game. With all your money going back to clients, you had your sister killed, then skipped town. It all goes to you. All forty-five million of it. But don't think we won't find you. You can't go anywhere we can't get you."

Garrison pressed the mute button.

"If you call Cole, we aren't going to solve the problem. We are going to be playing into the hands of whoever is doing this."

Austin took the phone from him and placed it gently back in the cradle.

"I know."

Cole had taken Austin's phone call and listened. He didn't agree with Nolebrow that Austin had a hand in killing her sister. The woman was running, and had been, for twenty-four hours. To plan and execute her sister's death required coordination, money and a cold heart. He didn't believe the woman had it in her mentally, physically or financially. With his gut as his guide, he sat down with Petrano and made the pitch of his career.

"You're asking me to put you on a plane to so you can confront this Uncle Carmichael since Lord knows I don't know his full name…"

"I—"

"Stop. Don't speak. If you are going to avoid incriminating yourself don't go acknowledging anything I'm saying. Furthermore," Petrano continued, "you told Austin Marks she needs to do the same thing."

"She's already on her way."

"You said it, not me. And one of two things will happen. If she is guilty by association, you are going to have the locals round her up and send her back in your custody. And if her uncle cracks, you're going to take him into custody, recognizing the entire extradition aspect is going to be a pain in the butt. So, you need my assistance in getting my counterpart down there to help out on this little affair."

"Yes sir. I'll be there just about the time you are giving your speech, which I still think is a bad idea."

"One sister is dead. The other sister inherits the money and still isn't cleared on the insider trading charges. On the surface, she's guilty."

"With all due respect sir, what's on the surface gets votes. But it's what lies beneath the surface that matters, like the truth."

Petrano raised an eyebrow. "We have motivation, yes? We have a woman, yes? We always identify persons of interest in murder cases, and Tracy Slade's death wasn't an accident. It was a hit and run. Unless you can provide me a reason otherwise, I'm running with what I have on Austin Marks if I don't hear from you by ten 'till the hour."

Cole let out a silent breath of air. "Thank you, sir."

"For what? You haven't asked for anything remember? As far as I'm concerned, this entire conversation was a lecture about not wasting fuel paid for by the state of California, so you better get back here as soon as possible. Got that?"

"Yes, sir." Cole could not help smiling at this boss's endorsement.

"Cole, do you still want a job when this is over?"

"If I'm alive, yes sir. And if it does work out alright, this might be the biggest victory for the office in recent memory," Cole said. "You will get the full credit."

Petrano shifted. "Okay. I'll give you a plane, the authority, and name-dropping power to do what you need to. But don't think I'm blind to the act you just pulled. I wrote the script on getting credit. And just so you are aware, I have been known to share some of that credit, especially to future attorney generals."

"Thank you, again, sir," Cole said, eager to leave the building.

He looked at his watch and did some quick calculations as he made his way down the elevator. Flight time on the Gulfstream would be nine hours. It gave him approximately an hour before Petrano made his speech. And he hope for Austin's sake it didn't mention her.

CHAPTER 62

Boggard answered his phone and listened to Cole's update. After hanging up, he immediately called his boss.

Stenson asked him for Cole's flight schedule to San Jose. "He plans on confronting both Ramon Carmichael as well as Austin, who is already on her way."

"Two in one," Stenson said approvingly. "Good plan."

Boggard told his boss about the intention to arrest the engineer at Dolphin, and correcting the code before more damages could be inflicted.

"It's likely the umbrella coverage of Dolphin will cover the renegade engineer," Boggard explained. He'd already been on the phone with corporate counsel from Dolphin, and knew where this was headed as well as his boss. The attorneys would negotiate behind closed doors, along with their insurers. In the end, a deal would be made to cover the clients, but also keep Dolphin afloat.

"Too much pressure and the company can declare bankruptcy, or sell itself." That meant getting out of any and all liabilities, sticking GreatLife with the bill.

"Agreed," said Stenson. "Just keep our team apprised so they can get the best deal possible. You've done a great job, son."

Boggard thought of the lives that had been lost, but also those that had been saved. Had Elaine not discovered the code, dozens, or hundreds of others might have died.

"Do you think the guys responsible will get the justice they deserve?" asked Boggard, feeling reflective. Tracy Slade was dead. Elaine was still in critical condition. The chances of Austin making it through this unscathed were looking slim, even if she were innocent.

"Yes, son. Justice will be served. You mark my words."

Hunger pains woke Cole, who had been dreaming about breakfast at his favorite childhood diner in his hometown of Depot Bay, Oregon. He searched the galley, methodically opening every drawer and cupboard. He'd expected to find instant coffee and crackers, but soon remembered this was the governor's plane. Duck champagne pate, smoked oysters, caviar and assorted crackers filled an entire section of one cupboard. In another were gourmet chocolates from Belgium, roasted macadamia nuts from Hawaii, and maple syrup from Canada. The fridge was stocked with wines from Germany, Italy, even Australia and sparkling wine and champagne from France. His body was craving protein, but he'd take a Gatorade.

He made his way up to the front of the airplane and asked the pilot if he had any real food on board. The pilot laughed and gave him directions to the smaller fridge behind the front seat of the plane. This was stocked with the food eaten by the crew. Sliced meats, cheese, bread, even an Odwalla superfood drink.

Cole took one of everything and called Snow, who gave him more details of Tracy's death.

"This woman was literally splashed across the sidewalk. That kind of thing takes precision timing and a lot of speed. I liked her attorney though," he added as an afterthought. "Hope he makes it. He's in the critical care ward."

"Unreal."

"The downed telephone lines have now rolled through the Rockies. Anything west of Utah is pretty much out. Also, the bad gas from Loron has spread to other regions creating havoc everywhere."

"Have you come up with anyone who can meet me on the ground yet?"

"Oh, yeah, hold on," said Snow. "Got a guy from the San Jose detective unit, Rodrigo Ueke. He'll meet you at the tarmac. He's helping, but it took the threat of an inter- governmental action to get his team on board. Carmichael is a sacred name in that town."

"He's not going to take a bullet for me, then."

"You got it. What are you going to do? You aren't armed with anything more than a theory and a possible co-conspirator, while the one we really had the evidence on is dead."

Cole didn't actually have a scripted plan yet. "Do you think she'll show?" he asked the detective. He was putting his entire career, and life on the line to fly down to meet her.

"Yes, and here's why. Austin is innocent. I believe that now, despite Nolebrow thinking that she could get someone to kill her sister. Unfortunately, innocent people always believe in the system. That's why they call people like Nolebrow, or show up at the station, then get completely screwed when false evidence is planted or someone makes crap up on the stand. Trust me. She's going to be there in San Jose when you show up."

Cole realized Snow wasn't talking about Austin exclusively. He, William Cole, was also one of the innocents, a person who still believed in the system.

The young attorney felt a wave of unexpected gratitude and growing respect for the hard edged officer. He knew parts of the system were broken, and by telling Cole that if she was innocent, the system would most likely betray her, and that included Petrano.

Cole would have to make the right call with Austin when he saw her, and if that meant letting her get away, then so be it.

CHAPTER 63

During the long flight, Austin and Clive had talked for hours, and he slowly graphed out a timeline. It started when she created Marks.

"How did these first customers find you?"

"It's hard to recall," she'd said, mentally worn out.

"Think back. It's important."

"They were almost all referrals."

"Not based on your reputation?"

"I was new to the area. I had no reputation."

Clive marked down all the names she could remember. He had her identify which companies wanted plans, and those that had an actual crisis. The hiring of the employees was next, then Justin, her former fiancé, and up to the present day.

"When did your uncle usually call?"

"He always called to congratulate me on new accounts, that sort of thing. Why?"

"Austin, I don't recall you ever announcing your clients in the press. Part of your deal has always been to be behind the scenes. True?" She agreed that it was but didn't catch the significance of what Clive was suggesting. "Okay. Next thing. You mentioned the companies on the white board you saw in Nolebrow's office. Can you recall the names?"

She wearily nodded and told him. After a few minutes, he scooted closer to her, placing the clipboard on her lap.

"Do you see anything unusual?"

"No. What am I supposed to see?"

"Look at the timeline. Here." He pointed to the date Asa was hired. "You have been going on the assumption all the lying and deceit happened after Asa started, but this shows you two things: one, it actually began years before and two, your uncle was privy to information you weren't telling him."

Austin's reaction was one of shock.

"Do you think my uncle is truly to blame?"

"Given what you've been told me, do you think it is all a coincidence?" She rolled her head back and forth on the leather, locking her eyes on Clive.

"You know, you have the goods on me now, if this goes off the rails."

She squinted. "How so?"

"I told you how I got the use of this plane. Knowing that the CEO of a publicly traded firm and his vice president of sales were conspiring to change the books, to pre-date sales closures to keep the stock up. I knew it. He confirmed it. I promised not to write about it, and now I'm using his personal jet."

"So you used extortion and blackmail? Please. Give me something that matters."

Her sarcasm made him smile, but it stopped when he saw the tear in her eyes. "I'm ruined, you know. No matter what happens," Austin whispered.

"Yeah. But, there is a halo in this pile of crap. You have someone who lost everything, money, wife, career, and learned to make a decent living being a gutter rat. I have some invaluable survival skills I can share. And even better, I have a place where you can live."

Austin's lips trembled. The stark, brutal reality of her new existence left her unable to speak, so she just nodded. He placed his palm on her cheek, brushing the corner of her eye with his thumb.

"I would never tell anyone about your secret," she murmured.

"I know. You're a much better person that I am."

"Yes, I know." She giggled then, and he smiled, his lips still apart when they kissed.

CHAPTER 64

Costa Rica. It had taken nearly nine hours of flying, but they had finally arrived.

The Gulfstream circled for its final approach into San Jose's Posado International airport.

Austin checked her watch. In less than an hour, Petrano would lay out the incriminating details of the supposed plot including Asa, herself and her sister. Not only would her business close for good, but public pressure might force Royce to resign, the board would be overhauled, and the stock would tank, ending in a takeover.

All of it was a classic, text book case study of crisis communications. One perfect for the right firm to come forward and help Dolphin out of its mess.

The pilot had arranged for a car and it was waiting for them outside the private hanger. In the dark, the city of San Jose resembled a patchwork quilt of black with white neon boarders and dark blue outline of water, its trim.

Austin squinted her eyes to read the dimly lit Spanish words on large, garish billboards lining the city streets. She looked around, hoping to find the current surroundings familiar, but a lot had changed in twenty years.

"Good architecture," Clive remarked absently. He held her hand tightly in his.

Consistent and firm. The man he's trying to be.

The car sped through the financial district and urban areas until the smooth road gave way to gravel. They rode in silence, and eventually the car took another turn, pulling into a long driveway lined with palm trees. Lights revealed a tall, iron fence with wire. At the gate, the driver called out and was admitted.

The gates slowly spread open, gliding forward on three-inch metal pipes. "No other guards?" he asked. She shook her head. It had been so many years, she had no idea of her uncle's environment.

To Austin's right, a path of crushed rock meandered through the area, stopping at slate steps that led to a regulation size tennis court. The man-made pond sat adjacent to the bank, in front of a large patch of grass that continued to slope down until it reached the main structure overtook the landscape, banyan trees flanking the arched doorway. Balconies decorated with craftsman metal fronted the windows of the home, vines painted the walls and wove through the iron.

Clive removed his hand. "Sorry," he said. "I need to activate this thing." He held it up. "It's a recorder pretending to be a very expensive pen," he quipped. "And no, I never used this with you, but it has served me very well. I expect it might do so now."

Clive and Austin approached the ornately carved double door. "Nice," he said, running his fingers lightly on the wood. She knocked and the door was instantly answered.

"Mi amiga," cried the housekeeper, greeting Austin with a slight bow, then a hug. "Come in, come in." The woman beckoned them inside. "This way. We have been so worried," she confided, walking Austin and Garrison down a long hallway and across an inner courtyard filled with climbing red bougainvilleas. "All those papers! Saying the most horrible lies about you."

Austin accepted her offer for water while Clive requested directions to the bathroom. Once in the library, Austin visually reacquainted herself with the room; the den of the man who stood accused of controlling her destiny through clients, companies and her sister. She moved toward the open veranda, wishing for the comfort normally associated with a warm, evening breeze.

Finding none, she turned back.

The decades-old leather furniture was comfortably worn and a natural part of the room's Spanish style. Hand-woven tapestries covered the walls, glints of gold and silver thread sparkling in the light, fitting perfectly beside original works of art from Frida Khalo and Diego Rivera. Within the large, wooden bookcases were leather bound editions of classical favorites in multiple languages, along with bronze statues and ornate wood carvings, precious items picked up from various countries around the world. Trophies did not line the walls. Only inanimate objects that gave no indication of the intimate side of the homes' owner.

My uncle is a collector of things, not people.

Austin walked to the desk. Silver picture frames captured pivotal moments in her life. One was a black and white photo of her walking. Another photo was of Austin at her debutante ball, her first date. The last photo was her out in the avocado orchard only yards away from where she stood.

"As you can see, the orchard hasn't changed much," her uncle said from the doorway. He held out his arms. The last place she wanted to be was in his embrace, but her inner child, the Latin girl at heart, walked forward. After kissing both his cheeks, she pulled back.

"You have been through so much." She nodded as Garrison walked into the room.

"Clive Garrison," he said, hand extended.

"Of course. Sit."

He walked to the other side of his desk. "We just heard about Tracy and the news reports stating you were missing." He made the sign of the cross on his chest and looked at a picture of mother Mary and Christ resting on a far bookshelf. "Do you have any idea why someone would want Tracy dead?" he asked.

"No," she said. "She'd been having an affair with one of my employees, but he's in jail. Besides, I can see him resorting to a lot of things, but not murder."

"You never know what someone might be capable of," her uncle replied.

Austin glanced at Clive. Not once, in all those hours on the plane, had they discussed Asa being involved in Tracy's death.

"Uncle, the police said she was run down in the middle of the street. They are pointing the finger at me because I will inherit all your money if Tracy is dead. I'm also implicated because Asa had access to the information on every client we had and he was making trades based on emails he created in my name. It appeared like I was asking him to do it. But it's all a lie. I would never do something like that."

"No, you wouldn't. But I would."

Austin froze. It was Clive who spoke. "Would what, exactly?"

Ramon sat in the chair behind his ornately carved desk. He folded his hands on the eighteenth century antique, his back facing the two-story bay window which opened out to the veranda.

"It was not supposed to have ended this way. Your sister should not have died, and I had nothing to do with that. But yes, you were to lose everything. All of it for one reason." He gestured outside his villa window. "To make you come back home."

Austin sank into the worn, leather chair behind her.

Ramon Carmichael turned, arms folded across his chest. "You had no brother. No heir for the lumber mill. Tracy didn't exhibit the traits we knew were required to run the business. You did."

"What traits?" she contended. "Being obstinate and fighting with my dad?"

"Determined. Headstrong. You could handle men twice your age with your intelligence. He knew you could do it."

"Certainly not after being disinvited to the funeral or being disowned by my mother."

"Wrong. Those things did not stand in the way of you getting the money due you. You rejected the inheritance, knowingly and purposefully, because you disliked the terms."

"What terms?" asked Clive. She glanced at him. It was a part of her life she'd never told him.

"I was to attend a designated college and return home here to Costa Rica to run the mill with the proceeds," she said crisply. "When the mill burned down, my uncle tried to convince me to use the insurance settlement to start a new one. If I didn't, I'd get nothing. So I chose to leave." She could tell from Clive's expression he didn't think the terms were all that bad.

"Correct. And dropped out of school and went to work. Your father was crushed--"

"Don't even say it," Austin commanded. "He took his own life, and I have lived with the blame of that for almost two decades. My mother hasn't spoken with me since, and my sister got me back in the worst possible way. And now, you are confirming that this whole thing was meant to force me to come back here again, Dad's—and your—ultimate way of exerting control?"

Ramon tried a smile. "You have millions of dollars at your disposal. You can start a new life. Never work again."

"Millions of dollars gained through dishonest acts? How did that all come about?"

The man's jowls dropped, along with his eyelids. "Your father took the insurance payout and put the majority in a fund to be managed by me. It had very specific instructions. Purchase money in critical industries."

"SanJo Investments," Clive said.

Her uncle nodded. "Named for the town where Tracy and Austin were born. When she married Royce, she told me of a way to change the code at Dolphin Software, to manipulate it. We could both make money. No one would get hurt." He shrugged. "It worked. Then the dollars kept getting bigger, and she wanted to take more risks. Bigger companies."

"Blendheim," Austin offered.

"And others. We made money short selling the company while buying up the competitors. You were handling many of those."

"And Asa?"

"Was convenient. The original twenty million is now worth about forty-five million. When I die, that money will now go to you."

"Why not my mother?"

"Your father never agreed with her decision to disown you over your decision not to join the business. Upon his death, she received a two million dollar life insurance policy. She doesn't even know about the fund."

"And you were going to turn this over to Austin and Tracy?" asked Garrison skeptically.

"Equally. As long as neither were convicted of a felony or dead."

A moment of silence occurred as Clive's eyes narrowed into a thin line, paralleling his mouth. "Your sister was setting you up," he concluded. "All the emails found on Asa's computers. Every last one tracing back to you. Your requests, his trades. He gets off free and clear, you take the fall and your sister inherits the entire amount."

"No. It's not possible."

"For almost fifty million," said Clive, "people will do a lot of bad things."

"And you," Austin turning back to her uncle, eyes glassy. "Every time you called me to ask about my current or upcoming clients?"

"He was using you too, Austin," Clive interjected. "The entire time."

"Trying to control my life, just like my father." She shook her head, her lips pursing. "Well guess what? I'm taking back control of my life, starting now."

Her uncle went to the balcony, hands resting on the metal. "Yes, and you can do it from here. Starting today, you can live a life of luxury. All of it yours, a new life with family."

Adrenaline pulsed through her as she said bitterly, "I have no family."

CHAPTER 65

The sound of two gunshots popped. Ramon Carmichael staggered back and was caught by Clive, who couldn't keep the large man from slinking to the floor. Austin dropped behind a couch, knowing the bullets had come from the courtyard and realizing she'd be in the line of fire if she went to help him.

"No, you don't, not anymore," said a voice, the Latin accent strong. "I'm to finish a job that started long ago." The sound of furniture scraping on the floor came from the far side of the room.

Austin glanced at her uncle. His chest was torn apart, his eyes already closing. Her self-defense skills were useless against a gun wielded by a skilled marksman.

"The brother of a man who caused such a colossal mess in the first place. But just to make sure of it...." four more pops sounded, and Austin looked up, seeing the man clearly, then ducked down again.

"What do I do with you?" the man asked.

"Nothing, hopefully," replied Clive. Austin leapt over the chair, straight onto the man's back, pushing him forward. A nearby lamp fell and broke, as Clive got up and kicked the man's head.

Pop pop pop. Clive reeled back, his arms flailing as the propulsion of the bullets sent him into the bookshelves. Austin heard the crashing of invaluable objects as she dove forward, digging her nails into the flesh of the killer until he screamed. But instead of dropping the gun, he punched her in the stomach, knocking her down. In a second, he was on top of her, straddling her chest, the gun to her cheek.

"Gotcha," he said triumphantly.

She caught a flash of Clive, wounded and blood splattered coming at the man from the side. He lurched forward, knocking into the killer's back. He tumbled over her head, his knee crunching her nose on his way down. By that time, Austin was up, on her knees, laboring to get the gun she knew was in her uncle's desk.

A hand grabbed her ankle, and she fell forward. Feeling the killer's palm on her shoulder, she gripped it, dropped down, collapsing her shoulders, and used his forward momentum to throw him directly over her. He met the coffee table head on, the glass shattering.

She closed her eyes, rolling forward into the glass, her objective to get the gun in the desk. It worked, but he got lucky, grabbing a fistful of hair, which he yanked back, exposing her neck. Instead of pulling away, she caught his wrist, taking him with her as she tucked her shoulder under his elbow and spun.

Snap! His elbow broke. The man screamed and she thought she had enough time to get to the desk. Then she heard the click of a gun and felt the wind of the bullet across her back. Two guns, this one with a silencer.

"I'll make you a deal, Ms. Marks," rasped the man. "Turn around and I'll only put a few bullets in you. That will allow an open casket. If not, I'll fire as many bullets as possible into the back of your head, destroying our face." She slowly turned to face him. "Always nice to see a person rise to the occasion."

"Why? Why are you here?"

"I said it before. Your uncle made a mess of things with his insider trading, but your sister made it a lot worse by destroying the Dolphin Software. That has cost my boss hundreds of millions of insurance money. For that, I made sure your sister died before she hit the ground."

"It was all about the money."

"No. Part of it was closure. Your father was the first to go. If he hadn't purposefully lit his own lumber mill on fire to get the insurance money, then I wouldn't have had to put the bullet in his head."

"You're lying."

He tightened his grip. "I take full credit for killing the man and making it look like a suicide. What I should have done was take care of you and your sister at the same time, but the boss wouldn't let me. It took time, but he finally gave me the go ahead."

Now! She rolled forward, feeling the spits of gunshots as she pushed off her hands, throwing her legs straight, her feet straight into the killer's chest. She staggered back as a bullet penetrated her right cheek, the burst of blood hot and sticky. Half-blinded, she used her left arm to knock the gun to his right and continued sliding her palm around his neck.

"If you ever consider using this move," Instructor Sean had always said, "don't think. Just do."

Austin cupped his chin in her strong grip, tilting it up, towards the ceiling. One quick breath lifted her slightly, and then she exhaled everything in her lungs, uncoiling, placing her heel behind the man's foot. As she did so, her victim's body unwound, first the neck, cracking in two places. His body followed, the spin twisting, ripping apart bone from muscle.

Austin released and let go of the broken body, which sank to the floor, lifeless. She heard the sirens just before she saw the red and blue glow in the distance.

And then she collapsed.

CHAPTER 66

"She is coming to," Cole said to Garrison. "It might be nice if I weren't the first person she saw." Garrison, his broken arm strapped to his side and a bandage covering his right ear, disputed the fact.

"You called in the calvary. She owes you her life, since I was helpless on the floor."

"You had a reason."

Garrison nodded. He'd passed out because of blood loss and woke in the hospital with medical staff speaking a language he didn't understand.

"Thank God you had that Monte Blanc pen on you. It recorded the whole conversation. We lifted it and gave Boggard a listen. He was about to take Snow's gun and track down Stenson Black himself. Suffice it to say that part of Black's plea deal included his firm paying for all of Austin's payroll costs for an extended period of time in exchange for a lighter sentence."

"I hope he gets an eternity."

"Accessory to murder will put him away for a while. Once we had that taken care of, Petrano made the recall announcements for the heart transplant devices. We took a page out of Austin's playbook. Her reassembled team created the scripts and deployed them to the same call centers she used."

"Who paid for it?"

"Stenson Black's insurance company of course."

"And Dolphin?"

"Royce exceeded our expectations," explained Cole. "He'd already shut down the system, but the key was fixing it. He asked me for help, so I got on the phone with Snow, who walked in with his guys and flanked the engineer, Greg Kale. The kid literally changed the software as they stood over him, guns at their holsters."

"What happens to Austin now?"

Cole shook his head. "Nothing. Austin didn't do anything wrong. She had the misfortune of hiring a bad guy and being related to an awful woman. She'll be able to go back to her life when she's recovered."

"Such as it is. You know the guy who attacked us? I remember seeing him at the Starbuck's down from Austin's office a few times, right when I'd started following her."

"He was Black's employee. His business strategy was to eliminate anyone who made his company suffer financial losses. Black believed in paybacks, and as we learned, it all began with Austin's father."

"At least she has closure on that. She wasn't to blame for his death."

They both watched Austin's eyes flutter.

"When Snow showed up at Campbell's door with a search warrant, he confessed to the backdoor deal with Asa to undermine Austin. With Austin out of the picture, Asa had been promised he'd take over Marks or be hired by Campbell as a partner. Together they'd assume or split all of Marks Communications clients. Now Asa will be heading to jail, his ill-gotten gains returned to a fund for the victims of the Blendheim and Interface tragedies."

Garrison whistled in appreciation. "A perfect irony."

"The real rub in this was Ramon. He was a major stockholder in these firms and had direct lines to Mackelby and Montegue. They confirmed he provided Austin's name and encouraged them to hire her. Montegue, Mackelby and Slade are now feeling the associated guilt of believing the worst about her."

"Not that her reputation will ever regain its previous luster," griped Garrison.

He only had one good arm but he wanted to put it around Austin, to shield her from misguided and cruel individuals; those like the man he once was. "One last question. How was Campbell able to feed Kell information when Asa wasn't around? There were some things that even Asa didn't know."

Cole took a sip of coffee, extending his pinky finger in Austin's direction. "The computers Snow's team confiscated from Austin's office had unique little devices attached to the side walls. Wireless sound monitors that intercepted all calls and most of the conversations in the office. Asa copped to installing them for Campbell."

"Illegal wiretap, extortion…" started Garrison. "That all adds to time in jail."

"Yes, and all because Austin took a few of his marque clients away and wouldn't pay homage to his certain brand of greatness."

Garrison shook his head. "Greed knows no bounds."

"And that was her sister's downfall. She learned about the inheritance in SanJo years ago. She bided her time, married well, but all the while, her eye was set on how to get Austin out of the picture. The first effort was helping Justin, Austin's former fiancé, return to his heroin addiction. It killed him, but didn't end up derailing Austin. Next up was getting someone inside her husband's firm to change the source code. She was sleeping with Greg Kale. Tracy figured Austin's firm was going to take the fall for insider trading, she'd be charged with a felony, and then walk with millions, just like Snow had hypothesized."

"Am I allowed to write a piece trashing Campbell and exonerating Austin?"

"It's too late. I called up Kell, who told me to give the information to a guy named Max. After I told Petrano about Campbell's role, he viewed him as the reincarnated devil. I let Max know Campbell's been arrested and bail rejected due to a potential flight risk. He's also on suicide watch."

"What about the concrete?"

"That took the President of the United States calling the heads of those countries where the betasydene was used. I'm not sure, but I suspect it will be carried out by consultants and paid for out of a line item in the budget that will never be revealed."

Garrison could only shake his head. *How little the people of the United States knew.*

"Last thing, I promise," Garrison asked. "How did you convince Petrano to let you take the government jet to nail Carmichael and rescue Austin?"

Cole turned to him, a smile on his face. "The week earlier, he'd told me I was going to be fired for working with Elaine to break into Dolphin's code. Giving me the plane would have been one more reason to let me go."

Garrison snickered. "I'm assuming you got a raise instead of the pink slip."

"And a slightly better title. What about you?" Cole asked. "I heard the *Mercury News* offered you a job."

Garrison couldn't bring himself to smile. He'd gotten what he desired, but the price had been very high. "Flattering, but I'm not sure I'm interested. That idiot Bernie Jax went for Austin's throat when it was convenient."

"Everyone did."

Garrison looked at Austin's still figure, lying so peacefully amid the tubes and needles attached to her body.

"You think she'll check out of the business world all together?" wondered Cole. That was exactly what Petrano was hoping, as it would make his initial statements about her appear more credible in the end.

"She's young, beautiful, and frighteningly intelligent. Despite everything that's happened, she's still smarter than ninety percent of the women in the world. Do you really think she's going to wake up and walk away from it all?"

Cole turned to Austin. "I've never had to make the decision between a life and a business. From what I now know of her background, she's never had a real life. Perhaps you could help her with that."

"What is Petrano going to do with the money in the SanJo account?"

"He's going to take all of it except the money used to start the account; the twenty million from the lumber mill payout. It's tax free, if she lives in San Jose, Costa Rica." They went silent as Austin's eyes fully opened. "How do you think you'd like living in Central America?"

Garrison smiled. "I'd love to have the chance to find out."

Cole touched Garrison's good shoulder. "Now that I've wrapped this up, I have a flight to catch."

"A vacation?" suggested Garrison.

"No. To visit the woman from Dolphin who uncovered all of this. Elaine Sylvies. As her attacker was shooting bullets, Elaine pressed her record and send button. We got the medivac up within minutes. She's alive, but needing some TLC."

"Sounds like an interesting story. Maybe one that should be written someday."

"Someday," replied Cole with a smile. "Take care Garrison. And take care of this woman. I think she's going to need you."

Garrison looked back at Austin. She focused her eyes on his, he smiled, opening his heart to her.

We are going to make it, Garrison thought, continuing to smile as her eyes slowly closed. Long after she fell back to sleep, Garrison stood there, keeping watch. It was a role he'd have as long as she let him. One that he'd earned, wanted, and would never take for granted.

The End

AUTHORS NOTE

This book is for Shandel Slaten Sutherland, who invited me to a lake in Northern California for vacation, and while floating, listened to my idea for a book based on my corporate experiences. When I struggled with a name, she immediately said "Global Deadline!" It took me another twelve years to write the novel, but her title was a guide and inspiration. Thank you Shandel.

ABOUT THE AUTHOR

Before she began writing novels, Sarah Gerdes established herself as an internationally recognized expert in the areas of business management and consulting. Her novels are published in sixty countries, and translated by publishers in four languages. Global Deadline is her fourteenth book. She lives with her family in Northern Idaho among a menagerie of farm animals.

BOOKS IN PRINT
Sarah Gerdes

Contemporary Fiction

In a Moment

Danielle Grant Series

- Made for Me (book 1)
- Destined for You (book 2)
- Meant to Be (book 3)

A Convenient Date

Suspense/Thriller

Global Deadline

Above Ground

Chambers Series

- Chambers (book 1)
- Chambers: The Spirit Warrior (book 2)

Incarnation Series

- Incarnation (book 1)
- Incarnation: The Cube Master (book 2)
- Incarnation: Immunity (book 3)

Non-Fiction

Author Straight Talk

The Overlooked Expert: Turning your skills into a Profitable Business, 10th Anniversary Edition

Sue Kim: The Authorized biography

Navigating the Partnership Maze: Creating Alliances that Work

Resources

Instagram: sarahgerdes_author

www.sarahgerdes.com

Made in the USA
Monee, IL
05 October 2024

66585424R00171